"I asked if you were okay."

Luke shrugged and gestured vaguely with the half-peeled cucumber still in his hand. "You seem flushed. Need me to turn the AC down?"

More like a cold shower. But Megan couldn't say that, and she couldn't admit that it had been so long since she'd been in a man's company that something as mundane as watching him chop vegetables was enough to get her hot and bothered. So she shrugged and turned back to the window. "I probably just got a bit too much sun at the splash park today, that's all."

He nodded, but she could feel his gaze lingering on her, as if he wasn't quite sure of her answer. No doubt he'd had plenty of chances to hone his personal lie detector abilities dealing with hordes of schoolchildren. Hopefully she was more adept at covering her feelings than they were.

* * *

PARADISE PETS

Dear Reader,

I'm so excited to be able to share a new Paradise story with you—one that is very close to my heart. You'll get to visit with some familiar friends from past Paradise books but also meet new faces, like single mom Megan Palmer. She's a young widow trying to do the best by her son, who happens to be on the autism spectrum. Between advocating for him, getting her degree online and now working from home, she's put her own needs aside for so long she's not sure she even knows what they are anymore.

I know all moms can relate to that constant balancing act—trying to be the best parent you can be while also handling all the other tasks of daily life. Add dating to the mix and things can get truly overwhelming. But Megan, like any mom, always puts her child's needs first and no one better stand in her way—not even her son's supersexy new principal.

Luke Wright—nicknamed Mr. Right by the gossips of Paradise Isle—may not have a ton of experience, but he certainly doesn't need one of the parents at the school trying to tell him how to do his job. And as much as he wants to help, letting a dog on campus—even a trained service dog—sounds like a disaster. But when his professional life and his personal life clash, he'll have to make a hard choice that no amount of teacher training days could have prepared him for.

I loved writing these characters, but as a former dog trainer and veterinary technician, I especially enjoyed researching and writing about service dogs. If you'd like more information on these amazing animals, I suggest contacting Canine Companions for Independence. You can find them at www.CCI.org.

I hope you will enjoy reading this story as much as I enjoyed writing it! And, as always, I love hearing from you! I can be reached on Facebook, www.Facebook.com/katiemeyerbooks, or my website, www.katiemeyerbooks.com.

Happy reading!

Katie Meyer

The Puppy Problem

—

KATIE MEYER

HARLEQUIN
SPECIAL
EDITION

HARLEQUIN®
SPECIAL
EDITION™

Recycling programs
for this product may
not exist in your area.

ISBN-13: 978-1-335-40805-1

The Puppy Problem

Copyright © 2021 by Katie Meyer

For questions and comments about the quality of this book,
please contact us at CustomerService@Harlequin.com.

Harlequin Enterprises ULC
22 Adelaide St. West, 40th Floor
Toronto, Ontario M5H 4E3, Canada
www.Harlequin.com

Printed in U.S.A.

Katie Meyer is a Florida native with a firm belief in happy endings. A former veterinary technician and dog trainer, she now spends her days homeschooling her children, writing and snuggling with her pets. Her guilty pleasures include good chocolate, *Downton Abbey* and cheap champagne. Preferably all at once. She looks to her parents' whirlwind romance and her own happy marriage for her romantic inspiration.

Books by Katie Meyer

Harlequin Special Edition

Paradise Pets

The Puppy Problem

Paradise Animal Clinic

The Marriage Moment
Do You Take This Daddy?
A Valentine for the Veterinarian
The Puppy Proposal

Proposals in Paradise

The Groom's Little Girls
A Wedding Worth Waiting For

This book is dedicated to all the people who have believed in me, even when I didn't believe in myself. Thank you for standing by me, come what may. Special thanks to my parents; my husband; my agent, Jill Marsal; my editor, Carly Silver; and everyone at Harlequin Special Edition.

Chapter One

No matter how old you were, being called into the principal's office was always nerve-racking.

That was the conclusion Megan Palmer reached in the fifteen minutes she'd been kept waiting in the reception area, perched on a worn plastic chair as a wall clock that looked older than she wearily ticked away the time. Her anxiety rose with every sweep of the second hand.

She really should be used to this by now. Ever since Owen had moved from a special school for kids with autism into a mainstream classroom, she'd been called in on an increasingly frequent basis to discuss her son's "difficulties."

That's the word they usually used—*difficulties*.

His teachers were concerned that her six-year-old was having *difficulties* adjusting, that he found transitions *difficult*, that he was having a *difficult* time following directions. Well, yeah, dealing with autism was difficult—for Owen. That's what always seemed to get lost in the conversation. It was always about how his behaviors affected the classroom, the routine, the other kids. Never about how hard he was working, or how incredibly overwhelming daily life could be for someone with a brain that was wired differently.

Megan knew exactly how it could be to deal with Owen. She'd been doing it all his life—most of that time as a single parent. But as her late husband had often said, the best things in life didn't come easily. At the time, Tim had been referring to his job as a soldier, defending the freedom of their country. But she figured it applied to a lot of things, and lately it had become her personal mantra.

Getting the news her husband had been killed by an IED hadn't been easy. Finishing school while grieving him hadn't been easy. Raising Owen wasn't easy. Transitioning him into a mainstream classroom hadn't been easy. The truth: each had been hard as hell. And she had a feeling today's conversation with Principal Wright would be the hardest yet.

But she was going to push for what she wanted—for what Owen needed—no matter how much educational red tape she had to cut through. She wasn't a little kid, and she wasn't going to let an elementary school principal intimidate her. She straightened her shoulders, rehearsed her well-researched arguments in her head, and ignored the little drop of nervous sweat trickling between her breasts.

"Mrs. Palmer, Dr. Wright will see you now," Ms. White, the school secretary, said. A middle-aged woman in slacks and a polyester blouse, she opened the little half door that divided the office into public and private areas. "I'll show you—"

"I know the way." *Too well, unfortunately.* Megan could probably give tours of All Saints Elementary School at this point. Blowing by the disapproving woman, she briskly stepped through the portal and walked down the short hall that led to the administrator's office. A left turn and there, three doors down, was her destination. The lion's den, as it were.

She knocked, perhaps a bit too firmly, and the door swung open a few inches, just enough for her to catch the principal's eye as he motioned her in, a phone pressed between his ear and shoulder as he typed furiously at the open laptop on his desk.

Megan stepped inside and took a seat in one of the two straight-backed chairs in front of the ancient, scarred wood desk while he returned his attention to whomever was on the phone. Frustration gnawed at her. Why call her back if he hadn't been ready—it wasn't as if this meeting had been her idea. But the man was probably used to women being eager to sit around waiting for a scrap of his time. Not because he was the principal of a small, private school, but because Luke Wright was drop-dead gorgeous.

It was a term she didn't often use for men, but it fit. Unlike the crusty old administrators she remembered from her school days, Mr. Wright—or "Mr. Right" as he was often referred by local gossipers—looked like he should be on the set of a Hollywood blockbuster, not sitting in a stuffy, overcrowded office in the tiny town of Paradise, Florida.

He was tall, at least six feet, with the lean athletic build of a swimmer or surfer. His hair was dark and thick, and just long enough to look a bit messy. In contrast, his beard was neatly trimmed. His necktie, purple with a pattern of small starfish, was perfectly straight. She'd had enough of these meetings to notice you could tell the time of day by his tie. Early in the day, it looked like it did now. By noon, he would have loosened it. By the end of the day, it would be hanging on the back of his chair, discarded with the jacket she'd never actually seen him wear.

Megan focused on the tie; it kept her from staring at his eyes. The eyes of a poet, she'd secretly thought the first time they'd met. They were dark, ringed with thick black lashes that any woman would envy, and they seemed too see way too much. His eyes made her nervous. *He* made her nervous. Her and every other woman on the island.

But unlike them, she couldn't afford to be sidetracked by the man's looks or his legendary charm. This was about her son. Everything in her life was about Owen now. He was the reason she'd busted her butt to get her computer science degree in half the normal time. He was the reason she'd taken a coding job that she could do during the day while he was at school, and at night while he slept. He was the reason she spent every other available minute researching therapies for children with autism. Owen was everything to her, and no one was going to keep her from doing what was right by him.

Luke knew he was being rude, but hanging up on the school's wealthiest donor wasn't an option. Not that he hadn't considered it a time or two—Mrs. Cristoff was nothing if not long-winded—and, unlike him, she seemed to have endless time on her hands. He, on the other hand, had a day of scheduled back-to-back meetings and was already running behind.

He didn't mind the chaos that came with a building full of schoolchildren, or the need to multitask. He was good at that. But he hated this part of job, the fundraising and political nice-making. He had too damn much to do to be discussing linen colors for the upcoming charity gala. But, of course, he couldn't say that without risking a huge chunk of his budget for next year. It also didn't help that Mrs. Cristoff lived across the street from him, which she believed gave her instant access at all times.

All Saints was a small school, and the tuition was low to keep it within reach of the island's working-class families. Donations kept the lights on, so he grit his teeth and assured Mrs. Cristoff that yes, he was sure chartreuse would look lovely. "In fact, why don't you call right now to arrange the rentals, so you can be sure to get the shade you want… Yes, right now… We can touch base later. Bye." He hung up and caught Owen's mom smirking at him.

That's how he always referred to her—"Owen's mom"—to remind himself that she was a parent of one of his students. It would be easier if she looked more matronly, but between her petite size and the smattering of freckles across the bridge of her nose, Megan Palmer looked more like a college coed than a woman with a school-age child. Too bad his body hadn't gotten the off-limits memo. Every time he saw her, his libido kicked into high gear. Today was no different.

Annoyed at the phone call, at the delay, and mostly at his own inappropriate reaction, he found himself taking his frustration out on her. "Something funny?"

If she was put off by his tone, she didn't show it. Instead, a full grin broke over her face. "Actually, I was just wondering if you had any idea what color chartreuse was."

"None." Despite the situation, her smile was contagious and he felt his tension ratchet down a few degrees. "Some kind of pink?"

"Green." Her blue eyes danced in amusement. "Actually, about halfway between green and yellow."

"Seriously?"

She nodded, the movement shaking free a few loose tendrils from the bun she always seemed to wear. He'd spent more time than he wanted to admit wondering what all that long blond hair would look like loose, how it would feel if he ran his hands through it.

"Is that a problem?"

His attraction for her? Definitely. But he didn't think that was what she was asking. "Is what a problem?"

"That whatever it is you were talking about is going to be green instead of pink? Wouldn't want you to end up with your house painted the wrong color or something."

She thought he lived in a pink house? He shook his head at the image. "No, it doesn't matter. Not to me anyway. I'm sure it's vitally important to Mrs. Cristoff, though. She's picking out tablecloths or something for the Scholar's Banquet, our biggest fundraiser of the year. She can have purple polka dots as far as I'm concerned." He grimaced; he shouldn't be venting to a parent. But Owen's mom didn't seem offended, her smile growing.

"Party planning probably wasn't part of your doctorate program, huh?" she asked, nodding at his diploma on the wall.

"Not exactly. Nor fundraising." Luke glanced at the file folder on his desk, the one with Owen's name printed on it, and sobered. He hated that he had to keep calling her in for these meetings. Hated even more that Owen was struggling so much.

He took his job as principal seriously and, if one of his students was having a hard time, he felt a personal obligation to help. The problem was that nothing seemed to be working for Owen. Luke had done some research on autism since the six-year-old had come to the school, but the information was all so general, so abstract. And Luke was growing increasingly worried that his elementary school wouldn't be able to offer the boy what he needed.

Since All Saints was a church-related private school, it wasn't required to follow ADA guidelines to accommodate special needs students. But that also meant no federal or state money to help with the costs of even trying. It was frustrating all the way around, and admitting defeat wasn't Luke's style. Regardless, he was running out of options. In the middle of his quandaries was Owen, a flesh-and-blood little boy whose pain was real.

As if reading his mind, Megan's smile vanished and what he thought of as her "mama bear face" fell into place. Concerned. Fierce. Ready for battle. "I assume there's been a problem in the classroom again?" Her words were clipped, but he sensed the apprehension behind them.

"The lunchroom, actually." He removed the incident report from the folder and passed it to her. "Owen got upset because there was a menu change. He threw his lasagna at the cafeteria worker."

Disappointment and embarrassment clouded her features as she skimmed the brief report. By the time she handed it back, her game face was in place. "I was promised that any changes to the menu would be communicated ahead of time. You know Owen gets anxious making choices, so we always decide ahead of time what he's going to order."

"I know, and I'm sorry." His regret was sincere. They had agreed to do that, and he planned to track down and deal with whomever had let things fall through the cracks. "But that doesn't excuse violence."

"Did he mean to throw it at someone? He has meltdowns, but I've never known him to be violent."

"I honestly don't know. But, frankly, it doesn't matter. The outcome is the same. We want to help Owen, but I have to consider the safety of the other students and staff, as well. And as much as we want to make this work, perhaps it is time to consider an alternate school environment for Owen." He hated saying it, because Owen really was a wonderful little boy most of the time. Nevertheless, his outbursts hadn't lessened and it was only a matter of time before he injured himself or someone else.

She flinched at the words as if he'd physically struck her. But, true to form, she didn't back down. Straightening her slight shoulders, she looked him square in the eye and said what no one at the school had yet dared to say. "No."

Megan felt her hands tremble, but she kept her head high as Luke Wright raised an eyebrow at her words.

"Excuse me?"

"With all due respect, Principal Wright, I know my son and what's best for him. He's making friends here, and he's growing both socially and academically. All Saints is where he needs to be."

"I sympathize with your concern for your son, but the truth is, his behavior is becoming more than we can handle." The compassionate look in his eyes did little to ease the sting of his words.

She'd expected this, but that didn't make it easier to hear.

"I know." Megan tried to keep her voice calm and authoritative, even as her pulse pounded a desperate rhythm in her temples. Leaning down, she felt more hair slip from her bun as she retrieved a packet of papers from her bag. "He's trying. But when things change, like they did today, it triggers his anxiety, and when he gets anxious he has meltdowns. We do have a plan in place for that, to prevent things from escalating. It works at home. It could work here, too. If you'd just let him bring Lily—"

He held up a hand, stopping her in midsentence. "No. We've discussed this before, and school is no place for a dog. Pets need to stay at home."

Megan bristled. "Lily isn't a pet. She's a trained service dog. Think of her like a personal aide for Owen." The idea of an aide had been floated before, but since All Saints was a private school, she'd been told she'd have to pay out of pocket. The cost was well outside her stretched-to-the-breaking-point budget. "Public schools allow aides for special needs children on a regular basis."

"But Lily would be an aide who might pee on the carpet or bite a child."

"Oh please. Lily's more potty trained than some of your students. And she doesn't bite." Unlike Owen, who had bitten a student at his last private school, resulting in his having to change schools. Paradise was a small town and if he was expelled from All Saints, she was pretty much out of options. The public schools for Paradise were on the mainland, and Megan wanted to avoid that kind of travel for Owen, if at all possible. She couldn't let him be expelled.

"Other schools have made it work, with no adverse outcomes." Technically, only three schools—at least, that she had found. All small private schools, like All Saints. But that didn't mean the idea wasn't a good one, just that it wasn't widely accepted yet. "I've brought a letter from the principal of one of them, detailing how having a service dog in the classroom has reduced behavioral problems and improved learning outcomes for his students with disabilities." She practically threw the paper on his desk as she continued, afraid if she stopped talking he'd tell her to take Owen and leave.

"This is an overview of the training Lily has had, and what she's able to do—" she added the glossy brochure "—and, finally, this is the log showing the improvement in Owen's anxiety and outbursts since getting Lily, as documented by his therapist." She dropped the thick stack of handwritten notes onto the pile and took a much needed breath of air. "I'm sure, if you'd just consider it, you'd see the benefit of Owen having Lily with him."

"Be that as it may—"

"Just read them." This time it was her turn to interrupt. "Please," she added, hating that she had to beg, that she was so utterly powerless. But then, it was a familiar feeling.

After a much too long silence, he sighed and nodded, the furrow between his tired eyes deepening.

"Really? I mean, thank you."

He shook off her gratitude and stood. "Don't thank me, I'm not agreeing to anything other than reading the information you brought. Beyond that… I just don't want you to get your hopes up."

Too late. Hope was about all she had some days, and she guarded it as fiercely as she did her son. Without faith, she'd never had made it this far, and Luke Wright had just given her fading optimism a fresh infusion of the stuff. "Of course not," she lied. "But I really think this could work. And I'm happy to answer any questions you have about how to implement things."

"I'll contact you after I've had to a chance to work through it. In the meantime, you may want to consider pursuing…alternative arrangements."

In other words, she needed to look for yet another school. As if she hadn't already researched to death every educational facility on the island. All Saints was the best. The public school system wanted him to attend a special program over an hour away, on the mainland. And the only private schools they hadn't already tried had already politely but firmly declined her inquiries. Besides, All Saints was academically one of the top schools in the state and, despite his challenges, Owen was extremely bright. He deserved the kind of education he would get here.

And the man who would decide everything was already standing, a not-so-subtle hint that it was time for her to go. Fine. She'd leave, for now.

"I look forward to discussing this once you've had a chance to read everything over." He nodded absently, but his gaze was already back on the spreadsheet program open on his laptop monitor. As far as he was concerned, the matter was settled. But Megan wasn't giving up. When it came to Owen, she didn't know how.

"So when should we meet?" She smiled, enjoying the befuddled look on his face when he registered her words.

"Excuse me?"

"When should we meet to discuss your thoughts on

the research material? About service dogs in the classroom?"

He sighed, and she knew she'd won the battle if not
the war. He opened a calendar app on his computer
and, after a minute of searching, clicked on a blank
space. "Let's do Monday right before dismissal, say
two thirty?"

She nodded and stood. It was only fifteen minutes,
but it was something. Extending a hand, she thanked
him, her mind already racing to the possibilities that
would open up for Owen if they could make this work.

As his hand enveloped hers, a jolt of awareness shook
Megan from her thoughts, tiny pinpricks of energy zing-
ing from her fingertips all the way to her toes. Her head
snapped up, searching for the source even as some long-
dormant part of her brain registered and cataloged the
sensation.

Attraction. Pure, physical, sexual attraction.

Jerking her hand back, she rubbed her palm on the
leg of her jeans, as if lust was some kind of contami-
nation that could just be wiped off. Yes, he was one of
the most attractive men she'd ever met, not to mention
intelligent and competent, but that didn't mean her hormones had permission to come out to play. Not now,
and not with this man. She had a mission to accomplish,
and nothing was going to stand in her way.

Chapter Two

Luke watched the door close and let out a breath as he sank back in his chair. He wasn't sure when, exactly, he'd lost control of the meeting, but he definitely had. Maybe around the time she'd started teasing him about his ignorance of color schemes.

He'd planned to list the reasons why Owen would be better served in a different, perhaps more specialized, environment. Maybe even start the withdrawal paperwork. Instead, she'd roped him into reading a stack of research and another meeting, neither of which he had time for. But he couldn't say no to her. Not because of his attraction—he was professional enough to set that aside. It was her fierce dedication to her son that got to him.

In his time as a teacher and now as an administrator,

he'd seen too many kids fall through the cracks. Kids who'd needed a bit of extra help but whose parents had been too busy or too oblivious to notice. Kids he'd tried to help. But even the best teacher couldn't take the place of a supportive family. He'd often found himself staring at the ceiling late at night, wondering what had happened to them once they'd moved to a different school and beyond his influence.

Owen would never be one of those kids, not with Megan Palmer ready to go all mama bear on anyone or anything that stood in her way. He admired her for it, and was grateful for Owen's sake, even if it made his own life harder. Hell, what was one more impossible dilemma in a job packed full of them? His nameplate said Principal but in reality the job was a mishmash of therapist, CEO, fundraiser, bookkeeper, and circus ringleader. Oh, and handyman, if you included the times he was called to unstick a window or to replace a loose doorknob. All for a salary that looked okay on paper but was almost entirely consumed by his titanic-size student loan payments.

Luke could have made more if he'd gone to a larger school in a more populated area. Places like New York State tended to pay a much higher wage to educational professionals. But you couldn't put a price tag on endless days of sunshine or small-town camaraderie. He'd discovered Paradise on a weekend fishing trip during his first year teaching and had been captivated by the tiny island perched on the edge of the sea. He'd squeezed in as many visits as possible between working and grad school. When a position had opened up at

All Saints, he'd jumped at the chance to move to Paradise full-time.

He was young to be a principal, with less experience than some on the board had wanted, but he'd convinced them to take a chance. Being willing to accept the less than stellar compensation package probably hadn't hurt. And now he needed to prove to them, and to himself, that he was up for the job. That meant keeping the parents happy, the students learning, and the donations flowing. It did not mean spending the weekend researching service dogs, or skipping lunch to have a follow-up meeting to discuss the situation. And yet that's what he had just agreed to do. Because doing the job was one thing, doing right by the kids—by Owen—was another.

The problem was that Owen Palmer's needs had to balance with the needs of his classmates, his teachers, and the school as a whole. Having a dog at school just wasn't tenable. A handful of paperwork wouldn't change that. Yet Luke found himself reaching for the information Owen's mother had left behind instead of clicking on the budget spreadsheet he should be wrangling. Maybe he could skim over the information now, and be done with it.

When the end-of-day bell rang two hours later, he was still reading and had a full page of notes scribbled on the back of the latest flyer announcing the fundraiser. Dazed, he stretched his neck from side to side. How had it gotten so late? He needed to be out in the hallways, supervising dismissal.

Technically, his staff could handle it, but he liked

to make himself available. Often a kid who didn't feel comfortable coming into the office would be willing to approach him in the more casual, albeit chaotic, setting. More than once, he'd learned of a bullying issue that way, and been able to nip it in the bud. Of course, dismissal was also prime time for parents to corner him, and although he made a point of taking every concern seriously, he couldn't help but notice a few of the single mothers manufactured reasons to start a conversation.

However, a few romantically minded mothers were no reason to shirk his duty to the kids, so he stood and, with a sigh, shut down his laptop and secured it in the drawer. Once the halls were clear, he'd put in a few more hours and then no doubt take it home to work the weekend. Oh well, it wasn't as if he had anything else to do. His modest house took little time to clean, a teen down the street looking to earn gas money had suckered him into paying for lawncare, and his social life was nearly nonexistent.

Not that there weren't offers—and not just from the single parents of his students. But the few times he'd taken a woman out it had felt more like a job interview than a date. He'd gone into it hoping for some laughs, conversation, maybe a good-night kiss, and the whole time his date had been sizing him up as future husband potential. No way was he ready for that. He had enough responsibility on his shoulders, thank you very much.

Having an administrator's position at his age was an amazing stroke of luck, but it also meant he needed to work his butt off to prove himself. If he messed up, there would be no allowances made for inexperience.

Going back down the career ladder tended to be a lot rougher of a ride than going up. Later, much, *much* later, when he was more settled in his career, maybe he'd be ready to settle down. Until then, he'd keep things casual. Surely, there were a few women left just looking for a good time.

A flash of blond hair, blue eyes, and long, lean legs appeared unbidden in his mind's eye. Again his palm tingled as if her skin had left a permanent imprint on his. If a simple handshake felt like a lightning strike, what would it be like to really touch her?

He shook the thought off. Megan Palmer was exactly the kind of woman he wasn't looking for. And by this time Monday, after he'd told her no for the last time, she'd be out of his life forever.

Today was just her day to deal with obstinate males, Megan decided with a huff of annoyance. She'd left the meeting at the school feeling at least somewhat optimistic about her powers of persuasion, but her confidence had been short-lived.

"I'm not hungry."

She sucked in a breath and counted to ten, keeping her temper in check as Owen stubbornly stared at her over a plate of chicken fingers. Homemade chicken fingers, from a recipe she'd found online. The food blogger had promised they were identical to the fast-food ones her son loved.

Owen disagreed.

Strongly.

His six-year-old palate was more sensitive than the

average consumer's, or maybe he was just upset that her home-cooked version didn't come with a toy like the ones from the drive-through. Regardless, he refused to touch them. Despite his claims to the contrary, she knew he was hungry. And an empty stomach in a small boy was the equivalent of a ticking time bomb. The hungrier he got, the worse his behavior would be. At this point, they were about five minutes away from a full-on meltdown.

He shoved the plate farther away, nearly upsetting his pint-size cup of milk.

Five minutes may have been too generous.

Megan moved the milk a few inches over and considered her options. She could continue to force the issue, and deal with the ensuing meltdown. Plenty of the parenting books piled on her nightstand advised exactly that. But the authors of those books had never met Owen. Techniques that worked for neurotypical children often seemed to completely fail when it came to kids like her son. Or maybe she was the failure and a better, stronger parent would be able to win this battle of wills.

The easiest thing to do would be to give in. To pack Owen in the car and take him for the real deal. The excitement might help him keep it together until he actually ate. Yet, as tempting as the idea was, any short-term relief would be overshadowed by long-term consequences. Parenting Owen required flexibility, yes, but she couldn't let him think of her as a pushover, either.

Firm but fair. That's what Owen's therapy team had advised, which sounded great in the office, but wasn't quite specific enough for this situation. She looked over at her son and her breath caught. His expression was defiant though his eyes were glassy with tears he was desperately trying not to shed. Her own stung in response to the toughness and vulnerability she knew warred within him. He'd had a hard day, too, and now he was tired, and hungry, and just as frustrated as she was. Lying politely under the table, Lily's head pressed against Owen's bare foot, showing that she, also, had sensed the rising emotional tide within him.

Your child isn't giving you a hard time; he's having a hard time.

She'd read that somewhere and, at the time, had viewed it as a lightbulb moment. Sometimes, though, like tonight, when she was preoccupied by a million things, it was easy to forget they were on the same team. Her job was to be his coach, not his enemy. Yes, that meant pushing him to do better, to be better, but in the end, their relationship mattered more than the food on the plate.

Rising, she moved to sit next to him instead of across from him, hoping he'd pick up on the change in body language. Even if he didn't, just being close enough to smell his grape-scented children's shampoo helped her find a last shred of patience. He was just a kid. And he needed her help.

"You don't like this food."

He shook his head, his shaggy bangs falling into his eyes. She really needed to bite the bullet and get his hair cut, but one issue at a time.

"Can you tell me why you don't like it?" He just looked at her, and she tried again. "Is it too crunchy?

Too hot?" Children with autism often had sensory issues, experiencing phenomena either more or less than
other people, while also lacking the language skills to
describe their feelings. "I could cut it up for you. Do you
want me to do that?" She was reaching now, but if she
could figure out why Own didn't want the food, maybe
she could fix it, or at least make it differently next time.

His eyes shut: something he did when he was on the
verge of a meltdown. Megan forced herself to be quiet
while he thought. Finally, he opened them and looked
right at her. "Red."

What? She looked at the chicken fingers, no doubt
lukewarm now, and tried to imagine how in the world
they could be too red when they were a lovely golden
brown. Maybe she'd misunderstood and he hadn't meant
the color. "Do you want me to read to you while you
eat?" Not their normal routine, but she was willing if
it would get him eating.

He rolled his eyes and pointed emphatically to an
empty space on the plate. "Red dip."

Understanding nearly clubbed her over the head.
"Ketchup? You need ketchup to dip the chicken in?"

He nodded, and she wondered how she could have
forgotten. He always dipped his chicken in ketchup, or
"the red dip," as he called it. Of course, a typical kid
would have simply asked for ketchup rather than refuse
to eat, but Owen wasn't typical. He probably hadn't
known what was missing, either—not a first. Like the
stereotypical absentminded professor, he could recite
endless facts about a topic of interest and yet not notice or retain more mundane information. One more

way in which his condition made everyday life just a bit more difficult.

But, hey, they'd worked it out, right? She retrieved the plastic bottle, squeezed out a generous blob onto his plate, and allowed herself a moment of self-congratulation. She hadn't lost her temper, she hadn't given in, and they'd found a way to work together.

Tonight, success tasted like homemade chicken fingers, and it was good.

Luke's bare feet pounded on the hard-packed sand at the edge of the water, his stride increasing even as his breathing grew ragged. He had a quarter mile left in his three-mile run and nothing as trivial as a lack of oxygen was going to keep him from finishing. No pain, no gain.

He raced for the lifeguard stand that marked his finish point, daring his body to make it just a bit faster than the time before. Lungs burning, he glanced at his watch as he passed the wood structure before allowing himself to collapse to his knees.

"You all right down there?" A teen sporting a thick coat of zinc oxide and a concerned look watched from the platform.

"Fine," he huffed. "Just…catching…my breath."

"Uh-huh," the boy answered, sounding skeptical. "You need to be careful of heatstroke in this weather. Had to call an ambulance for a guy last week because of it."

"I don't need an ambulance." This time Luke managed to string all the words together without taking a breath, hopefully proving his point. It had been an ugly run, several minutes slower than his typical pace, and yeah, he'd felt every one of the humid ninety degrees the weatherman had warned about. But he was in good shape and he'd stayed hydrated. He made a show of lifting his water bottle to his lips and draining what was left, making it clear he wasn't some dumb tourist who needed to be saved from himself.

No, he was a dumb native who should know better than to make his run in the middle of the day. Normally, he exercised in the morning, before the sun was high, like any sane person. But he'd had a sleepless night, finally dozing off a little before dawn. By the time he'd woken, it was late morning and hot enough to make the devil sweat. A sane person would have skipped the run, or at least postponed it until evening. Not him.

If he'd been trying to punish himself, he'd succeeded. His muscles were cramping, sweat stung his eyes, and he was embarrassingly close to upchucking the banana he'd eaten for breakfast. Mindful of the lifeguard as well as the sunbathers lining the shore, he managed to haul himself to his feet before a well-meaning townsperson decided he needed rescuing.

Moving slowly but steadily, he waded out into the gently rolling waves, letting the primal rhythms of the surf wash some of the tension from his body. He kept his gym membership current for the occasional bout of bad weather, but a run on the beach, even a really crappy run, beat the treadmill any day. And a dip in the ocean was a thousand times better than a lukewarm petri dish of a hot tub. And that was why he'd been so

eager to move to Paradise. Half floating, half swim-
ming, he let the current carry him and the stresses of
the past week away.

Well, most of them. It seemed even the powers of
sun, surf, and sand couldn't sway Megan Palmer out
of his head. He'd tried to focus on the budget last night
when he'd finally gotten home, but instead had ended
up wading through the rest of the literature she'd left
with him. Then, curiosity piqued, he'd spent another
few hours on the internet researching service dogs and
their work with autistic children. He had to admit, some
of the stories seemed nearly miraculous, and if Owen's
dog was half as helpful as the ones he'd read about, he
could understand why his mother was pushing so hard
for access to the classroom.

No yet completely won over, he was at least no longer
adamant about dismissing the idea out of hand. But it
wasn't the dog or Owen that had kept him tossing and
turning, tangled in sweaty sheets, half the night. It was
Megan herself. Her tousled hair, which he ached to run
his fingers through. Her clear blue eyes, the same shade
as the ocean that surrounded him now. And her skin...
Dear lord, he wanted to touch every inch of it, to taste
it, to bury himself in the sweet softness of her. Even
now, chest-deep in the chilly waters of the Atlantic, his
body reacted to the thought of her.

Frustrated, he turned against the current and shifted
into an efficient crawl stroke. He hadn't been able to
outrun the lust, but maybe he could drown it. Reach,
pull, turn, breathe...the steady rhythm had always been
enough to calm him. Exercise had gotten him through

the hormone surges and teenage crushes of puberty, and later the anxiety of college exams and job interviews. But this time, there was no peace.

He had no idea what to do about that.

Chapter Three

Saturday was her favorite day of the week. Weekdays were about school and filled with worry about how Owen was doing and whether or not she'd get a call to pick him up early. Sundays were for church—where she had to endure disapproving stares as Owen bounced and fidgeted in the pew until the kids were dismissed for Sunday school—and readying for a new week. But Saturdays, there were no obligations to meet, no one's schedule to obey. They could, and often did, spend the whole day just hanging out in the yard with Lily. And that was where they were now, Megan in a faded lawn chair and Owen knee-deep in a muddy hole.

Her phone started buzzing in the pocket of her cut-offs. Tugging it out, she glanced at the screen even though she knew who it would be. Her mother called every Saturday morning, no matter where she was in the world. Sometimes, like now, that meant they were crossing time zones, but thanks to modern technology her mother's voice sounded as clear as if she were down the street instead of half a world away.

"Hey, Mom."

"Hay is for horses," she responded automatically, as Megan knew she would. Her mother's gentle corrections were as predictable as her call schedule and, although they'd driven Megan to distraction as a kid, by her teens she'd found amusement in provoking them on purpose. "How's my favorite daughter?"

"I'm your only daughter, and I'm fine. How are you? Enjoying Brussels?"

Although her father's military career had ended two years ago, his technical skills and decades of experience had led to a second career as a consultant on nuclear technology. Instead of settling down, they still traveled the world. Megan was proud of them, but thought it would be nice for Owen to have grandparents around.

Tim's parents had moved to North Carolina shortly after his death, as if by escaping the state they could escape the grief of losing their only child. They sent Owen a card with a five dollar bill in it twice a year for his birthday and Christmas, but had never come back to visit.

At least her parents tried to create a sense of family, and Owen looked forward to their brief visits the few times a year they managed to make it into the same time zone. And they did love her. But long-distance love—no matter how strong—wasn't the same as having someone in your life day in and day out. And her father's career came first. Or, as he would phrase it, service to country came first. If they hadn't been willing to settle down when she'd been a child, they weren't going to do it now.

So Megan half listened while her mother described the amazing food and the less than amazing public transportation, only barely rolling her eyes when she referred to the furnished apartment they'd been given as "home." Her parents were firm believers in "home is where the heart is," but Megan wasn't so sure. Yes, home was about love and family, but she'd spent her whole life craving more, needing somewhere to spread roots that wouldn't be torn apart and dug up at a moment's notice.

"So, what do you think?" Her mother's question held an uncharacteristic note of impatience, making Megan think she must have repeated it more than once.

"Sorry, Mom, I lost the connection there for a minute," she fibbed. "What do I think about what?"

"Meeting us in the mountains for Thanksgiving. We could rent one of those vacation cabins in North Carolina or Georgia or wherever, and have an old-fashioned family holiday. What do you say?"

Megan bit her tongue, her thoughts tumbling too widely for her to voice them. Time with her family sounded wonderful, but would it be worth the fallout, behavior wise, of upsetting Owen's routine? Not to mention the logistics of a road trip with a first-grader and a dog.

As if reading her mind, her mother hastily added,

"We'd pay to fly you and Owen up, of course. Oh, wait, can Lily fly?"

Megan stifled a giggle at the mental image of the big Labrador with wings, flapping her way across the sky. "If you mean will the airlines let her on board, yes. As a service dog, she can sit in the cabin with us."

"Then it's settled. I'll start looking for reservations today."

"Mom! I didn't actually say yes yet."

"But you will, right?"

Megan wanted to be annoyed, but her mother's enthusiasm was contagious. And hadn't she just been wishing for more time with her family, for more shared memories? Sure, she'd hoped they would come to her, but a rented place in the Great Smoky Mountains was a lot closer than Europe. And that was how she ended up saying, "Of course, just send me the details." That's how it had always been, her mother diving headlong into a project and everyone else being dragged along before realizing what was happening.

They chatted for a few more minutes and Megan promised to check Owen's school vacation schedule and send her mother the dates he'd be off, not mentioning that there was a good chance he wouldn't even be at All Saints by then. No point in upsetting his grandmother with that little tidbit until and unless she had to.

"Well, I need to go. Your father made reservations for us for dinner and you never know when the tram is going to run. But I'll talk to you next week?"

"Of course. Love you."

"Love you, too."

Megan ended the call and glanced at the time, amazed as always at how exhausting her mother could be, even long distance. The woman had the energy of half a dozen mere mortals, and sometimes her fast-forward approach left Megan a bit disoriented. Still, she didn't hesitate to grab the phone without even looking at it when it rang again a second later, knowing the faster she agreed to whatever vacation detail her mother had forgotten to mention, the easier her weekend would be.

"Mom, I thought you said Dad was in a hurry?"

The line went silent for a beat and then a very male, very not her mother's, voice asked, "I'm sorry, is this Megan Palmer?"

Startled, Megan bobbled the phone trying to see the Caller ID, nearly dropping it in the process. The number was local, but not one she knew. For a split second, she considered hanging up and pretending she'd never said anything, but her ingrained Southern manners wouldn't let her. So she swallowed her embarrassment and replied, "This is she," as though she hadn't just called some strange man her mother.

"Oh good, I was hoping I would catch you."

Her stomach dropped as she realized this wasn't a sales call or a wrong number. No, the voice was familiar, though she couldn't quite place it.

"I'm sorry, who's asking?"

"This is Luke Wright, from All Saints."

Heat flooded her face. She'd worked so hard to be nothing but professional with Owen's principal, and now she'd gone and called him "mom."

"Oh, Principal Wright. I'm so sorry… I thought it was someone else."

"Yeah, I figured that out," he said, his amusement carrying clearly through the line.

Pride straightened her spine. Yes, she should have noticed who was calling, but it had been an honest mistake. He'd never called her directly before, and it was Saturday, for crying out loud. What reason would he have for calling her over the weekend?

Unless…unless he was in such a hurry to expel Owen that he didn't want to wait until Monday. Her brain froze at the thought and it took a second for her to realize he was waiting for a response.

"Um, what can I do for you?"

"Well, I read over the paperwork you left with me, about the service dogs, and had some questions. And, well… I was wondering if it would be possible for me to meet your dog."

"Owen's dog," she corrected automatically, her mind racing ahead to the possibilities. Did this mean he was open to Lily going to school? Surely he wouldn't ask to meet her if he was just going to say no, right? "When would be good?" She'd need to give Lily a bath, maybe spray her with some of that doggy perfume Owen had insisted she buy.

"Actually…" He chuckled, the sound giving her chill bumps despite the heat. "I'm in your driveway right now. I got the idea to come over, and then realized I should've called first. So, um, I'm calling."

He was there. In her driveway.

She looked down at her raggedy shorts and bare feet,

and then across the yard to where Lily and Owen—both covered head to toe in mud—were happily tunneling to nowhere, and wasn't sure if she should laugh or cry. In the end she did neither, and instead directed him to the gate at the side of the house.

A minute later, he rounded the corner, somehow looking impeccably dressed even in casual khaki shorts, a lightweight, short-sleeved button-down, and boat shoes. Self-consciously, she pushed the sagging strap of her stretched-out tank top back into place and forced a smile.

"Can I get you something to drink? I've got iced tea or water."

"Sweet tea?"

"Is there any other kind?" she quipped, pretending an ease she didn't quite feel.

"Not as far as I'm concerned." He grinned and she found herself reciprocating despite her discomfort. "I'd love one, if it isn't too much trouble."

"Not at all. I was about to get a refill anyway." She bent to retrieve her mostly empty glass from where it sat on the concrete slab next to her chair. "I'll be right back."

She debated calling Owen over to say hi and decided against it. He was lost in his own world and she knew that trying to force him out of it would take more effort than it was worth. Besides, she didn't want him overhearing her conversation with his principal. If things went badly, she'd explain it to him later, in private.

Waving the man toward her thrift-store patio furniture, she headed inside, careful to close the sliding door tightly against the oppressive heat. Even now, teetering on the edge of fall, her ancient air conditioner struggled to keep the house at a livable temperature. One more reminder of her precarious bank balance. She'd be happy to leave it all behind once she'd saved up enough money to move to a better house. Something with decent insulation and appliances that weren't older than she was.

But that, Megan reminded herself as she took out a second glass and poured the tea, all depended on her being able to work. She put in long hours at night, when Owen was sleeping, communicating with the overseas consulting firm that had hired her. Her plan had been to do the actual coding work during the day while Owen was at school. In reality, she'd been so tied up in knots worrying over him and how he was adjusting— or rather, not adjusting—that she'd barely managed to get anything done. And staying up even later to catch up was catching up with her. A glance at her reflection in the small window over the sink confirmed that the circles under her eyes would soon take over her face if she didn't get some sleep.

It all hinged on Lily being able to attend All Saints with Owen. She knew what a difference the dog made in his self-control. If he had Lily, he'd be fine. And that decision rested in Luke Wright's hands. Who, at this very minute, was sitting in her backyard. Surely he'd say yes once he saw how well behaved Lily was and the calming influence she had on Owen.

Even now, as she watched through the window, Lily was hovering over Owen, keeping a watchful eye on her small master as he played. But then, as if he could hear his mother thinking about him, Owen paused in his digging and looked up. Megan knew from the look on his face the moment he realized she was no longer on the patio and that someone else was.

And that's when the screaming started.

The first shriek had Luke bolting out of his chair and across the yard before his brain fully registered the sound. The cry was primal, triggering protective instincts he hadn't known he had. As he got closer, the screeching got louder, although he would have sworn a minute ago that that wasn't possible. What on earth could have happened? Bee sting? Fire ants? Pygmy rattlesnake? His mind raced in time with his pounding heart as he reached the boy, who was now curled in a ball, his face pressed against a concerned Labrador.

"Owen, are you all right?"

If he answered, it was swallowed up by the dog's muddy fur. At least the screaming had stopped, replaced by a low whimper that pulled Luke to his knees. Sliding in the mud, he looked for visible injuries, but it was impossible to see anything through the thick layer of dirt coating every inch of the boy's bare skin. He placed a hand on Owen's shoulder to calm him and was greeted by another round of screams.

Hell, he'd been left alone with the kid for all of two minutes and had managed to break him.

"Owen, it's okay. I'm right here." Megan appeared as if by magic, shoving past him in her rush to get to her son. "I just went in the house. I'm sorry, I should have told you." Owen's screeches continued, but the volume had lowered by a few decibels.

"I didn't see what happened." Guilt churned like acid in Luke's stomach. "I ran over as soon as he screamed. Is he okay?"

"He will be, if you'd back off." She glanced up at him from her crouch by the boy's side. "I'm sorry, I didn't mean it that way. It's just…could you give us some space, please?" Worry, and what looked a whole lot like embarrassment, troubled her eyes.

"Um, sure." He retreated to the patio and found the sliding-glass door ajar, an open invitation to mosquitos. She must not have taken time to secure it in her rush to get to Owen.

He just meant to close it, but what he saw through the doorway stopped him. The kitchen floor was awash in broken glass and iced tea, the ambler liquid slowly seeping toward the carpeted living area beyond. A glance over his shoulder showed the now quiet Owen still hunched over his dog, shaking his head at something his mother was saying and showing no signs of moving. Megan looked frustrated, but no longer panicked, which hopefully meant that whatever was wrong wasn't serious. Still, from what he knew of Owen, even a minor upset could take hours to recover from.

That was why he was more than a little surprised when mother and child walked through the back door only fifteen minutes later.

Megan, for her part, looked even more shocked. Mouth open, eyes wide, she looked from the now spot-less floor to where he stood at the stove with a spatula in his hand. "What did you…what are you… What's going on?"

Luke shrugged and flipped a perfectly toasted grilled-cheese sandwich. "I wasn't sure how long you'd be, and it was lunchtime, so I made sandwiches."

She blinked. "You made sandwiches?"

"Uh-huh." He gestured to the pan. "You do like grilled cheese, right?"

She ignored the question and asked her own. "What about the floor?"

"I cleaned it."

"You cleaned it?" she asked incredulously. "You picked up the glass and then…what, mopped my floor?"

He shrugged. "You were barefoot. I didn't want you or Owen to get cut."

"Or Lily," Owen piped up from the entranceway, where he was wiping the mud off the dog's fur with a microfiber towel. "She's barefoot, too. She's always barefoot."

Luke's breath caught. That was the most he'd ever heard Owen say. Even on a good day at school, the boy barely strung two words together. After a meltdown, he was often completely nonverbal.

Luke glanced at Megan to see if she was as shocked by Owen's speech as he was. But she seemed more surprised by his making lunch than by Owen's speaking up. Maybe Owen acted differently on his home turf. Or maybe the dog did make a difference. Even now the little boy kept one grubby hand fisted in the dog's fur, as if somehow drawing strength from the contact.

No, *strength* wasn't the right word. It was something

more subtle than that. *Peace*, maybe. The dog practically radiated a calm confidence that even a skeptic like Luke could feel.

Not wanting to shatter the moment, he kept his tone noncommittal and his gaze averted as he replied. "That's a good point, Owen. Broken glass could have hurt any one of you."

"Well, thank you, I guess." Megan bit her lip, looking wary. "But you didn't have to do that. I could have cleaned it myself."

"I'm sure you could have. But now you don't have to." He slid the last sandwich onto a plate and turned the stove off. "If you want to wash up, I'll put these on the table."

Owen obediently moved to the sink, stepping up on the green wooden stool no doubt put there for just that purpose. Megan moved to follow and then paused, confusion clouding her features. "There are only two sandwiches."

"I'm not really hungry. Besides, after Owen's reaction outside, I figured it might be better if I left." That, and he'd seen the status of her refrigerator and pantry. The food supplies were adequate but very basic. Maybe they were just close to grocery day. But unsure of her financial status, he wasn't about to take food from the mouths of a single mom and her child.

Her lips pursed as if to argue, though it was Owen who won him over.

"I'll share."

The little boy had suds dripping down his arms, mud smeared in his hair, and an intense look on his face. Of course, Owen was always intense. "Sharing is good. I get a sticker when I share."

Luke shook his head. "Yes, sharing is good but—"

"Let him." Megan put a hand on his arm, her touch hotter than the sizzling pan in front of him. Pulling him closer, she lowered her voice. "Spontaneous sharing is something his therapist is working with him on. It's a big deal. Please."

Megan hated to beg, but she would have gotten down on her knees if it meant keeping Luke from messing up this moment. An image of her on her knees before him, for a very different reason, flashed in her mind and her face grew hot. Where had that come from? She had no business even thinking such things with Owen in the room. Owen, who was having a breakthrough right this minute. She should be celebrating with him, not fantasizing about his principal.

Luke's eyes searched hers, but if he'd picked up on her wayward thought, he didn't say anything. Instead, he just nodded and grabbed a third plate. "Thanks, buddy. That's really nice of you."

She let out a breath. Crisis averted.

Turning back to Owen, she smiled brightly, letting her pride in his generosity push away any other thoughts. "That was so generous of you to share. Why don't you go put a sticker on your chart right now, before you forget?"

He grinned at her praise before darting off to his room, and her heart thumped an extra beat. Raising

Owen was hard, but moments like this made all the work worthwhile.

"Thank you," she said to Luke.

He shrugged and slid a small sliver of Owen's sandwich onto his own plate. "Will this be enough to count as sharing? I don't want him to go hungry just to be polite."

His concern touched her. "That should be fine. It's the thought that counts." Except for her earlier erotic thoughts about him. Those definitely did not count. They were just a weird stress reaction or something.

"Okay." Awkwardly, he folded himself into one of the chairs at her small kitchen table, his legs a bit too long to fit under it. He was too big for her kitchen, too big for her house. No wonder her thoughts kept turning to him; he filled the space in a way that went beyond the physical. He just had a presence—a very male one— that felt out of place in her little house. For so long, it had been just her and Owen. She wasn't even sure she remembered how to have a meal with another adult.

But she needn't have worried. Owen monopolized the conversation to an extent that she couldn't get a word in edgewise. Well, he and Luke, with Owen peppering the man with questions and Luke doing his best to keep up. All the while, Lily sat quietly at Owen's side, her head in his lap.

Several times Megan caught Luke watching Owen's interaction with Lily. Did he see the way Owen always reached for her before speaking? Had he noticed Owen getting upset when he dropped his fork, only to calm when Lily nuzzled his arm? Surely, he'd seen the way the dog had helped him cope with his earlier outside fear.

Or had the meltdown only further reinforced the man's belief that Owen needed to find a different school? The sandwich that had been so delicious a moment before turned to sawdust in her mouth at the thought. It was certainly possible that he'd come out here over the weekend because he hadn't wanted Owen returning to the school on Monday. Otherwise, why not wait to discuss things during the meeting they'd scheduled? Was he so eager to kick her son out that he'd made a special trip to deliver the news?

The anxiety she'd been keeping at bay began clawing its way to the surface, seeking an outlet. Nearly choking on it, Megan forced herself to swallow as she got to her feet. "I...just remembered I left something on the patio. I'll be back in a minute."

Outside, the heavy, humid air offered no respite from the fear weighing her down. Struggling to breathe past the panic, she scanned the small yard for a distraction.

Behind her, the door squeaked open and then shut, too softly for it to be Owen.

"Is everything okay?"

The sheer audacity of the question had her whirling to face him. "Why don't you tell me?"

"What?" Confusion shadowed his almost too perfect features. The look might have been comical in another situation. One that didn't stand to ruin all the progress she'd made these past few years.

"Are you kicking Owen out of school? Is that why you're here?" She fought to keep from shouting, all too aware of her son's proximity and the less than sound-proof nature of her flimsy windows. "Because if that's what you have to say, then no, everything is definitely not okay."

"Whoa, slow down." He raised his hands as if in self-defense. "That's not why I came here."

"It's not?" Her heartbeat, which a minute ago had been roaring in her ears, slowed enough for her to hear the cicadas chattering in the trees. "Then why?"

He shrugged, looking almost boyish. "I don't know exactly. But I was up last night researching service dogs—"

"You were?" Hope surged, crowding out her earlier panic. "You read the materials I left with you?"

He nodded. "That and a lot else. Google was pretty helpful, but I realized I wasn't going to be able to make a decision until I'd actually met Lily. Just because some other dog was amazing didn't mean your dog wouldn't be an untrained nightmare. I found plenty of stories about fake service dogs, you know."

Color flooded her cheeks at the accusation. "Lily is not a fake!"

"No, she's not," he conceded with a sheepish grin. "As far as I can tell, she's exactly what you say she is. But I had to find out. I couldn't just take your word for it. Trust has to be earned."

Megan nodded, for once in full agreement.

She didn't trust him any more than he trusted her. But, for Owen's sake, she was willing to try. "So does this mean Owen can bring Lily to school? Has she proved herself to you?" She suddenly noticed the mud marring Luke's previously spotless casual wear and cringed. "I mean, I know today wasn't a great introduction…what with Owen freaking out and the broken glass and…" Hell, she was making things worse.

Unperturbed, Luke rocked back on his heels as he considered. "Honestly, I don't know. I mean, how a dog acts in her own backyard isn't really indicative of how she'll behave in a classroom full of kids."

"Lily's wonderful in crowds." Surety filled her voice with confidence. She might question her own competence, but she had full faith in Lily's abilities.

Luke nodded, as if he'd expected that to be her response. "Well then, why don't we put her to the test?"

"What kind of test?"

"That's up to you. I'll give you and Owen and Lily the rest of the weekend to convince me she can handle herself in any situation. If you can prove to me that she's going to be an asset in the classroom, I'll agree to a trial run at the school." He arched one eyebrow. "What do you say? Are you up for the challenge?"

Her mind raced. A chance to keep Owen at the school, with Lily by his side? She'd agree to pretty much anything for that. Yet, even as she nodded her acceptance, another more primal part of her sounded warning bells. If thirty minutes with Luke Wright was enough to send her hormones into overdrive, how was she going to handle the rest of the weekend with him?

Chapter Four

Luke had thought he'd been pretty much everywhere in Paradise, which wasn't saying much given the size of the island town. But the splash pad was one place he'd missed. An omission that he was making up for now, thanks to his impulsively offered challenge. It wasn't bad, really, if you didn't mind 100-degree temperatures and screaming children darting in every direction. Thankfully, as a Florida native and professional educator, neither fazed him.

And he couldn't deny the lure of the place. There were gentle sprays of mist for toddler-size kiddos, water cannons swivel-mounted for the older kids' battles, a variety of dancing jets leaping in graceful but unpredictable arches, and, right in the center of it all, a giant bucket that dumped a miniature tsunami of water every few minutes. It definitely beat the childhood afternoons he'd spent playing in the lawn sprinkler. If he hadn't been still damp from cleaning off the mud from earlier, he might have been tempted to join in.

"Sunscreen?" Megan held out a tube of SPF 30 that promised long-lasting, waterproof protection.

"I'm good, thanks." He planned to observe, not participate. He'd staked out a bench under one of the colorful canopies along the perimeter of the park and had every intention of staying on it for the duration.

"You have to wear sunscreen at the splash pad." Owen squinted up at him, frowning. "It's a rule."

Megan shrugged in apology. "It is a rule, Owen, but—"

"But I didn't know about it. Now I do, so I'll put some on. I wouldn't want to get in trouble." Luke winked at Megan and squeezed out a healthy dollop of the coconut-scented lotion. "What about Lily, does she need some, too?"

He'd been joking, but Owen nodded earnestly. "Everyone does—that's how rules work."

Luke's jaw dropped as Megan carefully applied a tiny dab of sunscreen to the dog's nose before sending the duo to play. "Did you just put sunscreen on a dog?" He'd had several dogs growing up, and he couldn't remember any of them getting a sunburn, or even a tan, for that matter.

She nodded, amusement dancing in her eyes. "I did."

"Then either the heat has messed with your thinking, or I missed the newest trend in pet care."

"Neither. Owen used to fight me about the sunblock.

He hates the feel of it. I'd always put some on myself, even if I was staying in the shade, just to set a good example, but it was still a struggle. Then one day, as a joke, I put some on Lily. He thought that was fantastic and hasn't given me a hard time since."

"I take it back, you're a genius."

Her lips curved up at the compliment, but she shook her head. "I'm just a mom, doing whatever it takes to get through the day."

She was being too modest. He'd seen enough parents to know that she was one of the best, but telling her so would just make her uncomfortable. Better to change the focus back to the reason for today's outing. "So tell me, how does Lily make things easier? What is she trained to do?" He'd read about the various tasks service dogs could do, but only in a general sense. This was a specific dog, going into a specific situation—namely his school—and he needed to be prepared.

"Look and see." Megan pointed to a spot halfway across the splash park, where Owen was standing with his foot half on, half off a crescent-shaped sprinkler. "That's Owen's favorite part of the splash pad. He likes the way the water feels on his feet, and he likes the pattern the spray makes."

"Okay." Luke waited, sensing there was more.

"See the little girl walking up? She probably wants to play in it, too, but he likes having it to himself. Watch how he tenses up."

He wouldn't have picked up on it if she hadn't said something but, looking carefully, he could see a stiffness in the boy's posture that hadn't been there before. "I do."

"So does Lily. Or maybe she just senses it, or smells some chemical change… I don't really know. But she knows he is getting upset. Watch."

Sure enough, the dog, who a moment before had been sitting a few inches away from Owen, got to her feet and moved in closer until she was leaning into him, unmindful of the water jets now soaking her fur.

At her touch, Owen turned his gaze away from the approaching child and down to the dog. His hand reached to grip her fur, much as he had in the backyard earlier. With that contact, his ramrod posture softened, his shoulders dropping into a more relaxed position.

Megan smiled at the change, her own body language softening. "Lily is trained to pick up on Owen's meltdowns, or any emotional upheaval. If he gets upset, she provides physical pressure. If he's standing, like he is there, she will lean into him until he acknowledges her. If he's seated, she lays her head in his lap and presses down slightly."

"Like a weighted blanket?" He'd seen references to those in some of the literature on autism. Something about the pressure they provided was supposed to decrease the body's stress response and help children regulate their emotions. He'd thought it a scam, designed to con desperate parents looking for help.

"Sort of, yes. But when you add the emotional bond that Owen has with Lily, it's even more effective."

Luke rubbed the back of his neck as he admitted, "I didn't actually think those things worked."

"The blankets? Or service dogs for kids with autism?"

"Both, I guess." Damn, when had he gotten so jaded? "Maybe I need a service dog. One to alert whenever I'm being a closed-minded jerk."

"Nah, you seem to be pretty good at figuring it out on your own. You're here, aren't you?"

"For the duration."

"Which proves that you are willing to be open-minded. I can't imagine that standing around a splash pad, sweating to death, is your idea of a good time. Yet you're here anyway. Because of Owen. Because you care."

He nodded slowly, unsure of how to respond. Not only since she was wrong about this being a good time—he was enjoying himself just fine—but because he was afraid that his reasons for being there were more complicated than his professional concern for a student. And complications were exactly what he didn't need.

Megan ruffled her son's damp hair and surreptitiously checked that his seat belt was fastened securely. Since graduating to a high-back booster, he'd insisted on buckling himself in and, as much as she wanted to embrace each small step toward independence, she also wasn't going to take any chances with his safety.

Satisfied he was secure, she tossed the bag with his damp suit and towel on the floorboard before getting in herself. Luke, looking ridiculously cool and collected given the record-breaking heat, was already buckled into the passenger seat.

"Where to next?" he asked.

"You're sticking with this, huh?" After two-plus hours of splash pad chaos, she'd half expected him to make some excuse about a forgotten obligation and head home to salvage what was left of the weekend.

"You didn't think I was going to bail on you, did you?"

She flushed as the truth hit home. She'd been thinking exactly that. "Not exactly," she lied. "But you're a busy guy…" And babysitting a single mom, a difficult kid, and a wet dog couldn't be much fun for him.

"I'm not any busier than I was this morning when I agreed to give Lily a chance." His voice deepened and, for a second, she wondered if that was what he sounded like in bed. "I don't break my promises. If I say I'm going to do something, I do it."

"I'll keep that in mind." Great, now she was hijacking his weekend and had insulted his integrity. Perhaps her people skills had deteriorated more than she'd realized over the past few years. She hadn't exactly had the time for socializing or small talk. Still, that was no excuse for rudeness. She couldn't hold Owen accountable for his actions if she wasn't willing to do the same for herself. "I mean… I'm sorry. I shouldn't have doubted you."

He quirked an eyebrow at her apology, something she'd noticed him doing whenever she said something he hadn't expected. "No worries. But that still leaves the question of what's next."

Grateful for the change in subject, Megan put the car in Reverse and carefully backed out onto the street.

"Errands. Nothing very exciting, I'm afraid. I've got to drop off a few things at the post office and we've got library books that need to be returned." She told herself not to feel guilty. It had been his idea to observe how Lily and Owen interacted in everyday life. She just hadn't realized how boring that life was until seeing it through someone else's eyes.

"Perfect."

"It is?" she blurted. Yeah, her people skills definitely needed work.

"Yeah. I need to buy some stamps anyway, and I have some books on hold at the library, so I can pick them up while we are there."

"Oh. Okay." So maybe her life wasn't that abnormal, after all. Still, she had a hard time believing he didn't have other, better ways to spend his time.

Idling at one of Paradise's few stoplights, she tried to give him one last out. "You're sure I'm not keeping you from something? Because I'd understand if—"

His hand on hers stopped her midsentence. She looked to where his fingers, so much larger than her own, rested on hers on the gearshift before his voice drew her eyes to his face. "Don't."

"What? I was just…" Heck, what had she been about to say? The heat of his skin against hers had erased whatever point she'd planned to make. A horn blared and she yanked her hand away, missing the contact even as she accelerated under the now green light.

"Doubting me. I told you not to."

"I wasn't." It wasn't him she had doubts about. Her

second-guessing had nothing to do with him and everything to do with her own insecurities. "I just—"

"You've got to stop saying that."

"Saying what?"

"'I just.'" He'd mimicked her higher voice and grimaced. "Nothing good ever comes after that."

Megan opened her mouth to object but his narrow-eyed stare stopped her. "Fine," she huffed. "It's your weekend to waste." She'd carved out a reasonably good life for herself and Owen, and she wasn't going to let anyone make her feel badly about it.

"Believe it or not, I'm enjoying myself just fine."

She rolled her eyes and turned into the tiny Paradise post office's even tinier parking lot. Snagging a space near the front, she offered to leave the air running if he wanted to wait in the car.

"No way," he said with an easy grin. "Remember, I need stamps."

"Suit yourself."

Inside, Megan took her place in line, trying to mentally calculate how long each person ahead of her would take by packages they held. Owen wasn't a big fan of lines and, honestly, neither was she. She kept telling herself she'd set up a business shipping account so she could do this from home, but pickup cost extra and it didn't seem worth the money. At least, not until she was stuck in line behind a grandmother attempting to mail half a dozen packages, all unlabeled, to an equal number of places. Right now, shipping premiums seemed like an absolute bargain. At least Owen wasn't whining about how long it was taking. Not that she would have blamed him.

Glancing down to tell him as much, she realized that somewhere between the woman shipping individual bottles of essential oils—while describing the supposedly miraculous attributes of each in detail, loudly, and the forgetful granny still trying to figure out which package went to which grandchild—Owen had left her side.

That was fine; it wasn't as if he could get lost in a building not much bigger than the postage stamps Luke had come in for, and Lily knew to stay with him. Still, it wasn't like him. More curious than concerned, she scanned the small, crowded space only to spot him in literally the last place she would have imagined.

Owen, who barely spoke to anyone, who shied away from physical contact with other people, and who had a serious fear of heights, was six feet in the air, perched on Luke's shoulders, and talking with one of the postal employees.

Dying of curiosity, she gripped the thick manila envelope holding the contract for her newest and biggest project and wished she were close enough to hear what they were saying. The sight of her son gesturing animatedly while conversing with a complete stranger was more rewarding than any paycheck, but smiles and social breakthroughs wouldn't pay the electric bill and she'd promised to put the paperwork in the mail today.

So she stood and watched, and wondered what other surprises the weekend might hold.

* * *

Luke winced as little fingers fisted in his hair, but he didn't say anything. He'd seen Owen grip Lily's fur the same way to comfort himself, and if Lily could take it, so could he. Besides, he didn't want to interrupt the conversation. Keeping his own hands firmly anchored around Owen's ankles, Lily's leash looped around one wrist, he listened as the six-year-old rattled off statistics about different species of shark to the delight of a postal employee named Greg.

It seemed that stocking the shipping supplies was only Greg's weekend job. During the week, as part of his graduate studies in marine biology, he researched sharks and rays, which explained why he knew so much about the migration patterns of blacktip sharks. But Owen sounded almost as knowledgeable and, as good as the academics were at All Saints, Luke knew darned well the kid hadn't learned this stuff there.

Luke's own knowledge of sharks was limited to what he'd picked up from TV specials during Shark Week, so he just listened as terms like *dermal denticles* and *ampullae of Lorenzini* flew over his head, both figuratively and literally. When Owen had tugged at his hand and pointed up at a poster advertising an upcoming series of stamps depicting various aquatic life, Luke had assumed a childish curiosity and obligingly swept the kid up onto his shoulders to get a better view. Who knew he was dealing with a pint-size Jacques Cousteau?

"Hey, guys. What's going on?" Megan, apparently done with her business, appeared at his side.

He greeted her quizzical smile with a self-deprecating

grimace. "These two brainiacs are showing me up, that's what's happening." He tipped his head at the poster. "Owen wanted to talk about the newest stamp collection. When I couldn't hold up my end of the conversation, Greg here came to my rescue."

Megan's brow creased in confusion, triggering a giggle from Owen. "Greg's an ickyologist!"

"Ichthyologist," Greg corrected with a smile. "And not yet, but I'm working on it. I'm hoping to finish my doctoral research sometime next year."

"Ah!" Understanding eased the wrinkles between her eyes. "Talking sharks, huh?"

"Shark is about the only word I did understand. The rest was way above my pay grade."

"Don't feel bad," Megan assured Luke, her eyes twinkling. "He surpassed my knowledge on the subject a while ago. Thankfully the library has a great marine science section and sets aside any new shark books for Owen when they come in."

Glancing at the clock on the wall, she sent her son a pointed look. "Speaking of which, if we're going to get the new ones, we'd better get moving. They close early on the weekends." She paused, and her smile softened as she turned to Greg. "Thank you for…" Her voice faltered and Luke saw her swallow hard before continuing. "For talking with him. Not everyone would have taken the time."

"Hey, I was happy to do it. He's a great kid. You should bring him over to Harbor Branch sometime. We do tours, and if you call ahead, I'll see if I can take him back into the lab."

Owen bounced in excitement at the offer, nearly unseating himself from his perch. Megan simply nodded, her eyes shining, and took down the young man's contact information before leading the way to the car. Her pride in her son was obvious, shining brighter than the hot Florida sun beating down on the asphalt parking lot.

"Does that kind of thing happen often?" Luke asked once they were back in the car and headed for the library.

Megan glanced in the rearview mirror before answering, probably checking that Owen still had his headphones on and couldn't overhear.

"Almost never. In fact, I can't remember the last time he voluntarily spoke to a stranger. When I saw what was happening, I couldn't decide which was more shocking— him talking to someone he didn't know, or doing it from so high up in the air! He's afraid of heights," Megan clarified, slowing for a crossing pedestrian. "But he seemed totally relaxed on your shoulders."

"Well, I don't know about relaxed." Luke rubbed his sore scalp ruefully. "He was holding on for dear life. But he definitely seemed content enough, once he had someone who could keep up with what he was saying. How did he learn all that anyway?"

"Documentaries, books, the internet, museums... He's pretty obsessed. It's common for children with autism to have perseverations—special interests that they obsess about."

"Like dinosaurs or trains, or something?" Luke was pretty sure he'd read about that on one of the websites he'd looked at last night.

"Right. For Owen, it's sharks. Well, fish in general, but mostly sharks. You'd think in a coastal town, that would be socially acceptable, but he goes into too much detail for kids his age and they get frustrated."

"I can relate," Luke chuckled.

"Right. And adults don't generally want to sit and talk about fish with a six-year-old. That leaves him—"

"Lonely." Luke had come face-to-face with the feeling himself since moving to Paradise, but he was a grown adult making a career choice, not a little kid seeking acceptance. How much harder must it be for Owen?

"Yes. That's one of the reasons I think it would be so good for him to have Lily at school. He might not always know how to interact with people, but Lily does. She could act as a bridge between him and the other kids in his class."

Luke shook his head at her bulldogged tenacity even as he respected her ability to turn the conversation back to her own agenda. Besides, she did have a point. Right now, Owen was the kid who was different. But with Lily at his side, he'd be the kid with the dog. Definitely a step up in social status. And Luke was the one who could make it happen.

When Megan had first approached him with the idea, his only thought had been the liability. But now he could see how much was at stake. Not just Owen's ability to fit into the classroom, but his entire social experience and how he interacted with others would be affected.

Having Lily in the classroom really did seem to be the best way to help Owen. Although, Luke's sense of professional ethics meant he had to be sure it was safe for everyone, and he felt it on his shoulders like a physical weight. He wanted to do what was right for his school, and for Owen, and, God help him, he wanted to do something to ease the worry he'd detected in Megan's eyes.

"I promise you, if Lily proves herself this weekend, I'll be the first to welcome her to the school on Monday."

Megan nodded, her shoulders still stiff with the responsibility she seemed to always carry. His hand itched to reach out and rub some of that tension away, but he kept it fisted in his lap. Acting on the attraction he felt for her wasn't an option. Still, he hated to think of her dealing with all of this on her own. Owen at least had Lily to comfort him.

Who did Megan have?

Chapter Five

Megan wasn't sure when her anxiety had started to dissipate, but somewhere, between the splash pad, the post office, and the library, her nervousness had faded away, leaving her normally tough outer shell as mushy as the soft-serve mochaccino ice cream Luke had insisted on buying her. Scooping up a spoonful of the icy-sweet stuff, she wondered absently if the sugar high was clouding her thinking, or if it was normal to feel this relaxed when so much was at stake.

It certainly wasn't normal for her, of that she was certain. Worry and doubt were her near constant companions, to the point that she felt somehow irresponsible just sitting back and enjoying the moment.

Yet, there she was, sitting on slightly sticky bench, eating ice cream with a significantly sticky Owen, while

Lily lounged at their feet and Luke, the man who could make or break her son's educational future, fetched more napkins. And instead of freaking out, she was actually having a good time.

And not in the "things could be worse" way, or the "that went as well as could be expected" way. More a real, honest-to-goodness "having a good time" way. She paused, spoon halfway to her mouth, and tried to remember the last time that had happened.

"Is something wrong?" Luke's deep voice startled her from her mental musing and she self-consciously shoved the melting ice cream into her mouth to delay answering. Of course, she'd forgotten how patient he could be. Rather than accept her nonanswer, he leaned against the tabletop and watched her, his eyes never leaving hers as he waited for her to speak.

"No. I was just thinking." Avoiding his gaze, Megan focused on searching out one of the chocolate chunks hidden in the espresso-flavored ice cream.

"About what?"

Patient *and* persistent. Part of her wanted to be annoyed at his scrutiny—the part that was used to focusing on her son, her job, anything other than herself. But some tiny part of the person she'd been before all that found his attention invigorating. It was nice having someone express even casual interest in her thoughts and opinions. Nice enough that she found herself answering more honestly than she'd meant to. "I was thinking about how great today has been."

As soon as the words were out of her mouth, she realized how ridiculous they sounded. Running errands and standing around sweating to death while kids shrieked wasn't what most people would call a stellar day, ice-cream break notwithstanding. "Lame, I know."

Luke shook his head, shoved the last bite of his cone into his mouth, and swallowed. "Nah. Not lame. We'd all be happier if we took the time to appreciate the simpler things in life."

"Like running errands?" she challenged.

"More like sunny days and ice cream." He paused, his gaze lasering on her. "And friends."

"Friends." She repeated the word, the taste of it far sweeter than the mochaccino still coating her tongue. It had been far too long since she'd had a friend.

When she and Tim had first moved to Paradise, she'd gotten to know the other military wives. But those friendships had been too green, too new, to hold fast against the tsunami of grief when he died.

Or maybe the fault had been hers. She'd retreated into herself, like an injured animal going to ground while its wounds healed. Then she'd become consumed by Owen and his needs. Between the demands of parenting and going to school, she hadn't had time to think about friends, let alone to figure out how to make them.

Maybe now it was time. Emboldened by the idea, and the sugar coursing through her veins, she felt confident enough to ask the question that had been on her mind since Luke had showed up on her doorstep this morning. "So, one friend to another, can you tell me what you think so far?"

"About?"

She nodded at Lily, lying at Owen's feet, the remains

of a doggy sundae between her paws. "Lily. The experiment. Everything."

"Ah, that." He tilted his head as if considering.

If she hadn't been so worried about his answer, she'd have pointed out the gesture as a very canine thing to do.

"Honestly..." Luke began, "I'd say it's too soon to tell. She's an amazing dog. I'll give you that. And she's handling the crowds better than some humans I know. But it's only been a few hours, and we're talking about having her in school all day, every day."

Megan's heart sank. Logically, she could appreciate his answer, but she'd hoped for more. Still, it wasn't a no. So she swallowed her disappointment along with the last bit of ice cream and pasted a smile on her face. "Okay. I understand."

"Good. Besides, if I said yes now, I wouldn't get to spend the rest of the weekend with you."

Luke had meant the words to be playful, but one look at Megan's face told him he'd crossed a line with his remark. He'd wanted to reassure her, but somehow he'd ended up flirting instead. At least, that's what he was guessing from the deer-in-the-headlights look she was giving him.

His sun-fried brain tried to come up with a way to explain himself without digging in further, but he couldn't think with her looking at him that way. She was shocked, obviously, at his accidental come-on, but the blush spreading up her cheeks had him wondering if his boundary crossing had been entirely unwelcome.

Inappropriate, yes, but maybe not as upsetting as he'd initially thought.

Not that it mattered. He was her son's principal, and although his offer of friendship was genuine, it wouldn't—couldn't—go further than that. He had a job to do and could not afford to mess it up.

"I mean if I go home now, I'll have to spend the rest of the weekend doing paperwork and going over budgets. I hate budgets. Too many numbers."

"Oh, I see." Megan lowered her head and wiped at some sprinkles sticking to the table. When she looked back up, any sign of embarrassment or confusion was gone. And so was the sparkle in her eyes.

Damn. He'd really stepped in it. Once upon a time, he'd prided himself on his people skills, but his lack of a social life had obviously left him rusty when it came to chatting with a beautiful woman.

And, man, was she beautiful. He'd thought she was sexy in the straitlaced clothes she wore to their meetings at the school, but Megan in a tank top and shorts, with all that tanned skin showing, was mesmerizing. It was no wonder his brain had skipped straight from friendly to flirting—not that it was his brain driving that particular mishap. He'd been fighting a battle between reason and libido since he'd showed up at her house, and his rational side had all but raised the white flag when she'd licked a bit of ice cream from her lower lip. He hadn't stopped staring at her mouth since, wishing he was the one tasting her.

Thankfully, Megan seemed oblivious to the direction his thoughts had taken, at least until his blunder. He didn't need her reporting him to the board for sexual harassment, which meant he needed to hold it together and act like a professional adult, not a hormonal teenager.

Determined to do just that, he sat back under the guise of checking the time on the big clock on the First Coast Bank across the street. "So, what's next on the agenda?"

She glanced down at her watch and winced. "I probably should go to the grocery store and get something to make for dinner, but we've been out and about for so long already, that might be pushing it." Checking to be sure Owen was still more interested in his new library book than adult conversation, she continued. "His sensory issues make grocery shopping hard and, after all the activity today, he's going to need some quiet time. Honestly, we probably should just call it a day."

Luke could understand that, but he also wasn't ready to say goodbye. Thinking quickly, he made a counter offer. "All right, so no grocery store. Would he be okay going somewhere else, somewhere quiet?"

"Maybe. Why?"

"Well, you don't seem to have anything planned for dinner, and my surprise visit threw off your weekend. So how about I feed you dinner to make up for the inconvenience? My place isn't far from here, and Owen can watch TV or hang out in the yard with Lily while I cook. He gets his quiet time, and I get to avoid working on that budget project. It's a win-win."

He saw the hesitation in her eyes and couldn't blame her. Running errands together was one thing; eating dinner at a man's house was another. It was more…

intimate. Part of him knew that was why he'd asked her. Still, it wasn't as if they'd be alone. Owen and Lily would be there to chaperone.

Megan chewed her lip. "You a good cook?"

Sensing victory, he smiled in relief. "I know my way around a kitchen."

"Okay. But whatever you're making, I hope you have ketchup."

Megan didn't often regret a decision once she'd made it. But twenty minutes later, sitting on a stool in Luke's kitchen, she was definitely second-guessing letting him talk her into coming to dinner. Not that he'd done anything wrong. Exactly the opposite. He was being too perfect, and it was freaking her the heck out.

Resisting her feelings, or urges, or whatever it was that made her feel as if her entire body was electrified, was hard enough when they were in public. Here in his small but immaculate kitchen, sipping an amazing wine that he'd poured for her, it was nearly impossible.

She'd chosen a spot where she could watch Owen and Lily through the patio door to avoid staring at Luke, but that only occupied one of her senses. The rest of her was all too aware of the man. How could she not be? He was only steps away, so close she could smell the citrusy cologne he wore. His presence could fill a much larger room and, here in his small kitchen, there was no way to escape it. No way to escape him, or the dormant feelings he'd awakened in her. Longings she'd thought she'd buried with her husband.

It was just the domesticity that got to her, reminding

her of what life had been like when she'd been part of a couple. Simple things like preparing a meal together were what she'd missed most, and it was no wonder that seeing Luke chopping vegetables had her on edge. It was just a reminder of past feelings, that's all.

And yet, when he brushed her arm as he reached for a pot holder, it wasn't Tim she thought of. It wasn't Tim she wanted. The ribbon of need curling inside her wasn't responding to a ghost from the past but to the flesh-and-blood man standing beside her.

"Are you okay?"

Luke's question pulled her from her mental gymnastics, her brain whirring to catch up. "Um, what?"

"I asked if you were okay." He shrugged and gestured vaguely with the half-peeled cucumber still in his hand. "You seem flushed. Need me to turn the AC down?"

More like a cold shower. But she couldn't say that, and she couldn't admit that it had been so long since she'd been in a man's company that something as mundane as watching him chop vegetables was enough to get her hot and bothered. So she shrugged and turned back to the window. "I probably just got a bit too much sun at the splash park today, is all."

He nodded, but she could feel his gaze lingering on her, as if he wasn't quite sure of her answer. No doubt he'd had plenty of chances to hone his personal lie detection abilities in his dealings with hordes of schoolchildren. She hoped she was more adept at covering her feelings than they were.

Not that she *had* any feelings for him other than

friendship. Everything else was just hormones, an unwanted but temporary annoyance. Nothing to get worked up about, even if the warmth flooding her veins said otherwise. She didn't need or want a lover, but she did need a friend. And she was going to ruin any chance of that if she didn't stop acting like some starstruck teen, all tongue-tied and awkward. She could start by keeping up her end of the conversation.

With that in mind, she decided to appease her curiosity. "So, are you from around here? Paradise, I mean?"

He shook his head, looking up only briefly from the pan where he sautéed onions, mushrooms and garlic in sizzling oil. "Not Paradise, no. But not far. I grew up near Gainesville."

"So I assume you're a Gator fan then?"

"Of course. Went to FSU for undergrad and graduate school. Wait, don't tell me you're a Seminole?" He laid a hand on his heart as if being a fan of the rival Florida State University would be an unforgivable crime.

"And if I was?" She grinned, enjoying the banter.

"I may need to ask you to leave." A quick wink assured her his dramatics were all in fun. She found herself smiling despite her earlier discomfort.

"Then I guess it is lucky I'm a Gator grad, too. Technically speaking anyway. I just finished my computer science degree through their online program. So, although I haven't been to any football games, I do have a diploma to prove my allegiance."

"Well then, I guess you can stay."

"Good, because I'm starving and that smells amazing, whatever it is. What are you making anyway?"

72   THE PUPPY PROBLEM

"Pasta with a chunky tomato sauce." He added a can of diced tomatoes to the pan and stirred before lowering the heat and turning back to her. "I thought we could have that and a salad?"

The simmering sauce already had her mouth watering. No doubt it would taste nothing like the premade stuff she normally made. That, in itself, was a problem. The likelihood of Owen consuming a new food without an embarrassing scene was pretty much nil. Her stomach dropped. She should have anticipated this and insisted on going home for dinner. She still could…maybe fake a forgotten work phone call, or an upset stomach, and leave now. She was midway down that mental path when Luke intersected her thoughts.

"I figured Owen would want his pasta plain, right, with just some butter? I've seen him eat it that way in the cafeteria."

Dumbstruck, it took Megan a minute to do anything more than blink in shock. Here she was, drowning in self-doubt, and he was offering her a life preserver. "You don't mind?"

"Mind? Of course not. I'll just set his aside, it's no big deal."

Not to him, maybe. But at some point, Megan had found herself living a life where things like pasta, or her child's refusal to eat it, did seem like a big deal. Was that because she knew her son so well, or was it that she was so caught up in the small things that she'd lost perspective?

She'd thought he was throwing her a life preserver,

but maybe she didn't need one. Maybe what she needed more than anything was someone to remind her to enjoy the swim.

Chapter Six

Sunday mornings should never start with an alarm clock. And yet, not only had Luke set it before settling into a restless sleep Saturday night, he wasn't even angry when it went off. In fact, he was in a suspiciously good mood for a man who had stayed up working until the wee hours and was facing another night of the same. A sane person would be downright annoyed at how much time he'd lost to this ridiculous challenge. Yes, he prided himself on doing his best for the students, but that didn't mean he had to dedicate an entire weekend to just one student, even one with special needs.

But he was up, early, and there was a damn smile on his face!

Of course, it wasn't his work that had him rushing through a quick shower, or fighting the lineup at the

Sandcastle Bakery to buy doughnuts and coffee. It was the idea of spending more time with Megan Palmer. And that was the craziest thing of all.

Wasn't it?

He glanced around, noting how many of the small tables in the crowded bakery were taken by couples. Was it so unusual that he'd want that, too? Surely, it was natural to enjoy spending time with a pretty woman, even if she was the parent of one of his students. No, the problem wasn't that he was attracted to her; the problem was stopping himself from acting on it. The school board would likely frown on him dating a student's parent, no matter how pretty she was, or how much fun he had with her. And he wasn't the kind of guy to flaunt rules—even unwritten ones. Of course, if things didn't work out with Lily today and Owen transferred to a different school, that wouldn't be a problem anymore.

He shook his head, disgusted with himself for even thinking such a thing. More than anything, he wanted Owen to do well, to thrive. His growing appreciation for the boy's mother only strengthened his resolve to help the kid as best he could. If any family deserved a break, they did. And if Lily could prove herself, and he could give them the chance, he was going to do it. He just needed to remember that, and not the way her smile traveled all the way to her eyes when she laughed, or how she smelled like coconuts and sugar.

Thankfully, there was nothing in the employee handbook about being friends with a student's parent, which meant he didn't have to feel guilty about having had dinner with her last night, or for ordering an extra-large box of doughnuts to take to her house this morning. Friends shared food. Right?

"Anything else?"

Grace Keville, the bakery owner and Paradise native, patted the brightly colored box of pastries on the clean counter and patiently waited for an answer as if there weren't a dozen more people in line behind him.

"Just two coffees, one black and one...uh..." His brain churned to a stop. He had no idea how Megan took her coffee, although he knew she drank it. More than once, she'd come to one of their meetings carrying a to-go cup with the Sandcastle logo, which is why he'd had the idea of stopping. "I guess just make both of them black, and maybe throw some sugar packets and stuff in a bag? I'm not quite sure what she wants in it."

"Sure. Or you can tell me who it's for. If 'she' is a regular, I may know how she takes it."

"Seriously?"

Grace nodded vigorously, a single strand of her gray hair working loose from the chignon she always kept it in. "Paradise is a small town, and I've got a mind like a steel trap. In fact, I'll bet you a free bear claw that I get it right. That is what you normally order, right?"

He shook his head in amazement. "Wow, yeah, I do." He'd taken to stopping in on Friday afternoons, when it wasn't so busy, to get a snack before heading back to work until well past the dinner hour. "Okay then, it's for Megan Palmer."

Grace raised an eyebrow at the name, but if she wondered why he was taking Megan coffee on a Sunday morning, she had the good manners not to ask. Instead, she simply added a hefty dose of cream and a squirt of vanilla syrup to one of the paper to-go cups before pouring in the rich, fragrant brew that was as much of her bakery's success as the sugared creations filling the display counters. "There you go. Tell her I said hi. Oh, and you'll need these." She put a bundle of napkins imprinted with the bakery's logo in the bag, along with a set of plastic utensils.

"I will?"

"Mmm-hmm. Owen likes his doughnut cut up, so he can eat it with a fork. He doesn't like the feeling of the glaze on his fingers. Too sticky." She made the comment without censure, as if there was nothing out of the ordinary about a six-year-old boy unable or unwilling to touch a doughnut with his fingers. "And you'd better watch him, or he'll feed half of it to Lily." Grace said the last with a smile, her fondness for the boy and his dog overriding her typically prim demeanor.

Once again, Luke found himself amazed at the genuine feeling of community that pervaded Paradise. As an educator, he'd seen the general impact such a supportive community had on the youngest of its citizens. Until today, though, he hadn't really witnessed what that support looked like close up, on an individual level. But there it was, in something as simple as a set of plastic tableware. Some people might have rolled their eyes or mocked a child with the kinds of preferences Owen had. But to Grace Keville, he was a customer, and a neighbor, and therefore deserving of respect. Her open-mindedness was a refreshing reminder of how things could be—of how *he* could be.

Accepting the advice and the food, Luke made sure to leave a generous tip before threading his way through the growing crowd and exiting the shop.

Outside, the humid, salt-tanged air was a sharp contrast to the cool sweetness of the bakery. By the time he'd crossed the parking lot, he was wishing he'd worn shorts instead of khaki pants and a polo shirt. But it was Sunday, and Megan had mentioned last night that she and Owen were regulars at the church affiliated with the school. Paradise was casual enough that Bermuda shorts and golf shirts were considered acceptable attire almost anywhere. But as someone employed by All Saints, he felt a need to present a professional appearance. Also, the more business-like clothing would be a reminder to himself that this was all work-related. A reminder he sorely needed.

Driving the few blocks to Megan's house, he forced himself to focus on Owen and Lily, not on Megan. His research had showed that some other religious schools had made allowances for service dogs, but they were few and far between. Most had refused for fear of liability—that a special needs student would not be able to control their service animal—although he'd yet to turn up any actual lawsuits or injuries associated with service dogs on school grounds.

Truth be told, there just wasn't enough precedent to base a decision on. That left him relying on his own judgment. Normally that would be fine, he was good at his job and had confidence in his decision-making. But in this case, could he really trust himself to remain unbiased? The more time he spent with Owen, the more he wanted to help him, but he couldn't allow his feelings for one student to outweigh the safety of all the rest.

Beyond his concern for his students, there was another complication shadowing his judgment. Megan. Their budding friendship shouldn't—couldn't—be allowed to influence his decision. If he considered the flying sparks of attraction between them, he was also going to have to be very careful to separate the facts from his feelings.

Yet it wasn't concern over his professional ethics that had his pulse accelerating as he pulled into Megan's narrow driveway. That primal reaction could be chalked up to something much more basic. The simple human desire of a man for a woman. A desire he hoped he was strong enough to fight, and one that he wished like hell he didn't need to.

Megan heard the car in the driveway a fraction of a second before Lily let out a single welcoming woof. Luke was here. Again. Well, at least this time she was ready for him, as ready as she could be anyway.

When she'd come home from dinner last night, she'd been wired thanks to the sudden resurgence of her lifeless libido. Knowing sleep would be futile, she had poured all her nervous energy into cleaning the house.

She'd stayed up way too late but the house looked presentable if not perfect. Boys and dogs didn't allow for perfect. Still, she felt a sense of pride as she surveyed the freshly scrubbed floors and fingerprint-free surfaces. Pride tempered by exhaustion—the latter being a normal state for her. Glancing around one last time, she spotted her morning cup of coffee, still mostly full, on the counter. No wonder she was dragging.

The doorbell rang as she dumped the now cold liquid down the sink. Rinsing the mug quickly, she set it in the dishwasher and dried her hands on the seat of her jeans as she made her way to the door. Lily beat her there, her long tail wagging in anticipation. Nudging the dog and her own nerves aside, Megan opened the door.

Last night, as she'd scrubbed and mopped, she'd convinced herself that any attraction she'd felt for Luke had been an anomaly. A one-off thing due to the surprise of the moment or change in routine. A byproduct of too many Hallmark channel movies and romance novels. Nothing to worry about, now that she had a logical explanation.

But logic was no match for the wave of heat that washed over her the minute he walked in. And darned if she didn't get a bit weak in the knees when she caught a whiff of his cologne. Obviously the lack of sleep was getting to her. She had better wake up fast if she was going to keep herself in check.

As if reading her mind, Luke offered her a tall take-out cup bearing the logo of her favorite bakery. "Coffee?"

"Oh my goodness, yes, please," she answered, accepting the beverage with more gratitude than was probably normal for something as mundane as coffee. But caffeine had gotten her through late-night study sessions and endless days with a colicky baby. Surely, it could help her get through today, too. Then, once Owen had permission to take Lily to school, she could go back to her normal, boring life. At least, that had been the plan she'd come up with last night. Now, with Luke standing in front of her, it didn't hold as much appeal.

At least the coffee was the same as always. Perfect. She closed her eyes and savored it for a moment, letting the bittersweet brew work its magic. "Mmm…thank you. You have no idea how much I needed this." Taking one more sip, she reluctantly opened her eyes and found Luke watching her, his expression unreadable.

Uncomfortable with the scrutiny, she tried to find somewhere else to focus her attention and spotted Owen pulling one of his socks off. Again. "Owen, stop! We need to leave soon. You have to keep your socks on." She cringed at the hint of desperation in her voice, but this was not the way she'd wanted today to start.

Undeterred, Owen threw the offending item on the floor and moved to the other foot. "They can't wear them, they hurt."

Luke said nothing, but Megan felt the weight of his presence as she scooped up the socks and turned them right-side out again. Eyeing the clock, she took a deep breath and started over. "Let me see if I can get them on so they don't hurt, okay?"

Owen considered her words, the stubborn set of his jaw reminding her so much of his father. He had hated accepting help, too. Shaking off the thought, she focused on the task at hand. "I bet I can do it super quick, and then we can get going to church."

His frown deepened. "No, I don't want you to do it."

She sighed and looked at Luke. "I'm sorry. He has sensory issues, and if the seams of his socks aren't just right, he refuses to walk. I've gotten good at getting them on for him, but lately he's been wanting to do it himself. I'm proud of his independence but—" she waved the discarded socks "—it means we have a bit of trouble being on time."

"Gotcha." Luke nodded in understanding and then crouched next to Owen on the floor. "Hey, I get it, you're a big guy now, and you don't like having to ask your mom for help, right?"

Owen gave a small nod.

"That's cool. But if someone else helped you, just a little bit—maybe another guy—that would probably be okay, right? I mean it's good for guys to stick together, to help each other out, like on a team, you know?"

Owen considered this for a moment. "Like a soccer team?"

"Uh-huh. Or like a group of explorers, or a team of firefighters working together, helping each other."

Owen eyes widened. "Or in the military, like my dad. My mom says he helped lots of people."

Megan swallowed hard. She hated that Owen only had secondhand memories of his father, but at least they were good ones. She tried hard to make sure Tim's presence was kept alive as much as possible, but photographs and family stories were a poor stand-in for a flesh-and-blood parent.

"Exactly. Real men know it is important to help each other. And to let others help them. When there is an important job to be done, you can't let pride stand in the way."

Megan wasn't sure Owen could fully grasp the wisdom Luke was trying to impart, but something must have hit home because, after a moment's consideration, he reached to take the crumpled socks from her and held them out to Luke. "Okay, you can help."

Startled by the request, Megan moved to take over. "No, Owen, honey, he meant you should let me help you."

Luke motioned her back. "Nah, I got this. One guy helping another. Teamwork. Right, Owen?"

Owen nodded and eagerly held up one foot. Obviously, her assistance wasn't needed, or wanted, and as she watched Luke carefully align the seams of her son's socks, she wasn't sure how she felt about that. Part of her was grateful for Luke's skillful intercession. They might actually make it to church on time now, a minor miracle in itself. And it was a good thing for Owen to be able to put his trust in another adult. His therapist had often mentioned the importance of male role models, but it was still a bit bittersweet to have her son choose someone else over her. She'd just have to get over herself, though. This kind of progress was exactly why she worked so hard. Any small pangs of jealousy were nothing compared to the strides Owen was making.

Seemed he was making more of those lately, and his ever-patient principal was a major reason. That realization, and the fresh coffee, helped her wash down any remaining angst over her son's newfound independence.

"Do they feel okay now?" Luke asked.

Owen stomped up and down a few times, and grinned. "They don't hurt."

Luke, still sitting on the floor, beamed up at him.

"Of course not. I told you I could fix it. Next time, I'll show you how to fix them yourself. But for now, I think it's time to leave." He glanced up at Megan for confirmation.

"Uh, yes. Thank you."

Propelling himself upright with athletic grace, he shrugged off her compliment and headed for the front door with Owen and Lily.

Automatically, Megan grabbed her keys and followed, her brain focused on one single question. Today was the end of the experiment, so what had he meant by *next time*?

Everything seemed to be going well, right up until the vomit started.

Despite the delay caused by Owen's sock situation, they had arrived early enough for Luke to spend a few minutes chatting with Owen's Sunday school teacher, while observing Lily's behavior in a class setting.

Again, the dog impressed him, sitting or lying calmly at her young master's side, staying calm in the midst of a roomful of children. And Mrs. Dunn, the teacher—an older, no-nonsense woman in a floral dress and sensible shoes—had insisted that Lily was never any trouble, and that since the dog had started coming, Owen had fewer meltdowns in class. Megan had kept quiet, but her smug smile and raised eyebrow had telegraphed "I told you so" better than words could have.

They had found seats at the back of the church, in a mostly empty pew. A few people he knew from work had waved a surprised hello, but no one pointed out that he hadn't exactly been a frequent visitor. Then the choir started and he found himself too busy paying attention to worry about what people were thinking, seeing him and Megan together. He even enjoyed the sermon, especially when the pastor talked about how helping others was not only a duty but a true purpose. As a teacher, he could relate.

All in all, the entire morning seemed to be flowing smoothly. But just as the last hymn was ending, a panicked-looking teenager appeared in the aisle beside their pew. Pointing to Megan, she motioned for Luke to get her attention.

He hated to disturb her. As she sang, her eyes held a peace he hadn't seen before, but there was a good chance this was about Owen. Reluctantly, he tapped her elbow and tried his best to ignore the jolt of heat at the innocent contact.

Turning, her eyes widened at the sight of the teen. "Laura, what's wrong?"

The girl replied in a whisper, whether out of reverence for the service or a sense of privacy, he didn't know. Either way, it was impossible to hear her over the music. Megan moved closer, pressing into him in the confines of the pew as she indicated for Laura to repeat herself.

Understanding, the teen raised her voice, this time speaking loud enough to be heard over a jet engine, let alone the choir. That would have been fine if the choir hadn't finished the selection before poor Laura finished her sentence, informing him, Megan and the entire congregation that, "Owen puked everywhere!"

A strained silence filled the room as the two looked at each other, Laura's face flushing red in contrast to Megan's sudden paleness. Both looked mortified, but he knew Megan's real concern was for her son, not her own embarrassment. Thankfully, the pastor, upon realizing that whatever illness had occurred wasn't in the actual sanctuary, directed the congregation to bow heads in prayer, efficiently diverting the curious stares aimed in their direction.

"I've got to go," Megan whispered, already attempting to squeeze past him.

"I'm coming, too." She might need help if Owen was that sick, and he figured half a church service was plenty to start with, given his long absence. No need to overdo it.

Together they made their way out of the sanctuary and along a covered walkway to the building where the Sunday school classes were held. They found Owen sitting by himself at a table in the back of his classroom, Lily pressed firmly against him. The other students were coloring pictures of an ark and chatting among themselves.

"Oh good. Laura found you." Mrs. Dunn showed none of the teen volunteer's angst, only grandmotherly concern. He imagined that she'd seen her fair share of sick children and got the sense that nothing short of a plague of biblical proportions would fluster her. "Poor Owen isn't feeling very well, and I'm sure he'd rather be home than here. Probably one of those twenty-four-hour things. My grandchildren were both down with it last week. Hits hard but passes fast, and really, that's better than something that lingers, don't you think?"

"I suppose so," Luke agreed politely, as Megan checked her son over. "We've had a few kids in Owen's grade out with something, as well. It seems to be going around."

"Well, I'm glad to hear it's something short-lived, at least." Megan took hold of Lily's leash and placed a hand on Owen's forehead, smoothing away the hair from his pale face. "And I'm sorry about the mess. If I'd known he was sick, I would have kept him at home. I can help you clean up before we go."

"Nonsense. I've already taken care of that. You just get that boy home and in bed. And don't blame yourself. Little boys never admit to feeling sick. They just go-go-go until they can't anymore. I had four of them, so I know."

"Thank you," Megan replied as she guided a very subdued Owen toward the door. "For everything."

"No thanks necessary. And if you need anything, you give the Paradise Inter-Faith Ladies' Auxiliary a call. The number is in the bulletin. We'd be happy to bring over some soup or to make a run to the pharmacy for you."

"I appreciate the offer, but I don't think that will be necessary."

"Nothing wrong with accepting a bit of help. And, truth be told," Mrs. Dunn added, her voice a bit wistful, "most of us are old ladies looking for a way to be useful. Makes us feel good to have someone to take care of. Although—" she eyed Luke with an appreciative sigh "—you seem to have all the help you need, and in a better-looking package than I can offer."

Luke chuckled at her not so subtle appraisal. "I'll do what I can, and if she needs reinforcements, I'll make sure she calls." On second thought, he doubted he could *make* Megan do anything. But he'd call in backup himself if he had to.

As if reading his mind, Megan tossed him a defiant glare as soon as they were outside. "I've been taking care of Owen by myself his whole life. I don't need help—from you or the church ladies."

It wasn't that he didn't believe her… He did. She'd done an amazing job with Owen, on her own, as far as he could tell. Nonetheless, he heard the weariness beneath the tough words; saw the dark circles lurking under her flashing eyes. Yes, she probably could handle this and anything else by herself. But that didn't mean she needed to, or that she should.

Like it or not, Megan Palmer was going to learn that she wasn't on her own anymore. He'd said he would be her friend, and he didn't go back on his word.

Sighing with exhaustion as much as relief, Megan slipped out of Owen's room, careful to leave the door partially cracked open in case he called for her. The house was quiet, and she wondered if Luke had finally left. He'd driven her car home from church so that she could sit in the back with Owen. Then, instead of leaving, as she'd expected him to do—like she told him to do—he'd opened the door for her and followed her inside.

Six long hours later and he was still there. At least, he had been when she'd finally gotten Owen settled enough to fall asleep. Luke had left only once, just long enough to run to the store to pick up soup, crackers, and Pedialyte. He'd even thought to grab a sandwich from the deli for her and then insisted she sit and eat it while he read Owen a story. Making her way down the hall, she found herself hoping he hadn't left and admonishing herself for caring. Owen was out of the woods. There was no reason for Luke to stay any longer.

Yet he had. She found him in the kitchen surveying the contents of the refrigerator while fresh coffee hissed and sputtered its way through the ancient machine on her counter into the nearly full carafe below. Her heart skipped a beat. He'd stayed and he'd made coffee. To a caffeine addict like Megan, it was the sexiest thing he could have done. What would it be like to have a man like this around full-time, puttering in the kitchen, making her coffee?

As quickly as the thought came, she shooed it away. That kind of life wasn't part of her reality anymore. Never had been. When she and Tim had been married, he'd been deployed more than he'd been home, and had made excuses about helping in the kitchen, claiming he didn't know where she kept things. That hadn't stopped Luke, not that the men were in some kind of competition. She'd loved her husband very much, with a youthful passion that had made up for a multitude of minor differences. But time and responsibility had aged her and, in her current life, a man who knew his way around a kitchen was very much appreciated.

"Thank you. How did you know I'd want a cup of coffee?"

He grinned. "How do you know I made it for you? Maybe it's all for me."

She shook her head. "No way. My coffee, my coffee maker. I'd better get some."

He laughed at her intensity. "Fine, it's for you. I don't usually drink it this late, but I've never seen you show up to a meeting at the school without a to-go cup in your hand, no matter what time it is. So I thought you might be up for some."

Her breath hitched at the realization that he'd not only noticed her routines, but remembered them. She wasn't sure there was anyone else alive on the planet right now that knew about her 24/7 java habit. But he did. What did it mean that he knew her so well? And trailing behind that thought was an even more sobering question. What did it mean that no one else did? How pathetic was that? And why was she overthinking something as humble and ordinary as coffee? She needed to get a grip if such a simple thing had her emotions bobbing like a boat in rough surf.

Trying to hide her reaction, Megan busied herself by grabbing the pot before it was done and pouring a cup. The hot liquid sizzled as it hit the warming plate, mocking her impatience. "Owen's asleep. His fever broke, and it looks like Mrs. Dunn was right about it being fast to clear up. I think he's probably out for the count."

"Good. That means we don't have to eat in shifts."

"What?" She turned, mug securely in hand, pot safely back on the warming plate. "You're staying?"

She eyed the container of eggs in his hand. "And you're cooking?" Making her coffee had been foreplay, now he was making her dinner, too? He couldn't have done a better job of seducing her if he'd tried—which he wasn't. If her hormones were screaming, it was a testament to the length of her dry spell, not his intentions.

"Don't get too excited. I'm just making scrambled eggs and toast."

Her skin warmed; she had gotten excited, but not about the food. Taking care of Owen had distracted her—vomit wasn't exactly romantic—but now that the crisis was over, the attraction that simmered whenever Luke was around threatened to boil over. And who could blame her? The man was drop-dead gorgeous, and he had made her coffee. Even more impressive, when Owen had thrown up on the bed, it had been Luke who'd bundled up the bedding and put it in the washer while she'd given her son a bath. That level of kindness was above and beyond anything she would have expected, and a heck of a lot sexier than a bouquet of roses.

Nothing would come of it, of course. By tomorrow, life would go back to normal. For now, it couldn't hurt to enjoy the moment, to enjoy a man cooking for her, taking care of her. Besides, he was just so nice to look at. So that's what she did. She took her coffee to the little scratched-up table and sat and just looked her fill.

"You know," she said after the first glorious sip. "This is the second night in a row you've made dinner for me. I think I'm spoiled. Tomorrow night I'm going to wander into the kitchen and be very disappointed when I realize I have to actually cook."

"You deserve to be spoiled a little. When's the last time you had a night off from dinner duty?"

She shrugged. "Single parents don't get a lot of nights off, but sometimes I order pizza, or hit the drive-through. It's not a big deal."

He nodded, accepting her lie.

Though the truth was, his doing all this was a very big deal. And if she didn't convince her heart otherwise, she was headed for some very big trouble.

Luke beat the eggs more forcefully than necessary, needing some kind of outlet for the emotion running through him.

After his father died, his mother had raised him on her own. He'd thought that had given him insight, that he'd understood the challenges facing the single parents he dealt with as an educator. He knew about the financial difficulties and the logistical issues that came with working long hours to pay the bills. When it came to the emotional strain, however, he'd focused on the child's perspective. Logical, given he'd lived that life and, of course, at work he'd naturally be concerned with his students' issues more than their parents'.

Now, though, he was face-to-face with a parent's side of things. Part of him wanted to call his mother right now to thank her for everything she'd done to make their house a home all on her own. But more than that, he wanted to find a way to help Megan. She said what she did wasn't a big deal, but he'd heard the strain in her voice. He knew she was burning the candle at both ends, starting a career and taking care of Owen. That in itself was a round-the-clock job with no vacation or sick leave. And, after pouring herself into caring for her son, she had to take care of herself, too. If anything had to give, he'd bet it was that last item.

The worst part, there wasn't a damn thing he could do about it, other than make her some eggs that she was much too grateful for.

It wasn't like he could just show up and do Megan's laundry for her on a regular basis, not without looking like some kind of stalker. Besides, he had the impression she needed a friend more than a maid or a meal. As she'd pointed out, she could always order a pizza if she wanted food. But what she didn't have, as far as he could tell, was someone to share it with.

Despite all his good intentions about keeping things professional, he wanted to be that person for her. He wanted a hell of a lot more than that, too. Thoughts of what could happen after a shared dinner and drinks, of long nights that turned into early mornings, flashed into his mind like an erotic picture show. Gripping the spatula until his knuckles blanched, he forced himself back into the present.

The woman was exhausted and worried about her sick child and here he was fantasizing about her like some kind of sex-crazed teenager. Probably because, although their situations were worlds apart, the lack of a social life was one thing they had in common. The difference: he had a choice. If he wanted to go out with friends, or to hook up with someone, he could, and no one would be hurt other than himself. Megan didn't have that luxury. Everything she did revolved around what was best for Owen. As it should be.

That was why the best thing he could do right now would be to feed her, to discuss the Lily situation, and to get out so she could get some sleep.

As if on cue, Megan stifled a yawn. "Sorry, I guess I'm tired enough that coffee isn't going to make much of a difference." She narrowed her eyes at the mug, as if the caffeine's lack of effect was a personal affront.

"At least you'll be able to fall asleep tonight."

"Definitely." She drained her cup and leaned back in her chair. "But I imagine I'll be up checking on Owen a few times during the night. Just in case."

"Do you need me to stay?" Only after the words were out of his mouth did he realize what his offer might sound like. "I mean to help with Owen. We could take shifts or something."

She shook her head and smiled. "No need. I sleep with one ear open so I'll hear if he stirs. Besides, you've done more than enough already. Above and beyond the call of duty."

"I was glad to help." He set two plates filled with scrambled eggs and toast on the table, along with forks and napkins. "Butter or jam for the toast?"

"Jam, but I can get it." She started to rise and he put a hand on her shoulder to stop her.

"Sit. Eat. I'll get it."

She stilled under his palm, her breath catching before she nodded. "Okay. It's in the fridge, second shelf from the top."

Reluctantly, he moved away, savoring the soft brush

of her hair on the back of his hand as he let go of her. He'd love to spend time running his fingers through it, preferably while he kissed her thoroughly. Instead, he fetched the two jars of jam he found in the refrigerator and settled in the seat across from her, a safe distance away, before digging into his eggs. As long as his mouth was full of food, he couldn't say anything stupid. Like how attractive he found her. How sexy she was. How, if her son wasn't down the hall, he'd love to lick blueberry jam off her—

"Hey, are you all right?"

"Hmm, what?" With difficulty, he met her gaze, hoping his face wasn't broadcasting his thoughts.

"I asked if you were okay. You looked awfully intense there for a second."

Yeah, intense was one way to describe his desire for her. Also scorching, constant, and damned near painful. And the more he came to know her, the worse it got. Now, instead of just physical attraction, he was feeling things on a whole other level. He'd learned to control his hormones as a teenager. Trying to hide his emotions now was new territory, probably because until this moment no one had sparked such a deep chord with him. None of which he could share with her. So he lied, and hoped his short stint in church today canceled out any negative karma. "Just hungry, that's all."

Megan smiled nervously, moving her fork around her plate without actually eating. "Oh. I thought you were maybe thinking about our agreement. That maybe you'd made up your mind."

He swallowed, relieved and yet disappointed by her

assumption. Of course she'd assume he was thinking about that. Her mind was always on her son. For her, there was no other reason for him to be there. Despite his offer of friendship, she still saw him as a means to an end. It wasn't a flattering realization. But this wasn't about him, which was why he'd made the decision he had.

Megan's stomach churned; her interest in food forgotten as she watched emotions flicker across Luke's face. Maybe she shouldn't have pressed him. For crying out loud, she could have at least let the man finish his dinner before bringing it up. Weren't men usually in a better mood with a full stomach? But she was a ball of nerves and, between her lack of sleep and the emotional and physical toll of caring for a sick child all day, she'd run out of emotional reserves to be patient any longer.

Seconds passed and still he didn't answer. The coffee that had seemed so heavenly a few minutes ago now threatened to burn a hole in her empty stomach. Acid and bile rose in her throat. For a split second, she thought she'd caught Owen's bug, but knew the burning was just a physical manifestation of her angst.

Finally, after finishing his toast in two bites, he spoke. "I did. Decide, I mean."

"And?" Her fingers gripped the table, pressing into the scarred wood. His answer meant everything. Did he understand that?

"And… Lily can come."

For a second, Megan was afraid she'd heard wrong, that she'd wanted to hear yes so badly that she'd imagined it. But his smile was all the confirmation she needed. "Really? I mean thank you! You won't regret this."

His eyes sparkled as he stood to clear the table. "Yes, really."

She followed him to the sink. He rinsed the plates and she put them in the dishwasher, the mundane task at odds with the excitement building within her. "I can't wait to tell Owen. When can Lily start?" She dried her hands on the worn checkered dishcloth Luke handed her, her mind going a mile a minute. "Is his teacher going to be okay with this? Should I schedule a conference with her or something? Or maybe I should—"

"Whoa!" Luke put his hands on her shoulders, as if to physically restrain the energy flowing through her. "Slow down. Given how Owen's feeling, I'm guessing he isn't going to be at school tomorrow anyway. Once he's better, Lily can come with him. As for everything else, I thought we could sit down and hash out the details together."

Megan flushed, as much from the physical contact as her excitement for Owen. Luke was so near and her emotions were so close to the surface. A dangerous heat warmed her, spreading from the skin beneath his strong hands down her body. It would be so easy to lean into him. Without thinking, she stepped forward, waited for him to back away, to break contact. Instead, his fingers tightened their grip and his eyes narrowed. The same intensity she'd seen earlier was back, and this time it was focused on her.

Her skin tingled under his scrutiny like it did whenever lightning hit too close. An apt comparison to a moment that was equal parts thrill and terror, where she knew she was in danger yet couldn't move away.

"Megan..."

His voice was strained, and she knew it was because of her. She wasn't the only one feeling...something. She didn't want to stop and name it. There would be time to overthink and pick it all apart later. Right now, she just wanted to feel. To share an important moment with another adult human being.

Hesitantly, she raised one hand to his face, tracing the line of his jaw with her thumb. His neatly trimmed beard was rough, scraping her skin, and she relished the sensation. She'd forgotten how different a man's body was. Exploring his face with her fingers, she moved on to the contrasting softness of his lips. As she brushed lightly over first the top and then the bottom, Luke's breath hitched and his eyes closed. Within her, a confidence blossomed, fueled by his reaction.

Boldly, Megan rose on her tiptoes, fisting her hand in his shirt for balance, and kissed him. His lips, which had felt so soft against her fingertips, were firm and warm against hers. He let her lead, but there was nothing passive about him.

Her last coherent thought, before sensation overtook reason, was that he wanted this as much as she did. She let the realization flow over her and then be washed away, overpowered by the wave of heat, need, and sheer awareness that surged through her like a rip current pulling her out to sea. She tried to remember to breathe, to hold herself up, but the strength of her own wanting disoriented her.

She clung to him with both hands, holding on to his hard, warm body like a lifeline, needing an anchor. His hands were on her, as well. Instead of steadying her, they excited her more as they skimmed her arms, then up and down her spine, moved through her hair and across the sensitive spot at the back of her neck. All the while his lips and tongue drove her to a place she didn't recognize, didn't remember. Had she ever felt so purely physical, so aware of every nerve ending, every brush of skin against skin?

Wanting—no, *needing* more, she released her death grip on his shoulders and slid her hands to his waist. Tugging at his shirt, she pulled it from his pants and burrowed her hands underneath. Luke hissed as she made contact, her fingers skimming across his flat abdomen and along his ribs, then back again. She smiled against his lips; pleased she had such an effect. But her pleasure was short-lived. Luke pulled back, using his own broad hands to still hers. "You're killing me," he groaned roughly, his tone sending shivers down her spine.

"I had no idea men were such delicate creatures, that a kiss could be deadly." For half a second, Megan wondered at herself. Since when did she flirt with men in her kitchen? But that was a question for later, for whenever her brain came back online. Now was for feeling, touching, doing. Not for thinking. She tried to pull him to her, seeking his mouth, but he maneuvered her so that her face ended up buried in his neck instead. Fine, she could work with that. She nibbled at his throat and then used the tip of her tongue to gently taste him. She was rewarded with a nonverbal but very clear response, and the feel of his hardness against her made her want to see what else he liked. It was obvious he clearly liked this. So why was he trying to stop her?

"Megan." His tone was harder now, although his voice sounded stressed. "Honey, please know that I am going to hate myself for saying this, but we have to stop."

She liked the endearment. Everything that came after it, not so much. Tipping her head back, she looked him in the eye, squinting against the stark kitchen lighting. Somehow, the harsh brightness did what his words couldn't and her brain started to sputter back to life, reminding her of their current situation. This was her kitchen. The one only a short hallway distance from her sleeping son. Her sick, sleeping son. "Owen? Did you hear him?"

Was that why Luke has stopped her, because he'd heard her son calling for her, and she'd been too far gone to notice? Untangling her hands from his shirt, she stepped back, fear and embarrassment crowding out any remaining desire. What had she been thinking? She hadn't been, that was the problem. For heaven's sake, she was a mother! She couldn't just turn off her brain because there was a hot man within arm's reach.

"Megan, calm down."

"I am calm," she objected. If her clenched fists betrayed her words, he was smart enough not to mention it. "Also, for future reference, the phrase *calm down* has never actually made a woman more calm. Ever." Leaving him with that tidbit, she turned and headed for Owen's room.

Luke grasped her arm, his fingers on her skin a blazing reminder of the heat they'd just shared. "He's fine. At least, he hasn't made a sound. I was listening for him."

And she hadn't been.

Maybe he hadn't meant it that way. Probably not. Still, the implication was there. This was exactly why she didn't date. Not that fooling around after sharing scrambled eggs was a date. Clearly, she wasn't capable of adding one more thing to her already overloaded life. Obviously, other women could balance motherhood and a sex life, but she couldn't even handle a freaking kiss without losing track of all her responsibilities. And that wasn't fair to her son.

"I think you had better go now."

"Wait, I didn't mean—"

"This was a mistake, that's all. Please, let's just forget it happened." As if she'd ever be able to forget that kiss. No way. But that didn't mean she wanted to discuss it to death, either.

"Fine." He nodded, his tone making it clear things were definitely not fine. "What about Owen?"

She bristled. "He has nothing to do with—" she gestured between herself and Luke "—this."

His jaw clenched. "I mean what about him bringing Lily to school? We were going to go over the details, remember?"

Yeah, she remembered now. He'd wanted to set

"guidelines" or something like that. "Send me an email. I'll look at it in the morning. Right now, I'm going to go check on my son and then get some sleep." Or more likely, lay awake and ponder all the ways tonight went wrong. "I'm sure you won't mind letting yourself out."

Without waiting for an answer, she turned her back on him and whatever had just happened, and walked on shaky legs down the hall and back to her normal life.

Chapter Seven

Luke was still fuming the next morning. He wasn't upset with Megan. Yes, he was disappointed that she'd refused to talk to him last night after they had kissed, but he also knew she'd been emotionally and physically spent. He would wait to hash things out after she'd had a chance to regroup.

No, his anger was entirely self-directed. He'd blown it big-time. Megan had been vulnerable, needy, and he'd been insensitive. He didn't regret the kiss, he was still a guy, but he should have handled things better. He should have stayed in control, found a way to slow things down without slamming on the brakes and freaking Megan out. Normally, he was pretty good at handling himself, but when she'd started to undress him, he'd nearly lost his mind. It had taken all his willpower to hit pause for a minute and put some space between them. He'd wanted to regain control, not to scare her away completely.

Her icy tone had made it clear she either hadn't understood or hadn't cared. And now, with Owen sick, he wouldn't get the chance to see her today. Instead, he was supposed to email her. Fine, he could be professional about it. But that didn't mean he had to be happy about it.

"Dr. Wright?" Ms. White, the school secretary, peeked her head around his office door.

"What is it?" he grumbled.

She frowned at him. At least two decades older, she was not the least bit intimidated by his surly attitude. "Mr. Edwards is here to see you. Unless," she continued primly, "you'd like me to send him away?"

Damn, he'd forgotten about Grant coming. "I'm sorry. Yes, please send him in."

She smiled, as quick to forgive as she was to rebuke. "Happy to."

During his research into service animals in schools, one of the administrators he'd spoken with had offered to share their waiver of liability form. After how well Lily had behaved this weekend, Luke wasn't anticipating any problems, but it was his job to make sure all the bases were covered, just in case.

That was why he'd asked Grant Edwards, a fishing buddy and contract lawyer, to look it over and make any needed changes. The plan had been to meet with him first thing this morning and then have Megan sign whatever they came up with when she arrived with Owen. After everything that had happened this weekend, the appointment had slipped his mind. He supposed he could include the forms in that email Megan had asked for as she'd kicked him out of her house.

Hell. He rubbed a hand over his eyes, feeling a headache building.

"Man, you look rough."

Luke looked up to find Grant staring down at him, a cocky grin on his face.

"Gee, thanks. Nice to see you, too."

Ignoring the sarcasm, Grant settled into the chair across from Luke's desk as if he had all the time in the world. There was something disconcerting about his being decked out in a fancy suit instead of the old T-shirt and board shorts he wore whenever they went fishing. But under the expensive clothes, the attitude was the same. Full of life and confidence to burn.

"So, seriously, what's up? Hangover? Sick? Woman troubles?"

"None of the above," he lied. "Just a headache, probably got too much sun this weekend or something."

"Yeah? Doing what? I didn't see you at the pier on Sunday."

The kiss with Megan flashed back into Luke's brain, searing him with heat all over again. "Went for a run Saturday and got a bit overheated, so I stayed inside on Sunday."

"That's right, now that you mention it, I heard you were seen at church Sunday morning." Grant leaned back, obviously enjoying himself. "I've never known you to skip fishing for church. Work, yes—you definitely work too hard. But church? Only one thing I've ever known to get a man to trade a fishing pole for a Bible, and that's a good-looking woman."

Luke stifled a groan. He so did not need this right now. "I do happen to work for All Saints, you know. It's good for me to put an appearance in now and then."

"Maybe," Grant conceded, pretending to ponder the idea. "From what I heard, you did indeed make an appearance, for the first half. But then were seen exiting quickly, hand in hand with a woman. A pretty one, too, according to my sources. And it just so happens that that very same woman is the one you asked me to draw up the papers for." He grinned, knowing he'd hit home. "So it seems my theory stands. The only reason a man trades fishing for religion is if there is a woman reeling him in. Trading one catch for another, you could say."

Luke opened his mouth to argue, but closed it again. Grant was too good at reading people; he'd see through a bullshit story. It was one of the reasons the guy was so good in the courtroom. He'd never explained why he'd made the switch to contract and real estate law, but it certainly hadn't been for a lack of success. More likely the tame stuff paid better than working for the county prosecutor. Grant clearly hadn't lost his touch, and Luke needed some serious resolve to keep from squirming under his friend's affable cross-examination.

"Fine, what do you want to know? Although I'm warning you, the actual facts are probably much less interesting than whatever stories the Paradise gossip network has started spreading."

"No doubt," Grant agreed with a chuckle. "I've heard everything from a run-of-the-mill fling to you being her long-lost husband returned from the grave. Obviously, in that version, her husband wasn't actually killed but was instead working undercover as a spy."

Luke groaned. This was why he didn't date. He spent thirty minutes with a woman in public and was now a returning war hero back to claim his lost bride. "Tell me you are exaggerating."

"Maybe a little. But not much."

"Well, let me assure you, none of what you heard is true."

Grant frowned. "Not even the fling? I was kind of hoping that one was true."

"Fake news." A single kiss didn't count as a fling, right?

"So you haven't slept together? Or kissed? Made goo-goo eyes at one another over a romantic dinner?"

The lighthearted tone didn't fool Luke. Grant would keep digging until he hit pay dirt. Uncovering the truth was what he did. It was just damned annoying to be on the wrong end of his shovel. "Listen, you can't talk about this with anyone, okay?"

"Would I do that?" Grant put a hand over his heart in mock distress. "Your lack of faith wounds me."

"Dude, I'm serious. Her kid's a student, and I don't want to mess up my job here."

Grant straightened, lawyer face in place. "Do your terms of employment prohibit fraternization with the relatives of students?"

Luke shook his head. "I don't think so. At least, nothing obvious. But that doesn't mean the board of directors wouldn't unofficially frown on the idea. Getting rid of a first-year principal isn't hard, and I don't need them gunning for me."

Grant was silent for a moment. "I guess I see what you're saying, but still, why don't you let me take a look at your employment contract, so you know what you're dealing with."

"I don't think it matters anymore. She made it pretty clear last night that this isn't going to be an ongoing thing."

"Aha! So it was a thing!" He pumped a fist in the air. "I knew it."

"Not really. I mean, we spent some time together, but it was about her kid—at least, at first. You saw the waiver, she wants her kid's service dog to come to school, and I needed to see the dog in action before I could make an educated decision."

"Right, but something other than dog walking must have happened to get you this twisted up."

"We kissed."

"Okay, now we're getting somewhere. What happened after the kiss?"

"She kicked me out of her house."

"Yikes."

"Yeah. I wanted to talk, but she told me to email her, and then said to let myself out." He hung his head, hating to ask but needing to know. "You think I blew it?"

"She told you to email her? Yeah, man, sorry. That's definitely a shutdown."

"I figured. Probably for the best, given everything."

Grant nodded, allowing him the out. "So what are you going to do now?"

The only thing he could do. "I'm going to take a look at those forms you brought and then I'm going to email her."

Megan stood at the counter, debating pouring another cup of coffee. She'd already had three and it was only 10:00 a.m. She didn't need any more caffeine. What she needed was a distraction. Anything to keep her hands busy so she didn't keep checking the email app on her phone.

She hadn't heard from Luke yet. What had she expected after the way she'd treated him last night? First, she'd pounced on him, crossing both professional and personal boundaries. Then, after practically eating him alive, she'd acted like he wasn't worth the time of day. She hadn't even said goodbye. Just walked away like… well, like a not very nice person.

At this point, no news was probably good news. After everything, she wouldn't blame him if he retracted his offer to let Lily come to school. Worse, it was entirely possible he'd ask her to remove Owen from the school entirely. All because of her.

She'd jeopardized everything. And for what? For a few minutes of feeling good? Had she become that lonely, that desperate, for physical contact, that she'd gamble her child's future away? It made no sense. She wasn't a risk-taker, and she never lost control, not ever. Even after Tim died, she'd kept it together, made the arrangements, and moved on with her life.

There was no explanation for her behavior. But couldn't sleep deprivation make people act out of character? She'd certainly been exhausted, but she'd been tired for the past six years and this was the first time she'd groped someone in the kitchen. Maybe she was having some kind of midlife crisis. Although, at not yet thirty years old, it seemed unlikely. And dwelling on the situation wasn't going to help. Neither was sitting around, waiting for him to email her, like some soppy teenager. "It's not like I don't have plenty to do around here, right, Lily?"

Ever patient, Lily simply stared up at her before settling down again next to the ceramic dog bowl Owen had picked out for her the day they'd brought her home. Her empty dog bowl.

"Oh, sorry! You want your breakfast, don't you?" Normally, Owen fed Lily before he had his own breakfast, but because of his stomach bug, she'd just given him some watered-down juice and told him stay in bed. That was an hour ago, and between the change in routine and ruminating on the whole Luke situation, she'd not thought to do it herself.

"See, Lily," she said, opening the kibble canister and finding it nearly empty. "This is exactly why I need to stay away from Luke Wright. I obviously can't handle a love life and everything else. One kiss and I nearly forget to feed you." She scooped Lily's normal ration into her bowl and, feeling guilty, added a few dog biscuits from the jar on the counter. "We don't need anyone else anyway, right, girl? The three of us are a team, one for all and all for one."

The reference to teamwork made her think of Luke's little pep talk with Owen yesterday about accepting help. Ugh. She didn't want to think about him, or about what he'd said. It was good advice for a six-year-old, but she was an adult, and she wasn't used to needing other people.

She did, however, need to get more dog food. That had been on her weekend to-do list, but between ice cream and dinner at Luke's on Saturday, and then Owen getting sick yesterday, it had slipped her mind. One more sign that she wasn't cut out for a social life.

"So, how are we going to manage this, Lily?" She didn't want to drag Owen out of his sick bed, and even if she had someone to call to watch him, she didn't like leaving him when he wasn't feeling well. Frustrated, she poured a cup of coffee she shouldn't drink and tried to think. This was a simple problem, and she was a modern woman. Surely, she could figure something out.

Megan thought better when she cleaned, so while her brain puzzled over the problem, she started another load of laundry and then emptied the dishwasher. She'd moved on to wiping down the microwave when an idea came to her. Grabbing her phone, she quickly checked on Owen before placing a call.

The Paradise Animal Clinic wasn't far from her house, and they carried Lily's dog food, a premium brand recommended by her trainer. Maybe, since they were so close, she could arrange to have the food delivered to her house for an extra fee.

When the receptionist picked up, Megan quickly explained her request. "I can give you my credit card over the phone, and I'm happy to pay a delivery fee," she added, crossing her fingers.

"We don't normally do that," the young woman replied uncertainly. "I'd have to ask the doc."

"Would you, please?" She had no real reason to expect such a favor, but this was Paradise, the tropical version of Mayberry. The kind of place where personal service still existed. At least, she hoped so. A minute later, the hold music clicked off and a different voice came on the line.

"Hi, Megan, it's Cassie. Olivia said you were asking about a delivery?"

"Yes. I mean, I know you don't normally do that kind of thing, but Owen's sick, and I'm out of Lily's food. I thought maybe if you could spare someone—"

"Oh no, is Owen okay? I hope it isn't that stomach thing going around at school. Emma had it last week. I swear I've never seen so much puke in my life."

"Yes, it is, and he's doing much better now, thank you. I just don't want to drag him out of the house if I can avoid it."

"I don't blame you. Let the kid rest. If you can wait until this evening, I'll bring the food by myself. Is there anything else you need? Soup? Crackers? A bottle of wine or some chocolate for yourself?"

Megan laughed, her heart lifting. "Just the dog food. And this evening is fine."

"Okay. Well, I have to run, we've got a litter of puppies that just came in for their first vaccines. Just call and tell Olivia if you think of anything else you need. Otherwise, I'll see you later."

Pleased with her success in solving the dog food dilemma, Megan turned her attention to the project she'd promised her most recent client.

Several hours later, she'd made good progress. Owen was feeling better, too, and had joined her at the kitchen table with his coloring books and crayons. He was so intent on his artwork that he didn't even look up when the doorbell provided an unexpected but welcome distraction.

"I'm going to see who's at the door. I'll be right back. Okay?"

Owen nodded and continued coloring. He didn't like being interrupted. She, however, was ready for a break. Rolling her shoulders to work out the kinks, she headed for the front door, expecting a salesman or perhaps a package she needed to sign for. Instead, she found Cassie, Lily's veterinarian, standing on her doorstep with a large takeout bag in her hand and a sack of kibble at her feet. "Cassie! I didn't expect you until tonight."

The strawberry-blonde shrugged, her freckled nose scrunching as she smiled. "I know, but I actually had time for a real lunch break today, so I figured I'd come by now, if that's okay?"

"Of course! Would you like to come in?"

"I'd love to." She hefted the takeout bag. "I hate eating at my desk, so I took the liberty of picking up enough food for all of us, in return for you letting me enjoy a meal at a real table."

Megan nearly dropped the dog food bag she'd just picked up. The petite veterinarian had always been friendly at Lily's checkups, and they'd run into each other at All Saints, where Cassie's daughter was a grade ahead of Owen. But they weren't what Megan would consider friends.

"You didn't have to do that—"

"I know, but I did anyway." She grinned. "I remember what it's like to be a single mom. Admit it, more often than not, lunch is whatever bits of food your kid left on the plate."

Megan couldn't help but return the smile. "Guilty."

"Besides," Cassie continued, lowering her voice, "I have an ulterior motive. There is some very interesting gossip going around about you and a certain school principal, and I figured this was my chance to get the straight scoop."

Megan stopped halfway down the hall, panic rising. "What? What kind of rumors?" Had Luke told someone about what had happened last night? Embarrassment flip-flopped in her stomach, followed immediately by anger.

"Nothing terrible." Cassie patted her shoulder before moving past her toward the kitchen. "It's all sort of ridiculous, really, just speculation. You know how people get. Once they saw you together at church, people started thinking—" She stopped, spotting Owen, and Megan was left wondering what exactly people were thinking.

"Hey, kiddo, you remember Dr. Cassie from the animal clinic, right?"

He looked up, his eyes widening in recognition. "You're Emma's mom. Is Emma here, too?"

Cassie shook her head. "Sorry, Emma's at school. I

came to bring Lily her dog food, and I brought lunch for you and your mom."

"Oh." Much less interested in food than a potential playmate, he returned his attention to the coloring book in front of him.

"Hey, Owen." Megan put her hand over his, stilling his crayon. "What do you say to Dr. Cassie for bringing you lunch?"

He squirmed. Social niceties didn't come easily to him. "Sorry?"

She held back a chuckle. "That's a polite word, but try again. Why do you say when someone brings you something?"

"Oh yeah." He briefly turned in Cassie's direction, not quite managing eye contact, but almost. "Thank you." Returning his attention to the paper in front of him he asked, "Now can I color?"

Reminding herself that small victories would add up, she decided to accept his not quite perfect manners for now. "Sure. Are you hungry?"

He shook his head, and Megan didn't push. It was no surprise his appetite wasn't quite back yet, after yesterday. Rising, she turned and found Cassie had already found plates and was dishing out the food. "Wow, you're efficient."

The other woman shrugged. "I'm a working mom, we have to be, right?"

"Good point." Megan helped herself to half a sandwich and one of the bowls of steamy soup. "Do you mind if we eat outside? I know it's hot but…" She angled her head in Owen's direction.

"More privacy. I get it."

Heading back the way they'd come, she called to Owen over her shoulder. "I'll be out front with Dr. Cassie if you need me." Then to Cassie said, "Thanks. He often seems like he's in his own world, but he has an uncanny ability to tune in right at the worst times."

Outside, the humidity was brutal, but the covered porch was shady and boasted a secondhand swing she'd refinished herself.

Settling onto it, Megan motioned for the veterinarian to join her. Cassie had brought thickly carved turkey on crusty sourdough bread, with homemade potato chips and sour pickle spears, so, for a few minutes, they ate in silence. But as soon as Megan finished the last bite of her sandwich, Cassie pounced.

"So, spill it, lady. What's going on between you and Paradise's most eligible bachelor?"

"Nothing."

"Uh-uh." Cassie shook her head. "I can't go back to the office without more info than that. I'll be eaten alive."

Megan blinked. "You want me to give you a scoop so you can spread more gossip?" And she'd just started thinking that maybe Cassie could be a real friend. She started to stand, but Cassie, looking stricken, grabbed her wrist.

"No, I was kidding. It was a joke. A bad one, obviously. Trust me, I've been the subject of enough gossip to last us both a lifetime. I'm not looking to create more. In fact, that's why I came over today."

"I thought it was to deliver dog food and to escape the office."

Cassie grinned. "That, too. But mostly I wanted to give you a heads-up and to see if you were okay. I know what it's like to have people speculating about your love life… Emma's father wasn't exactly a stand-up citizen and, when I got pregnant, he left town. What had happened, and what I was going to do about it, fueled the rumor mill for a long time."

Megan sat back. Maybe there was more to Cassie than she'd realized. She'd certainly never heard this story, but then again, it would have been before she'd arrived in Paradise. "I'm sorry, that had to be hard."

"It was." She shrugged. "It made me never want to date again, both because I had lost my faith in men but also because I didn't want to give people a reason to talk about me."

"It is pretty freaky to know that people are gossiping about me," Megan admitted. "I mean what can they even say? That we sat by each other at church? It's not like they saw us—" She clamped her mouth closed, realizing what she'd been about to let slip.

Cassie leaned in, her eyes sparkling. "Saw you what?"

"I thought you didn't like gossip," Megan protested.

"I don't. But this isn't gossip. It's girl talk. I hate gossip, but I'm a big proponent of girl talk."

Is that what this was? It had been so long, Megan had forgotten how nice it could be to share things with another woman. Doing so now felt risky, but she was dying to tell *someone*. "You aren't going to repeat this?"

Cassie traced an *X* across her chest. "Cross my heart."

"Fine. I mean, it's not like it's a big deal or anything. We were just spending time together so he could get a feel for how Lily helps Owen, with the idea of maybe having Lily go to school."

"Okay…"

"That's why he was at church with us. But then Owen got sick, and we came back here. I figured Luke—"

"You call him Luke? You guys are on a first-name basis?"

Megan waved a dismissive hand to shush her. "I figured he would leave once we got back, but he didn't. He stayed. He even washed all the sheets Owen had vomited on."

"Tell me this story doesn't end with puke and laundry," Cassie begged. "'Cause as sweet as that is, that he helped, it's kind of gross."

"True. He also made me dinner after Owen was feeling better and finally went to sleep. And then…well, we kissed."

"Whoa. Dr. Wright—I mean Luke—kissed you?"

Heat flooded Megan's face. "Actually, I kissed him."

"Oh wow! That's even better. I knew I liked you!" She gave Megan's arm a squeeze. "So now what? Are you guys seeing each other? Is he even allowed to date one of the school parents? Is that why you want to keep it quiet?"

Megan shook her head, trying to ward off any more of Cassie's questions. "Now, nothing. I don't know if he's allowed to date me, but it doesn't matter. The kiss was a onetime thing."

"Did he say that?" Cassie's eyes narrowed. "Because if he took advantage of you and then dumped you, you could report him to the school board."

"No, it's not like that." Megan's hands twisted the napkin in her lap. "I told you, I'm the one who kissed him. And then I realized what a mistake it was and I asked him to leave. Actually—" she bowed her head "—I kind of kicked him out."

"And that's it?" Cassie asked incredulously. "Surely he must have had something to say about that."

"I didn't give him a chance. When he tried to change the subject, to talk about Lily going to school, I told him he could email me."

"Oh. Wow. Okay, so I guess the next question is, did he? Email you, I mean."

"I don't know. I turned off my email notifications."

"Well, go grab your phone and turn them back on," Cassie ordered. "Because I have a very strong feeling this isn't over yet."

Megan reread Luke's email for at least the tenth time, which was dumb, since she'd understood it perfectly the first time. It was clear and to the point. Nothing personal. Nothing to indicate they had anything other than a professional relationship. Still, she was glad she'd insisted on waiting until Cassie had left to open it. She'd promised to call her new friend if she needed to talk, telling her she'd be the first to know if anything of importance happened.

She was pretty sure this bare bones email, more a list of instructions than anything, didn't count.

As per our agreement, Owen will be permitted to bring his service dog, known by the name Lily, to school on a trial basis. Please note the following stipulations:
- She is to be kept on a leash at all times;
- She is to use a designated area for relieving herself, and any waste must be properly disposed of;
- All vaccination records and county licensing information must be kept on file with the school;
- This agreement may be revisited at any time, for any reason.

Please sign the attached liability forms and return them along with copies of the above-mentioned medical and licensing information as soon as possible.

Also, please plan to attend with Owen and Lily the first day, to help with any issues that may arise during the transition.

Sincerely,
Luke Wright, Ph.D.
Principal

Megan wondered absently if his email program used a standard signature, or if he'd purposely typed out his credentials to impress her. Not that she cared. She was more concerned with that final bullet point, the one saying he could basically change his mind at any time, for any reason. So much for thinking she could stop worrying. That one line meant she'd be on edge until Owen graduated.

Her fingers twitched over the keyboard as she contemplated how to respond. She couldn't exactly say, "Attached are the signed forms you requested. Also, sorry about kissing you and then freaking out."

In the end, she went with simple and to the point.

I appreciate this opportunity. Health permitting, Owen and Lily and I will be there tomorrow. I have attached the signed forms you requested. Let me know if there is anything else you need.
Sincerely,
Megan Palmer

That should satisfy him, and if he did decide to talk... well, she'd left an opening. A small one, but still, "need" could have many meanings. And if not, she hadn't embarrassed herself by delving into things better left unsaid.

Shutting her laptop, she stood and stretched. She'd gotten a decent amount of work done, but she'd have to do more tonight if she was going to spend all day at the school tomorrow. Now, though, she wanted to give Owen the good news.

"Hey, buddy, can you come here for a minute?"

Owen looked up from the Lego creation he'd been building. Some kind of outer space fire station, with a plastic figure in a NASA spacesuit riding around the block buildings on top of the fire truck he'd gotten for his birthday last year. "What is it?"

"I have some important news. Good news," she added.

That got his attention. Dropping the truck in his hand, he stood and scrambled through the jumble of toys to join her on the couch. "Tell me!"

"Well, I just got an email from Mr. Wright, and he said it's okay for Lily to come to school with you. Would you like that?"

For a second, he just sat there, eyes wide, mouth open. She'd have taken a picture if she could. But as soon as she thought it, he was back in motion, bouncing up and down on the couch like it was his personal trampoline. "Whoa, easy on the couch, buddy. Keep that up and you might launch yourself right into space. Then who would Lily go to school with, huh?"

Abandoning the couch, but not the motion, he leaped to the ground where his acrobatics continued. Laughing, she watched him, loving the sheer joy in his eyes. "So, are you going to tell Lily, or am I?" she teased.

He grinned. "I am!" Still mostly airborne, he crossed the room and knelt beside the sleepy dog. As always, his motions slowed when he was with her. When Lily had first come home with them, Megan had worried he'd be too rough with the dog, too boisterous, but it had never been an issue. She had a feeling it was more Lily's calming influence than her own words of caution that had done the trick, but that was okay. After all, that was the whole reason they'd gotten a service dog.

"Make sure you tell her to be on her best behavior," she advised Owen, watching him whisper to the seventy-pound canine. "Principal Wright said we can bring her on a trial basis."

"A trial?" He looked up at her, confusion clouding his face. "She has to go to court?"

"Court?" It took her a minute to make the connection. "Oh no. Not that kind of trial. A trial basis means we are going to try it out to see if it works. If it does, she can keep going to school with you. But if it doesn't… like, say, if you start playing with her instead of listening to the teacher, then she'll have to stay home."

He considered her words, his expression serious. "Lily won't mess up. She's always good. I'm the one that gets in trouble. But I'll try hard, I promise."

An ache grew in the middle of her chest, stealing her breath. "Oh, honey, I know you will. You just keep doing your best, and that's good enough for me."

He nodded. It was a phrase he'd heard from her many times.

Because at the end of the day, that's all either of them could do. Just do their best and hope it was enough.

Chapter Eight

The sound of the first bell echoed over the din of children's chatter as students made their way past Luke's office to their classrooms. In five minutes, the tardy bell would ring, and another school day would begin. The routine was the same every time, and yet today felt different. He felt different. Keyed up. Unless something had changed, Owen would be back in class today, which meant Lily would be coming with him. And, as he'd requested, so would Megan. He felt fairly confident about his decision regarding Lily, but he didn't have the foggiest idea how to act around Megan.

It wasn't like they'd broken up or something. They hadn't even dated. He could handle that. He'd never planned to be anything more than friends. But after the way she'd spoken to him, he wasn't sure they even had that anymore. That shouldn't be a big deal. Except the two days he'd spent with her and Owen had been the best days he'd had since moving to Paradise.

Pathetic, but true. He liked Megan's sense of humor, her deep-rooted sense of loyalty, her toughness. And he really liked how she felt in his arms. Most of all, he liked how he felt when he was with her. She made him feel alive, in touch with the world beyond his work. And now, for reasons he still couldn't quite understand, it was over.

He wasn't sure he could go back to a Megan-free life. Two days, and he was addicted. Now he had to decide if it was better to go cold turkey and avoid her as much as possible, or to give in to his urge to check on how things were going in Owen's classroom. If he avoided her, would she think he was angry? Was he angry?

Maybe a little. At least, he had been. She was the one who had kissed him, and yet she'd acted as if he were the one to blame. So, yeah, he'd been upset. But he was a big boy and knew that everything wasn't about him. Now he was more concerned than anything. From what he could tell, she didn't have a lot of people she could count on, and it wasn't in his nature to just walk away.

Mind made up, Luke left the office just as the tardy bell was ringing. His footsteps sounded loud in the suddenly empty hallway. As he made the short trek, he reminded himself to focus on Owen, not Megan. His students were his first priority. His feelings for Megan, whatever they were, could wait until he was off the clock. There would be plenty of time for that brand of self torture later.

As soon as he opened the classroom door, he saw her. She was kneeling next to Owen's chair, one hand on his shoulder and the other on Lily. And he realized, watching them together, that there was no way to compartmentalize his concern for Owen and his feelings for Megan. Yes, he wanted more than anything for Owen to be successful. But Owen's success was in huge part due to his mother, and her support. And one of the things he admired about Megan the most was her dedication to her son. It defined her. There was no way to separate it from her, or her from Owen. They were a unit, a family.

And he was on the outside.

"Principal Wright. I didn't know you'd be visiting us today." Owen's teacher, Ms. Feltz, met him at the door, and then directed the class to say good morning. He smiled at their chorused greeting. He might not have everything he wanted, but he did have a whole school full of kids that needed him and, most of the time, respected him. That was worth a lot.

"Good morning to you all. I suppose you have noticed the newest, furriest member of the class?" Giggles and nods responded. "Good. Well, I know she's a super cute dog, and you all want to meet her, but as Mrs. Palmer and Owen are going to explain, she's here for a special reason. She's a working dog, and just like it is your job to pay attention to Ms. Feltz and follower her instructions, it's Lily's job to pay attention to Owen and follow his instructions." Owen straightened in his chair at Luke's words. "You already know you aren't allowed to play around and distract your classmates from their work, and that goes for Lily, too. Let her do her job, or she won't be able to keep coming, okay?"

Laughter gone, they nodded. He made eye contact with each child, hopefully impressing upon them the seriousness of the situation. When he was as sure as he could be that they would at least try to do as he asked, he turned the floor over to Megan. "Mrs. Palmer is here today to help Lily get settled in, and to make sure everyone is comfortable. So listen to her and, if you have any questions, you can ask her or Owen, or Ms. Feltz."

"Thank you." Having Megan smile at him was like feeling the warmth of the sun on his face after a month of rain. He wanted to stay, to hear what she'd say to the children, to see her smile again. But he had no logical reason to remain, and a full day of meetings and phone calls ahead of him. He'd made the right decision by coming to the classroom. He'd gotten his fix. It would have to be enough.

For now anyway. Because she'd smiled at him, maybe he hadn't quite ruined everything after all.

If Megan had had any illusions that her life was tough, by midmorning Tuesday she'd reconsidered. Yes, juggling motherhood and a career on her own required some serious sacrifice, but it could be worse.

She could be an elementary school teacher.

Now that was tough.

Kids were constantly moving, asking questions, dropping pencils or needing bathroom breaks. The noise was nonstop, and she quickly developed a new appreciation for how hard Owen had to work to keep it together in such a high-stimulus environment. No wonder he came home exhausted each day. She was reaching that point herself and the school day wasn't even half over.

"Mom," Owen whispered, tugging on her sleeve. "What happens if Lily needs to use the bathroom?"

They'd been over this at least three times already, but for some reason Owen was still fixated on the question. That happened now and again. It was almost like his mind got stuck and no amount of reassurance seemed to help. She just had to wait it out; eventually he'd move on. Until then, he'd worry, sometimes obsessively. "Remember, I said that she goes out every three hours. You'll walk her to the spot I showed you, behind the school."

"What if I get lost? Or I forget? What if she has an accident on the floor?" His horrified expression made it seem like having an accident in the classroom was the absolute worst thing that could happen to someone. And maybe to him it was. "You won't get lost, it's just down the hall. And if you forget and she needs to go, Lily will let you know, just like she does at home."

"What if I don't notice? Like, if I'm busy taking a test or something?"

Ms. Feltz glanced their way, sending a wordless reminder that the students were supposed to be working quietly. Even if Megan could figure out a way to reassure Owen, this wasn't the time or place for what would assuredly be a long conversation.

"Listen, let's take her right now and then you won't have to worry."

"Now?"

"Yes. I'll go with you and make sure you remember how to get there, okay?"

"But I'm not done with my worksheet!"

Ms. Feltz sent another, sterner look their way.

Crap. Not good. "Fine, you finish your work, and I'll run out and take her myself. You can go with me next time."

"Thanks, Mom."

Taking Lily's leash, Megan tried to be as unobtrusive as possible as she navigated between tables to the front of the room. Still, she attracted quite a bit of attention and decided she'd ask about Owen moving to a spot closer to the door tomorrow. That would at least make these little trips less disruptive.

That still left the issue of Owen's anxiety about the task. She wasn't sure what to do about that.

"Penny for your thoughts."

Luke's voice came from somewhere behind her. Spinning, she somehow tangled Lily's leash around her ankles, tripping herself up and confusing the poor dog.

"Here, let me help you with that." His hand on her shoulder was probably meant to steady her, but the memories his touch sparked were more unsettling than the sudden loss of balance. Standing on one leg, she quickly unwrapped the leash and took a much needed step back. Space was a good thing. She just wasn't sure there was enough of it in the universe to keep her from reacting to this man.

He let his hand fall back to his side, a sheepish grin on his face. "Sorry, I didn't mean to startle you."

"It's fine." Megan shifted the leash from one hand to

the other, hating how awkward this was. What a difference a day could make. One dumb decision, one loss of control, and now everything was different.

Before, when he'd just been Owen's principal, she'd sometimes been anxious because she was worried about her son and his education. Now, she still had that to deal with, but there was this big barrier between them, one she'd thrown up. Necessary, but uncomfortable. She didn't know what to say, or how to be around him. How did you go back to a purely professional relationship with someone after something like that?

Seeing she had her balance, Luke motioned for her to continue walking, falling into step beside her. "Is everything going well in the classroom?"

"Just fine. Why?" What had he heard? Could the teacher have contacted him with complaints already? Owen had been a bit loud, and the other students did seem a bit distracted, but it was the first day. "Just working out the kinks, figuring out a routine, that kind of thing," she explained, trying not to sound defensive.

"Good. I just wondered…you seemed pretty pensive. When I saw you leaving with Lily, I was worried."

"Oh no, I'm just taking her for a bathroom break. Owen was in the middle of something, so I'm taking her myself." They'd reached the end of the hall and she paused. Was the conversation over or was he going to follow her outside? Did she want him to? She hated this…this feeling of uncertainty. "So, I'd probably better do that. Take her out, I mean."

"Right. Of course." He stepped forward and pressed

down on the heavy metal bar that activated the door. "Ladies first."

She stepped past him, careful not to accidentally brush against him. At least outside she could put more distance between them, have a bit of breathing room. Lily, unconcerned by human drama, made her way briskly to the grassy area that ran between the back of the school building and the faculty parking lot. Once there, however, she took her sweet time. Apparently every grass blade needed to be smelled individually before she could choose her spot.

Megan mentally willed the dog to hurry. The sooner Lily was done with her business, the sooner she could escape whatever awkward conversation Luke was planning. The chaos of the classroom suddenly seemed like a refuge in comparison to the noise in her own head.

"I'm sorry."

Once again, Luke's words had her spinning around in surprise. At least this time she hadn't hog-tied herself in the process. Of all the possible ways she'd imagined this conversation could go, him apologizing to her hadn't been on the list.

"Why?" she blurted, confused.

"Because I somehow upset you, and I didn't mean to do that. I never meant to make you uncomfortable."

Her brain tried and failed to make sense of his words. "You didn't do anything. I'm the one who should be apologizing. I was the one who made advances. And then I was so rude to you." She shook her head, remembering. "You didn't deserve that, I'm sorry."

"No apology needed, and I'm glad to know it wasn't

something I did." He grinned that slow burn of a smile that made her insides melt. "For the record, I didn't mind your advances one bit."

Her heart skipped a beat as his meaning hit her. "Then...why did you stop me?" She glanced around, making sure they were still alone.

He stepped closer, lowering his voice so she had to strain to hear him. "Because it was either stop while I still could, or lift you onto that countertop and have my way with you. And as appealing as that was, I knew it wasn't the right time or place."

The expression on Megan's face when she realized what he was saying told him the desire flooding his senses was far from one-sided. She could deny it, but words wouldn't erase the dilated pupils and flushed cheeks, or the flutter of pulse he saw at her throat.

Unfortunately, that was all the reaction he was going to get. Just as she opened her mouth to speak, a giggling group of kids came around the corner, followed by the school's PE teacher.

"Coach Destefano." He gave a small salute to the woman and received a wave in return. "Tennis today?" The courts and a small storage shed housing some sports equipment were the only things on this side of the school, other than the parking lot itself.

"You got it. Got a few kids with a real decent swing. I'm thinking we might be able to put a team together this year."

"Great. Set up a meeting and we'll talk." He could probably find some funds somewhere for that. Maybe hit up the local tennis club for sponsorship. Florida had plenty of professional players; maybe he could get one to make a donation. Adding more fundraising to his to-do list wasn't appealing, but he knew how beneficial after-school sports could be. Making a mental note to look into it, he waited until the coach and her class were out of earshot before turning back to Megan.

Too late. She was gone.

Disappointment flared but didn't diminish the triumph he'd felt when he'd seen her reaction. Nothing was truly resolved between them, yet he had a better feeling for where he stood. Where they would go from here, he didn't know. There was a lot to consider. His job, for one. Maybe he'd take Grant up on his offer to look over the paperwork he'd signed with the school board. Nevertheless, even if he was in the clear legally, that didn't mean there wouldn't be ethical issues to consider. To say nothing of the optics of it all.

Paradise was a nice town, but there were times he wondered why the place even had a newspaper since the rumor mill ensured everyone knew everything that happened to anyone well before it could hit the printed page. In a big city, no one would care about his dating a student's parent. But in Paradise, it would be big news. Was he willing to deal with that? Was Megan? What about Owen?

Luke shook his head, as if to physically shake the swirling thoughts into some kind of order. He was getting ahead of himself. Just because Megan felt some attraction to him didn't mean she wanted to do anything about it.

What if she does?

That question circled through his head the rest of the school day. Somehow, he managed to get his work done, though his customary focus seemed fractured. Ms. White, with her usual directness, asked if he needed to take a sick day after he asked her the same question three times and still didn't remember the answer. He'd assured her he was simply tired, and then gotten a lecture on the importance of sleep and the benefits of warm milk with a splash of bourbon at bedtime. She'd said that last part with a conspiratorial wink, warning him to keep her advice to himself as not everyone understood the medicinal benefits.

Luke had agreed, struggling to keep a straight face. He'd heard stories about the amount of "medicine" consumed at the monthly card games she and the other grand dames of Paradise attended. He was pretty sure there were fraternity parties that were less rowdy. Still, her concern touched him, so he nodded with an appropriate amount of gravity and assured her he'd take her secret to the grave.

He'd hoped to catch a few minutes with Megan in the cafeteria at lunch, but had been stuck dealing with a student found vandalizing school property. A bit of a harsh term for doodling a heart with a boy's name in it on her desk, as he'd pointed out in a private email to the teacher who'd sent her to his office. The poor girl had been humiliated at having her crush exposed, so he'd just given her a warning and a bottle of all-purpose cleaner to remove her artwork. Not a big deal, but it meant he'd had to eat a sandwich at his desk instead of stealing a few minutes with Megan.

Now it was almost time for the dismissal bell, and he wasn't going to miss his chance again. Assuming things had gone well today, she wouldn't be back in the classroom on Wednesday. Then who knew when he'd get to see her next. He wasn't sure what, if anything, was going to happen between them but he knew for a fact that letting things drop, without any further contact, didn't feel right.

He made it to Owen's classroom two minutes before dismissal, and chose to wait outside rather than to disrupt the class. His earlier visit had been explicable, but a second might arouse suspicion. Or maybe he was overthinking things. Either way, he waited and watched, the small glass window in the old oak door giving him a clear view. She'd moved, he noticed. Now Owen was at the first desk, closest to the door, with Lily between him and the wall. It made sense. Lily was now out of the way, where she wouldn't be accidentally stepped on or tripped over by a distracted student, and boy and dog had easy access to the exit.

He was wondering whose idea it had been to switch when Megan looked up and caught him watching. She started. For a moment, he was afraid she'd be upset at the intrusion. But then a small smile softened her expression and he relaxed, nodded in return. Just then, the bell rang, and instantly the atmosphere changed. Children jumped out of their seats as if on springs, scrambling for backpacks and lunchboxes. Moving aside, he let the jostling herd pass through the open door. A few students said hello to him, but most were too intent on making an escape to notice he was there.

Once the initial chaotic flood receded, he cautiously poked his head through the doorway. "Is the coast clear?"

"Mostly," Ms. Feltz answered, a grin on her face. "I suppose I should try to get them to be more civilized at dismissal but—" she shrugged "—I figure as long as they behave themselves during class time, I won't fault a little extra enthusiasm when it's over. Some days I kind of feel like running and shouting myself."

He chuckled, picturing the fortysomething woman with the beginnings of gray in her hair scrambling with the rest of them in the mad dash for daylight and freedom. "I know exactly what you mean. And," he reassured her, "don't worry, I won't keep you. I just wanted to check in with our furry friend here to find out if we should expect her back tomorrow."

Megan looked from him to the teacher and then at Owen and sighed, the sound carrying in the now quiet classroom. Something tightened in his gut. After seeing Lily in action this past weekend, he hadn't expected there to be any problems. The look on Megan's face seemed to say otherwise.

"For the most part, things went very smoothly." Ms. Feltz jumped in, her matter-of-fact tone easing the tension in the room.

"But?" he asked. Megan wouldn't look so concerned if there wasn't more to the story.

"We had a bit of trouble with figuring out the best way to handle her potty breaks." Megan answered for her. "Owen's not quite comfortable taking her on his own yet."

"I was busy!" Owen insisted defensively. "The other kids might finish while I'm gone, and then I won't know what to do."

Ah. So the issue wasn't Lily, it was Owen. That was something he'd failed to consider and, from the look of frustration on Megan's face, he wasn't the only one. Even the normally steadfast Ms. Feltz seemed at a loss. "I told him I wouldn't penalize him if he needed extra time to care for Lily but..."

But given Owen's rigid thinking, that hadn't done the trick. "I see. So, if we set aside that issue for the moment, would you say Lily was otherwise helpful?"

His question, meant for all of them, was answered by Owen himself. "Yeah. When my pencil broke, I got mad. It was the new red one. My favorite," he explained. "I wanted to throw it, but Lily told me not to."

"Um, okay." Luke looked to Megan for help. He'd learned that service dogs could perform some amazing tasks, but he was pretty sure the ability to speak English wasn't one of them.

"I think what Owen means is that she nudged him, or put her head in his lap. She's trained to distract him when she senses he's getting upset." Megan reached down and stroked the big dog's head. "It's pretty effective."

"Right, that's how she tells me. And when Jake was standing too close to me in line, Lily got between us so I didn't have to push him away."

"No pushing," Megan replied automatically. "Use

your words. If someone is in your space, you need to ask them to back up."

Good advice. He imagined Owen did his best to follow it, but given the number of times the boy had been sent to his office for discipline issues, he hadn't been very successful. If Lily was helping with those issues, she deserved to be there. "So the only issue is the bathroom breaks, is that right?"

Three heads nodded in unison. "Okay, so what if he took her... I don't know, when there is free time or something?"

"What? I don't want to miss recess," Owen objected.

"Oh, right." It was a logical solution, but from a kid's point of view, it probably seemed like a punishment. Not what he was going for. "Sorry, just trying to brainstorm." He absently scratched his head. There had to be a way around this. "How often does she need to go out?" he asked, trying to grasp the scope of the problem.

"During a school day? Once, maybe twice, to be safe," Megan responded.

"It doesn't take long, right? I could ask around. Maybe one of the staff would be willing to do it." Hell, he'd do it himself if need be, although how he'd find the time to duck out twice a day, every day, he wasn't sure.

"No." Megan shook her head. "The staff here works hard enough, and I'm pretty sure their job duties don't include walking dogs and picking up poop."

Luke rocked back in surprise. Megan was the last person he'd expected to object. After all the effort she'd put in to making this happen, he couldn't believe she was giving up now. He was about to tell her so when she made him an offer she couldn't refuse.

"This was my idea, so I'll do it. Like you said, it won't take long, and one of the benefits of working from home is being able to set my own hours. I'll just run over and take her out myself. If that works for everyone else, I mean." She turned to Owen's teacher. "I promise, I won't do anything to disturb the class."

The woman smiled, obviously relieved to have a possible solution. "That sounds fine to me."

Now all eyes were on him, waiting for his final decision.

A chance to have Megan on campus every day? Hell yeah, that worked for him. He only had one question.

"When can you start?"

Chapter Nine

Megan couldn't believe how easily they'd fallen into the new routine. She'd drop Owen off in front of the school each day and he'd proudly walk Lily into the building and on to class. Then, about two hours later, she'd come back, pick up her visitor pass at the front office, and quietly sneak into the classroom to get Lily. Five minutes later, she'd return and leave. A few hours later, she'd repeat the process, and then finally come back to pick them both up.

So far, the strategy was working. Owen hadn't had any more trips to the principal's office and, even better, the other kids were warming up to him now that his behavior was more predictable. For the first time he was making friends. In fact, the only hitch in the system was the hit to her work schedule.

She hadn't quite anticipated how much her concentration would be affected by the constant stopping and starting. And even though nothing on Paradise was particularly far from anything else, four round trips added up to hours being cut from her work day.

She'd taken to working in the park across from the school to save the drive time, but using her phone as a wi-fi hotspot wasn't ideal, and the weather wasn't going to hold out forever. Fall was well upon them, and although the temperatures didn't drop drastically this far south, the periodic cold fronts could trigger nasty thunderstorms. The weather had seemed okay when she'd left the house this morning, but now angry dark clouds raced across a slate-colored sky. Hesitating at the front door to the school, she considered her options.

"It looks pretty miserable out there, doesn't it?"

She turned, grinning when she caught sight of Luke approaching. Over the past few weeks, she'd gotten used to him popping up out of nowhere. She didn't see him every time she came to the school, but often enough that she no longer thought the run-ins were accidental. He was seeking her out and, despite herself, she was flattered. Besides, she honestly enjoyed his company. There had been no more talk about the night they'd kissed. Instead, they had fallen into a comfortable friendship, sharing funny stories about their day or commiserating over the stresses of their very different but equally demanding careers.

She still felt a tingle in her belly when she was around him. But he was a handsome man; she'd have to be dead not to feel some attraction. And unlike in her empty kitchen, there was no risk here of her giving in to temptation. As long as they were in public, she was safe to enjoy his company. After all, no matter how hot he looked or what his deep voice did to her insides, Megan wasn't going to accost him in the middle of a school hallway.

So she let herself enjoy their little encounters and refused to feel guilty about it. What she was feeling less than thrilled about was the current weather. "Yeah…that wind is vicious, and I didn't think to bring a jacket." She looked down at her T-shirt and jeans and shrugged. "I guess I'll work at the diner today and hope I don't wear out my welcome." She had done it a few times when rain had driven her indoors, but hated taking up a table for hours during the lunch rush. The library and coffee shop, while quieter, were on the other side of the island.

"Or you could just work here. The coffee at the diner is better, but our prices can't be beat."

He'd offered to let her camp out at an empty desk in the administration suite before, but she'd always turned him and his offer of free coffee down. Everyone had already made so many accommodations for Owen; she didn't want to be even more of a burden. Besides, she wasn't sure how much work she'd get done with Luke around. Her thoughts tended to drift to less than professional topics in his presence.

Still…she did have a lot of work to do and a bustling restaurant wasn't a distraction-free environment, either. As she considered, a clap of thunder shook the building and the heavens opened up. The world outside shrank;

her view of the park across the street now blocked by a solid wall of water.

"Unless you've got a snorkel in that bag of yours, I think you're staying here for a while."

"Just a phone and my laptop, so I guess I'm stuck." She watched the storm for a moment; awed by its power despite the inconvenience it created. "But just for today."

"Whatever you say," he agreed. Too easily. If she didn't know better, she'd think he was glad she was stuck here for the afternoon. The thought made her nervous, which was silly. He was just being nice. Friendly, even. That was all. He wasn't going to make a move on her in his place of business. Unbidden, her mind returned to the first day she'd brought Lily to school, when he'd told her he'd wanted to have his way with her. A shiver that had nothing to do with the weather ran through her.

"You're cold," Luke said, noticing. "I've got an old sweatshirt in the office if you want it."

She didn't correct him. "Thanks, but I'll be fine. I just need a place to sit, and maybe some of that free coffee."

"Right this way." He led her through the outer section of the administration area toward the private space where his office was located. For a moment, worried that's where he was headed, she considered turning around. Call her a coward, but she'd rather brave the storm than risk spending the next couple of hours only a few feet away from Luke. Thankfully, he continued down the hall and opened the door to a room she hadn't noticed before.

The walls were lined with bookshelves heavy with an assortment of supplies and textbooks. In the center of the room, taking up nearly all the remaining space, there was a long conference table surrounded by standard office chairs that, despite their blandness, still somehow managed to look out of date. A bank of windows on the wall opposite the door boasted old-fashioned roll-up shades, currently closed. Still, she could make out flashes of lightning behind them as the storm gathered steam.

"What do you think? It's technically our conference room, but as you can see, it's more a storage area than anything. Most of the teachers prefer to meet with parents in the classroom and the staff meetings are held before or after school, which means it's all yours whenever you need it."

"Wow." A place to work uninterrupted for hours at a time? "This is perfect." Thunder crashed again, closer than before, making her jump.

"I think your standards may be too low," he said with a chuckle, "but it's dry at least. You've got the wi-fi password, and the coffee is in the teacher's lounge two doors down, so you'll have plenty of caffeine. If you need anything else, just knock on my door."

She shook her head, determined not to impose any more than she already had. "You go do principal stuff, and don't worry about me. I'll be fine on my own." She always was. But as he left, closing the door behind him, she wondered if fine was good enough. Because, for the first time, she wasn't sure it was.

* * *

Luke had never been so glad for a thunderstorm in his life. For weeks now, he'd watched Megan truck across the street to the park bench that had become her personal office. She'd never complained, but even this far into fall, the heat could be brutal. When she came for Lily's afternoon break, she usually looked flushed and sticky. The one time he'd noticed her rubbing her neck, she'd straightened and mumbled something about it being awkward to type without a real table. His frequent offers to stay and work at the school were always rebuffed, with her insisting it wasn't necessary.

Maybe not, but she deserved more than just the necessities in life. If it was within his power to make things even a bit easier for her, he wanted to do that. And yeah, maybe if she were around more, he'd finally get the nerve up to ask her out. He'd thought about it often enough—sometimes it was all he could think of. But although they seemed to have returned to a semblance of friendship, he could sense the barriers she'd erected. She wasn't ready for more than that. She might never be. So he grabbed whatever brief moments he could and waited for some kind of sign.

He wanted to believe that her agreeing to stay at the school today was that sign, but he was pretty sure Mother Nature, not any romantic interest, had spurred that decision. Still, she was there. It wouldn't be that strange if he dropped in to check on her at some point and then casually suggest they go out for dinner sometime, right? Or maybe dinner was too much. Maybe drinks. Or coffee. Start small, and see how things went.

It was a solid plan. Except, of course, for the very real chance that his mounting interest would scare her off. Was he willing to risk it? Especially since there were myriad reasons why he shouldn't pursue her at all. His job, her busy lifestyle, the fact that she'd reacted very badly the one time they'd crossed the line from friendship to something more. Yeah, he had plenty of rationale for leaving things as they were, not rocking the boat. And one good reason for moving forward.

Megan.

She was the first thing he thought of when he woke up, and what he dreamed of at night. He'd even started timing his meetings around her dog's potty schedule, for crying out loud. And, like a junkie who needed more and more to get his fix, those few minutes in the hallway weren't cutting it anymore.

If they were dating, he'd have the right to call her in the evenings, or to drop by. They'd get the chance to have real conversations. He'd picked up bits and pieces about her life, but he wanted to know more. He wanted to know everything about her. And most of all, he wanted to have another taste of her.

That thought pushed him over the edge. Shoving up from his desk, he stalked down the hall to the closed conference room door. Rapping once, he pushed it open and found her chewing on the end of a pencil as she squinted at her computer screen. She didn't look happy.

Maybe this was a bad idea. The timing was off. She hadn't even seemed to notice that he was there. He could just leave and try another day.

Then again, she might go back to working at the

park. This might be his only chance. He was going to hate himself if he didn't take it.

This very well might be now or never. And never wasn't an option he was willing to contemplate.

Not wanting to startle her, he cleared his throat as he entered. No reaction. Again, he considered leaving. Again, he rejected the idea. At this point, he just wanted this whole thing to be over with, even if she turned him down. At least he'd know, and maybe then he could stop obsessing over her.

Giving up on the subtle approach, he approached the table. "Hi."

That was terrible, as far as pickup lines went, but she looked up, so he'd take it.

"Oh. Hi." She pushed at the strands of hair that had fallen over her eyes, shoving them haphazardly back into the loose bun she always wore. He'd overhead one of the female teachers referring to the style as a messy bun, or a mom bun, but whatever it was, it was sexy as hell. Or maybe that was just Megan in general. Yeah, pretty sure that was it.

As Luke stood there staring at her like a loon, her expression grew concerned. "Is everything all right? Did someone complain about me being here?" She started to close her laptop. "I can leave. I'm sure the storm will be letting up soon." Another crash of thunder made her wince. "Or not. But—"

He caught her hand, stilling it before she could put her computer into her bag. "Stop. Everything's fine. I was just…checking on you." Now he was the one wincing. "In a totally non-stalker-ish, supportive-of-your-independence kind of way."

She stared at him, a strange, almost painful look on her face.

Great, he'd offended her.

She laughed suddenly, bending almost double and shaking with the force of it. He probably should be offended, her amusement was definitely at his expense. But seeing her let loose was more than worth the blow to his ego. She always maintained an edge of control, even in the most casual environment. Only when she'd kissed him had he glimpsed the real Megan, the one who didn't feel the need to weigh every decision, to consider every action. And now, again, he was seeing her. As she gasped for breath, her eyes sparkled as she giggled uncontrollably, and he was awestruck.

"I'm sorry," she finally managed to say, wiping the tears from her eyes. "But that was probably the most ridiculous thing I've heard in a long time."

"No worries. You looked like you could use a laugh. If I'd known sticking my foot in my mouth would have that effect on you, I'd have done it a long time ago."

"And why is that?" she questioned, a smile still on her lips. If he didn't know better, he'd have thought she was flirting.

"Everyone needs a bit of fun now and then. And," he said, biting the bullet, "you're beautiful when you laugh."

Her face froze, and he felt her armor slip back into place, the walls go up. Desperate not to lose the moment, he plowed on. "I actually came in here to ask if you'd like to go out for coffee. With me."

She dropped her gaze and reached for her computer, avoiding his eyes. "No need, the coffee here really isn't that bad. I had a cup just a bit ago."

He wondered for a second if he'd been unclear. Maybe she hadn't realized he was asking her out, not inquiring about her caffeine status. Her shaking hands and the blush of pink climbing up her cheeks told him the misunderstanding was deliberate.

He could leave it be, back off and go along with the charade. Or he could go for broke.

"Megan." He waited until she looked up at him. If she wanted to turn him down, she was going to have to say it to his face. "I want to spend more time with you. Personally, not professionally."

"I…I don't understand."

"I'm asking you out. On a date. Coffee. Dinner. A movie. Whatever you want."

Indecision clouded her sky blue eyes. "Do you really think that's a good idea?"

"The truth?" He shrugged. "I don't know. But I do know I can't stop thinking about you."

Her blush deepened and she tried to look away.

"Don't." He lowered himself into the chair beside hers and cupped her cheek, turning her eyes toward his. "Don't run away from this."

Megan's pulse was pounding so loudly in her ears she could barely make out Luke's words. But his meaning was clear. He was right. She was running. Not just from him, but from the feelings he brought to the surface, feelings she'd thought were gone forever. Did she want to go down that road again? She'd nearly lost herself in the pain of losing her husband, but she'd held strong because of Owen. If she and Luke tried and things didn't work out, she'd be risking not only her own heart, but Owen's, as well.

Taking hold of that thought, she let out a breath. "People will talk. You know they will. We sat in the same pew and half the town had us eloping by the end of the week. If we go out on a date, it will start a feeding frenzy among the gossip groupies."

His fingers traced the curve of her jaw and up to her ear. "I don't care."

It was so hard to focus while he was touching her like that, but she had to try. "You don't mean that. Besides, I care. I don't want Owen having to deal with it."

His hand stilled, letting her know she'd made her point. But then his grin returned and his fingers began working their magic again, this time finding their way to the nape of her neck. "So we keep it a secret. That could be fun."

He pulled her to him, closing the small gap until her thigh pressed against his knees. "I'd love to take you out and show you off, but if privacy is what you want, I can definitely work with that." The husky tone of his voice had her body tingling in all the right places, making it hard to think of a reason to say no. Or maybe she just didn't want to say no. His strong hand began gently kneading the knots of tension at the base of her neck and she groaned.

His pupils dilated at the sound, his breath hitched. She loved the effect she had on him, even as she fought her own response. "No one will know?" she whispered, desire nearly strangling the words.

"Not unless you want them to."

"Okay." She said it quickly, before she could change her mind.

Her sudden agreement seemed to surprise Luke. One eyebrow raised, he searched her face as if expecting a trick. "Really? You're sure?"

No, she wasn't sure. But for once she was going to leap before she looked. If—or more likely when—things went badly, she'd deal with it. With their reputations and Owen's feelings protected, all she was risking was her own pain. And with Luke's lips so close to hers, his touch and scent filling her senses, she was willing to deal with that later for just a little of how he was making her feel right now.

Putting that all into words would ruin the moment, so she showed him instead.

Angling forward, she found his mouth with hers. Last time, she'd been tentative, hesitant, easing her way into the kiss. This time, she skipped past it all. She'd waited weeks to taste him, and she wasn't waiting any longer. Greedily, she licked, nipped, and explored his mouth, and he met her hunger with his own. The hand at her neck held her steady while his other hand moved to her thigh, tracing small circles higher and higher. Eyes closed, she tried to move nearer, needing to be pressed against him but boxed in by the arm of the chair and the edge of the table.

Sensing her frustration, he shifted and gripped her waist, lifting her up while kicking the chair out of the way. For an instant, she was floating, carried in his strong arms, and then she felt the hard wood of the conference room door against her back. Click. The sound of the lock was loud in her ears. Had anyone else heard it? Were some staff member standing in the hallway right now, listening?

"Stop," Luke growled.

"Stop what?" she asked, squirming as he nipped at the sensitive skin above her collarbone.

"Thinking." He licked the spot he'd just grazed, and she gasped at the contrasting sensations.

"I'm not supposed to think?" she managed to ask before his mouth covered hers, silencing her with a very thorough kiss.

He lifted his head. "Not right now." He kissed her, and this time she felt her knees start to buckle. "Just feel."

As if to convince her, he pressed his body against hers, pinning her gently with his hips while his hands roamed up and down her sides, leaving goose bumps in their wake.

Mmm...he was right. Feeling was better than thinking. Giving in, she reached for him, pulling him ever closer.

His mouth returned to Megan's skin, setting her on fire each place his lips landed. She fisted her hands into his shirt, holding on for dear life. The only thing she was capable of thinking now was that they were both wearing way too many clothes.

He must have had the same thought. "How unprofessional would it be for me to strip you down and take you against this door?" he asked, sneaking a hand under her T-shirt.

She gasped as he cupped her breast, arching toward him even as she vetoed the idea. "Very."

His hand stilled and then eased back to her waist. His breathing was ragged, his muscles rigid beneath the starched fabric of his shirt. For a moment, they just stood there, forehead to forehead, as the world slowly came back into focus.

"At least this time you can't kick me out," he teased once they were both breathing normally.

Ugh, she still couldn't believe she'd done that. But he was overwhelming, and having her barriers knocked down at the time had freaked her out. Especially when she'd been the one knocking them down.

"You're doing it again." His voice was light though his stare was serious. "You have a very bad habit of overthinking things."

"Sometimes." Might as well own it. "When things are complicated."

A wicked little smile crossed his face. "Well then, how about I simplify things. I like you, and I'm pretty sure you like me."

She nodded, biting her lip.

"Then that's all that matters. Like I said, simple."

She wanted to believe him. But somehow, she didn't think it was going to be quite that easy.

Chapter Ten

Luke had never thought of himself as a masochist, but encouraging Megan to work in the empty conference room during the day had turned into a kind of self-torture. Sitting in his office all week, knowing she was just down the hall, was a painful temptation. The few stolen kisses they'd managed had only primed his desire, until it threatened to spill over in public, which he had promised wouldn't happen. The only saving grace in all of this was that he knew Megan was dealing with the same frustration.

What they needed was a few hours of actual privacy. The problem was how to make that happen. Not only was there Owen to consider, but they both were incredibly busy. She had a big coding project she was working on for some client in Mumbai, and he had people breathing down his neck about the annual fundraiser banquet coming up. Each year they put on a holiday-themed event, hoping to hit people when they were looking to make end-of-year tax-deductible donations. Last year's totals had been less than stellar, and although it wasn't official, he'd be willing to bet that was a big reason the board had decided to bring new blood into the administration. Namely, him. And if he wanted to keep his job, he needed to be sure this year's gala and fundraising totals weren't a repeat of last year's.

He was an educator, not a party planner, and it chafed him to have to spend so much time and energy dealing with catering decisions and seating arrangements—Mrs. Cristoff had called three times about that already today—when he had a million other, more relevant, issues to address. But he was a realist. Those donations were the reason All Saints was able to keep tuition affordable for the island families it served. Without them, he'd have to either cut salaries or charge parents more, and neither option appealed to him. He just wished the people with the money would write the checks based solely on the importance of the cause instead of needing to be wined and dined before they pulled out their wallets.

Fair or not, the gala meant he was swamped with more work than he could fit into a twenty-four-hour day, and that meant no sneaking over to Megan's after dark, like he had originally hoped. But tonight that was going to change. If they weren't going to be a couple in public, then they had to make time to be together in private. That was why he'd spent the entire day chained to his desk, pounding through as much work as possible just to take the evening off guilt-free.

Normally he made a point of "accidentally" bumping into Megan at least once during the day, either in the lounge where she'd switched the generic coffee for freshly ground beans she brought in herself, or in the halls when she was walking Lily. He'd gotten good at coming up with excuses to stop by the conference room, as well, usually under the pretext of storing or retrieving supplies from the packed shelves. He'd fetched and retrieved the same stack of manila folders three times, all to have a few minutes alone with her. But he was willing to skip that ruse today in favor of uninterrupted time with her tonight.

Forcing Megan from his mind, he clicked through his email, taking notes and sending responses where appropriate. Several were from parents inquiring about homework assignments or upcoming exams, and he forwarded those to the appropriate faculty member. He'd just landed on the email requesting approval of a field trip idea from the science department when a knock sounded at his door.

Frustrated by the interruption, he bit out a "come in" and returned his attention to the monitor in front of him.

"Is now a bad time?" Megan's hesitant query had his head snapping up in surprise.

"No, not at all." He grimaced, knowing he'd sounded short. "Please come in. My bark is worse than my bite, I promise."

She blushed at his word choice, and he realized the

accidental innuendo. Closing the door behind her first, she moved to the side of his desk.

Taking her hand, he pulled her into his lap and nipped at her lush bottom lip.

"Hey now," she laughed, wrapping her arm around his neck. "I thought you said you didn't bite."

"I lied." He did it again and then, since he was already there, kissed her thoroughly. When he came up for air, she was plastered against him, as if she couldn't get close enough. Stroking her back, he tipped his head so he could see her eyes. "Now that that's out of the way, what brings you to my office?"

Her eyes twinkled. "Other than this, you mean?"

"Hey, if you just couldn't make it through the day without touching me, I'm okay with that. I just was wondering if there was something else you needed."

She shrugged and laid her head on his shoulder, effectively hiding her face from him.

"Megan, honey, what is it?"

"Nothing. I just…well, you never stay in your office all day. I thought maybe you were avoiding me."

"What?" He sat straighter, shifting her so she was facing him again. He saw embarrassment but also fear in her eyes. Hell. Of course she'd think that. He'd been practically stalking her for weeks, and then today he'd gone MIA without any warning.

"No! I was just busy. I thought if I buckled down, I could knock out enough work to justify an evening off. I should have said something."

"Oh. Okay." She nodded but he could tell she wasn't fully convinced. "I get it, work comes first." She gave him a smile that didn't quite reach her eyes, and got to her feet, smoothing her clothes into place.

"I was trying to clear my plate so I could spend time with you."

That got her attention. She paused, half turned to the door. "You were?"

He nodded. "I was going to ask if I could come by tonight, after Owen's asleep." He let the implications of that hit her.

"Oh." She bit her lip. "What about the neighbors?"

"I'll park down the street and walk." He would scale a mountain if it meant having uninterrupted time with her. "So what do you say, can I come over?"

She grinned. "You'd better. How about nine?"

"Sounds good."

She started to leave then turned back, one hand on the doorknob. "Oh…and, Luke?"

"Yes?"

"Don't be late."

Megan practically sauntered back to her spot in the conference room. Not only was Luke not avoiding her, he was coming over. They were finally going to get some time together away from prying eyes. Anything could happen.

And just like that, the confidence she'd felt a moment ago congealed into a thick layer of anxiety. What had she just agreed to? In the heat of the moment, it was easy to forget all the baggage she carried, but now, sitting in a borrowed chair staring at a computer screen, she felt the weight of it. She wasn't some twenty-year-old, without a care in the world. She was a mom. She liked to think she still looked good, but pregnancy and nursing had changed her body. Motherhood had changed her soul. Dating, and all that went with it, had a whole different feel than before.

If you could even call what they were doing dating. A few stolen kisses and casual conversation wasn't exactly a relationship. That wasn't his fault; she was the one that had wanted to keep things secret. She still did, for good reasons. But suddenly it felt weird. Like it wasn't really happening. Once upon a time, she had shared the ups and downs of her love life with friends. But one by one they'd faded out of her life as her world shrank. At the time, she'd accepted it, maybe even embraced it. More people meant more complications.

But now that she had her head above water, she could grasp all that she'd missed. Agreeing to see where things went with Luke was a huge step, but it was time to make another one.

Picking up her phone, she found the number she wanted and called. Reaching out was scary, but she'd been brave enough to walk into Luke's office and confront him, and that gave her confidence.

"Paradise Animal Hospital, this is Olivia, how can I help you?"

"Hi, Olivia. This is Megan Palmer. I was hoping I could speak with the doctor? Or leave her a message?"

"Of course. Is everything okay with Lily?"

"She's fine. I was actually calling about a personal matter." Feeling foolish, she continued. "It's not urgent, but I don't have her cell number, so…"

"No worries. Let me just check if she's available." A click and then the sounds of classic rock and roll echoed over the line as she waited. A minute later the music abruptly ended and Cassie came on the line.

"Megan. What's up? Need me to drop off more dog food?"

She smiled at the woman's cheerful enthusiasm. "No, thanks. I was actually wondering if you had some time to talk."

"What kind of talk? I've got about ten minutes until my next appointment, or I could stop by on my way home."

"Well, remember how I said you'd be the first to know if anything changed…regarding a particular someone?"

A pause and then a high-pitched squeal that had Megan holding the phone away from her ear. "Okay," Cassie proclaimed, "that's definitely an in-person conversation. I'll be there as soon as I finish up. And I'm warning you, I'm going to want details."

True to her word, Cassie arrived on Megan's doorstep only a few minutes after the clinic closed. Still in her scrubs, she had a bottle of wine in her hand and a smug smile on her face.

"I hope you like merlot. A client gave me this a while back after I helped deliver her dog's puppies. I kept forgetting to bring it home, which works out, since this kind of news deserves celebrating."

Megan took the bottle and led Cassie to the kitchen.

"It's not like that, really. I mean, there isn't anything official to tell you."

Cassie started opening and closing cabinets, her back to Megan. "So give me the unofficial version. I don't care." She reached up to a high shelf and pulled down two stemmed glasses. "But pour first. It's been a long day."

Guilt had Megan pausing, corkscrew halfway into the bottle. "Are you sure you can stay? If you're tired, we could talk another time. You'd probably rather get home."

Taking the bottle out of her hands, Cassie finished uncorking it and filled both glasses. "I wouldn't be here if I didn't want to be." She took a deep sip of the ruby-colored liquid and sighed. "Besides, Alex is off tonight, and it's good for him to have some alone time with the kids." She took another, smaller sip. "And it's good for me to have some time where I don't have to be the doctor or the boss or the mom."

Now that, Megan could identify with, at least in in a theoretical way. She raised her glass. "I'll drink to that."

The wine was rich as it flowed over her tongue. But it was Cassie's friendly smile that warmed her insides. She'd missed this and hadn't even known it. Gratitude filled her. "Thanks for coming."

"Are you kidding? I'm dying to hear the latest update." She set her glass down. "I meant it when I said I want details. Remember, I'm a married lady, I have to live vicariously through you if I want some excitement in my life."

Megan raised an eyebrow. She'd seen Cassie's husband, a deputy with the local sheriff's office. Tall, dark, and handsome, he was the sexy cop fantasy brought to life. "I don't buy that for a minute. In fact, I would bet money you'll be creating your own excitement later tonight."

Cassie blushed. "Maybe. Still, I want to hear everything."

A glance out the glass door showed her Owen was still happily digging in the sandbox, his toy dinosaurs lined up beside him. Lily, a few feet away, had likely been assigned the role of assistant archaeologist. Confident her son was out of earshot and would stay that way for at least a few minutes, she motioned Cassie to join her at the kitchen table.

"I'm not quite sure where to start."

"Then skip to the good parts," Cassie suggested, wiggling her eyebrows.

Megan chuckled. Maybe it was the wine, maybe it was Cassie's blunt personality, but somehow she wasn't as nervous talking about this as she'd expected. "All right. So, since Lily started attending school with Owen, I've been going by there twice a day to take her out for her potty breaks."

Cassie made a face. "Please tell me that your dog's bathroom habits are not the good part."

Laughing, Megan shook her head. "Be patient."

"Fine, but if this doesn't get better, I'm going to need more wine."

"It does," she reassured her. "Anyway, like I said, I'm at the school twice a day, plus pickup and drop-off, of course. And, naturally, Luke is there, too."

"Being as he's the principal, that makes sense. Get to the part I don't know."

"Well, we've been talking a lot. He always seemed to show up in the hallway when I was there, or have some reason to be outside at the same time I was walking Lily. At first I thought it was coincidence."

"Please—" Cassie pointed a finger at Megan "—tell me that man was stalking you in a good way."

She shrugged. "Maybe. Probably. Either way, it was nice. He's fun to talk to."

"Nice to look at, too. But you didn't call me up because he's a good conversationalist. So, out with it, what happened?"

"Fine." Talking quickly, Megan outlined the lead-up to her working in the conference room. Then, taking a big gulp of wine for courage, she got to the point. "And then I kissed him."

"And did he kiss you back?" Cassie smacked herself on the forehead. "What am I saying? Of course he did."

"He did," Megan confirmed. "In fact, if the entire staff and student body hadn't been on the other side of the door, I think he would have done a lot more." Heat crept up her cheeks. "It got pretty intense."

Cassie fanned her face with her hand. "Hot and heavy in the conference room. Please tell me you didn't kick him out this time."

She shook her head. "No, but I made him agree to keep it a secret."

"Okay. I can kind of understand that, given how fast gossip flies around here."

"Exactly."

"So, now what? Are you two still making out on campus? Seeing each other outside of school hours? What?"

"Yes. No. I don't know." She looked down at her almost empty glass and considered a refill. "But he's coming over tonight, after Owen goes to sleep. It's the first time we will actually be alone and I'm not sure what he's expecting to happen."

Cassie considered that for a moment. "Well, unless you think he's going to try to force you into anything—"

"Never."

"Then the real question is what do you want to happen?"

"I don't know." And that was the reason she'd called Cassie. "I haven't dated in years. I don't know how to do this."

"If you mean the mechanics, I assure you nothing has changed," Cassie said with a smirk. "It's still insert tab A in slot B, if you know what I mean."

"You're terrible," Megan protested, laughing despite herself. "I mean I don't know if we are moving too fast, or if that's even a thing these days. We've never even gone out on a date and yet…"

"You don't think you can keep your hands off him." Cassie smiled. "Been there, done that, have the maternity clothes to prove it."

"Yikes."

"Yeah, that was my reaction, too. Alex and I hadn't been together long, sort of like you and Luke. I didn't plan for us to sleep together but…well, you've seen him." A dreamy smile briefly softened her expression before she turned serious again. "Obviously you're smarter than me, since we're having this conversation now instead of after seeing two pink lines. But I'm going to ask anyway. Have you thought about birth control?"

"Um…" Megan swallowed hard. She hadn't, not really. "I'm not on the pill or anything, but I assumed we'd use a condom if things got that far." Was she really having this conversation?

Cassie nodded in approval. "Always a good choice, especially since you don't know his history. Do you have any?"

She shook her head. She'd had no reason to buy such things until today.

"Well, if he's a typical guy, he'll come prepared. But make sure he does, before things get to the point of no return, if you know what I mean."

"Got it." Practical stuff covered, she drained the last droplet of wine. "But it probably won't come to that. I mean, I don't even know if he wants to sleep with me. Maybe he's expecting to come over and just watch a movie or something."

"Maybe, but I doubt it. If you're at this point, I can only assume he is, too. But if it doesn't feel right, put on that movie and wait until it does."

"How will I know if it's right?" She knew how to work with data and numbers, but this was unfamiliar territory. How was she supposed to make such a big decision without any kind of objective information to base it on?

Cassie laughed and stood, gathering up her purse

and keys. "Oh, you'll know. And when it is, it'll be amazing."

Megan walked Cassie to the door and said goodbye, grateful for her new friend's advice even if she wasn't sure how helpful it was. Apparently, there was no metric to rely on, no set timetable or clear signal to say when it was right to move to the next phase. Instead, she'd have to rely on her instincts, which, when it came to matters of romance, were rusty from years of neglect.

Still, despite her confusion, Megan had little butterflies of anticipation swirling in her stomach. Maybe Cassie was right, and she needed to just go with what felt right. Wasn't Luke always telling her she was overthinking things? What worked for her on a coding project or when creating a grocery list might not be the best approach for a romance. She just didn't know if she could turn off that analytical side long enough to try to find out.

Over the next few hours, she somehow managed to get Owen fed and bathed and ready for bed, even with her brain in overdrive. It got even worse after she tucked him in. Standing in front of her closet, she realized she had no idea of what to wear. Was a dress too formal for what wasn't even really a date? Jeans and a T-shirt didn't seem right, either. Exasperated, she considered calling and telling Luke not to come.

Except then she'd have to give a reason. He wasn't likely to accept her inability to choose an outfit as a valid excuse. Mostly because it wasn't.

She could text Cassie. But that was ridiculous. She

was a grown woman and fully capable of dressing herself.

Marching back to the closet, she grabbed her favorite skinny jeans and a coral scoop-necked blouse. Turning back to the dresser, she dug through her top drawer until she found a matching bra and panty set. Maybe nothing would happen tonight, but a girl couldn't be too prepared.

She hurried through a shower and was almost finished with her makeup when her phone buzzed, signaling an incoming text message.

I'm here.

Her hands shook as she typed out a response.

I'll be right there.

Quickly she brushed on light coat of mascara, and then tiptoed down the hall. She found Luke standing on the front step with a bottle of wine, and couldn't help but laugh.

"What's so funny?" He glanced around. "Do I have shaving cream on my face or something?"

She motioned him inside and shut the door as quietly as she could. "No. I'm sorry, it's just that I'm going to start to get a complex if people keep bringing me booze."

He narrowed his eyes. "Who else is bringing you wine?"

"Why, are you jealous?" She took the bottle and

carried into the kitchen, just as she had earlier that afternoon.

"No."

Considering his scowl said otherwise, her confidence shot up a notch. "I think you are. But," she added, taking pity on him, "you have no reason to be. Cassie Santiago had some a client had given her and shared it with me."

"I see," he said, the muscle along his jaw visibly relaxing. "That was nice of her."

"It was," she agreed. "And, for the record, you're the only man making late-night deliveries." Might as well get that out in the open. They'd never actually said they were exclusive, and she wasn't going to take things any further without knowing.

"Good. I didn't really think otherwise. But I'm afraid I don't share well." He took her hand and pulled her to him. His embrace was possessive—she could practically smell the testosterone—and despite her independence, she'd always been a sucker for an alpha male. Looking up, she sought his eyes. "Me, either. And I know we said we would just see what happens, and we aren't officially dating, but if there is anyone else—"

He shushed her with a press of his lips to hers. "There isn't. And there won't be, as long as we're still… involved. Promise. I'm old fashioned that way."

"Not too old fashioned, I hope." She licked her lips where the taste of him lingered, just enough to whet her appetite. She wanted to feast on this man. All of him. Her earlier worries were burning away from the heat he ignited in her. One small kiss and she felt the fire building inside, demanding she feed it. And just as Cassie predicted, she knew exactly what she wanted, and she wanted it now. "Because we don't have a chaperone."

"Thank goodness for that," he muttered, leaning down to kiss her again, slowly, thoroughly, exploring and teasing until her knees weakened.

She gripped his shoulders, letting his strength support them both, and gave in to the sensations washing over her. Time and space collapsed to this moment in this man's arms.

"Hold tight." His breathless command had barely penetrated when she felt her feet leave the ground. Instinctively, she wrapped her legs around his waist for balance, keeping them in place when he set her gently on the kitchen table.

"That's better." His breath tickled her ear when he spoke, her perch bringing her up to his level.

"Mmm-hmm," she agreed, using her legs to tug him closer, creating a delightful friction between her legs where their bodies met.

He kissed his way from her ear to her neck, pushing her blouse aside as he worked his way down. "I told you I wanted to get you on this table."

She arched her back, giving him better access. "Is reality living up to your fantasy?"

His hand dipped beneath the low neckline, cupping her breast. "Oh yeah. But if this is going where I hope it is, we may need a bedroom."

His thumb rasped across her nipple and she bit her lip to keep from moaning. "You think so?" she teased once she could speak.

He nodded, his mouth busy doing something amazing to her earlobe.

"Well then, what are you waiting for?"

Luke didn't need to be told twice. Releasing her breast, he gripped Megan's hips and lifted her easily, loving how well she wrapped around him. Quick steps took him down the hall to her bedroom, the only room of the house he'd hadn't been in. The furnishings were simple: a dresser missing a knob, an overstuffed chair with an assortment of clothes draped across the back and, most important, a queen-size bed centered under a low window.

Goal in sight, he was across the room in three strides. The caveman in him wanted to throw her down and strip her as quickly as possible. Instead, he stopped just short of the bedside and released his grip, letting her slide slowly down his body until her feet hit the floor. "Are you sure?" He needed to know this was fully her choice before they were in the bed, neither of them thinking straight. "We don't have to do this."

She stared at him, lips swollen from his kisses, hair mussed. "What? Don't you want to?"

"More than my next breath. But if you need more time—"

"Then all I need is to know if you brought protection."

Relief surged through him. "Yes, ma'am." He reached into his back pocket, withdrew his wallet and one of the condoms he'd stored there earlier. "Scout motto— Be Prepared."

She took the packet from him and tossed it on the bed. He reached for her, but she moved back, bumping into the mattress. Before he could protest, she grabbed the hem of her blouse and pulled it over her head, revealing a blue lace bra that barely covered her full breasts. He swallowed hard, temporarily frozen. When she reached behind to undo the clasp, he stopped her. "Let me."

She hesitated, and then dropped her arms to her sides. Stepping to her, he traced the strap over her right shoulder, gently sliding it down before dipping a finger under the sheer fabric covering her nipple. She whimpered as he teased her, and then moaned when he ducked down to suck her through the lace. Her responsiveness stirred his blood, sending it south to where he strained against his pants. But this wasn't about his pleasure—not yet. She was trusting him with her body and he would make darned sure she didn't regret it.

Releasing her now rock-hard nipple, he moved to the other side, using his left hand to pull the thin fabric down and give his mouth direct access. He licked and sucked, the fingers of his right hand working the other breast. Her breathing grew ragged, and he felt her thrust against him. Even fully clothed, he could feel her heat.

He felt her fingers at his belt, clumsily working the buckle. "You're killing me." Her frustrated whisper only encouraged him. Moving her hands aside, he reached for the button of her pants, kissing his way down her belly as he undid them. She shuddered as he eased the denim down her thighs.

"Up," he directed, lifting her until she was sitting on

the edge of the bed. Kneeling in front of her, he freed one foot and then the other from her jeans. His hands massaged her feet then her calves, kneading gentle circles as he felt her muscles relax. Only then did he move between her thighs, pressing a kiss to the scrap of fabric covering her before moving it aside.

He teased her, using his tongue and fingers, slowing whenever she approached climax, driving her higher but not letting her go over the edge. Not yet. He needed to be inside her when she let go.

Megan's hands fisted in his hair as she writhed beneath his mouth. Sensing she was nearly there, he explored her with his fingers and found her more than ready. Still, he teased a bit longer, waiting until she bucked beneath him before rising to his feet.

Her eyes fluttered open, confusion on her face, and he smiled. "I'm not done, don't worry." Quickly, he shucked his clothes, the sight of her driving him to hurry. She was the sexiest thing he'd ever seen, her flushed skin exposed by the lingerie he'd pushed aside somehow even hotter than if she'd been completely nude. He found the condom where she'd thrown it and quickly rolled it on. He thought about moving her to the center of the bed, but he didn't want to wait another second. Instead, he positioned himself back between her legs and pressed against her, letting her feel him at her entrance.

Her legs wrapped around him, pulling him closer, but he resisted. "Look at me." It took her a few seconds, but when her gaze met his, he thrust into her waiting body. He kept eye contact as he slowly withdrew, noted the desperation in her face, heard her whimpered frustration as he left her empty.

"Please…" she begged.

"Please what?" He shifted ever so slightly, stimulating her without moving any deeper.

"Please…don't stop." Her body arched up to him, and he couldn't hold out any longer even if he'd wanted to. Grabbing her thighs, he lifted her, adjusting his angle and then pushing forward, filling her over and over, watching her head roll side to side as she rode the waves of pleasure with him. When he felt her closing in, he increased his rhythm, and when she finally climaxed, the squeeze of her muscles pushed him over, too.

Stunned by the intensity of his release, he settled there, body shaking, as air heaved in and out of his lungs. Beneath him, Megan lay nearly motionless, eyes closed, even as he felt her spasm around him as she rode the aftershocks. When he thought he could move without falling over, he pulled out and used a tissue from the box on the nightstand to dispose of the condom before climbing up beside her on the mattress.

"Are you okay?" He ran a hand gently over her body and felt her shiver. "Cold?"

"Mmm…maybe a little." She snuggled against him. "But I feel too good to care."

He kept one arm around her and pulled back a corner of the bedspread with the other. Holding her tight, he rolled them both onto the exposed sheets before covering her up.

"Nice move." She giggled and pressed closer. "Actually, all of your moves are pretty good."

He pretended to frown. "Just good? Not amazing, or excellent, or the best you've ever seen?"

Her eyes twinkled. "You know, it's hard to really judge based on a single example. I might need a repeat performance to form a truly accurate opinion."

His body stir and he grinned. "I think we can make that happen."

Chapter Eleven

Megan woke the next morning sore in places she'd forgotten she had. Luke had made good on his promise of a repeat performance, and then, out of condoms, he'd found other ways to "improve his score," as he'd put it. By the time he'd left a few hours before dawn, she'd been more than willing to award him top marks before a final kiss goodbye.

A hot shower eased the kinks from her muscles and cleansed the scent of sex from her body. But nothing, not even the mundane chore of emptying the dishwasher or making breakfast, could wipe the satisfied smile off her face. Even Owen, not the most observant when it came to emotional nuance, had commented on it, asking why she was so happy.

That he didn't normally think she was happy gave her pause. "I'm always happy, buddy."

"Nope." He shook his head, too long bangs falling into his eyes. She'd have to convince him to let her cut his hair soon. A dilemma for another day. "Some days you are mad, or sad, and mostly you are just..." He struggled, his face crunching as he sought the right word. "Regular. You're usually just regular."

She chewed on the word and decided he was right. But that wasn't a bad thing. "I think most people are regular a lot of the time," she finally replied, using his terminology for lack of anything better.

He nodded, his eyes back on his cereal bowl. "Yup. But today you aren't regular. You're happy."

"I guess I'm just glad it's Saturday," she hedged. Not a lie, just not the whole truth. Thankfully, her son's newfound social awareness didn't seem to pick up on her prevarication. Or he just was more interested in the sugary cereal she only allowed on weekends than he was in her elevated mood. Just as well, she was still getting used to it herself.

A knock at the front door provided a welcome interruption from any further questions. Carrying her mug she answered it, her pulse stupidly ticking up in hope that it was Luke. But, of course, it wasn't. That wasn't their arrangement. Instead, Cassie was on her front step, again bearing food.

"I brought scones," she said by way of a greeting, as if it was perfectly natural for her to show up unannounced early on a Saturday morning. "Cinnamon are my favorite."

"Mine, too." Megan held the door wide for her, and then led the way to the kitchen, now empty. Owen's cereal bowl was in the sink and a glance out the back door showed him tossing a ball to Lily. "I know you said you wanted details, but you could have just called."

"I could have," she agreed, pulling two pastries out of the bag and placing them on the plates Megan handed her. "But you might not have answered. I figured it would be harder to avoid me in person."

She laughed, knowing Cassie was right, and grateful her new friend didn't hold that against her. "And you brought baked goods as backup?"

She shrugged. "I'm not above bribery."

"I'm glad." The cinnamon scones really were her favorite. "Can I get you some coffee?"

"Sure." Cassie accepted a cup and took a sip before starting her questioning in earnest. "So, how was it?"

"How was what?" Megan stalled, taking a bite of her scone. Sugary goodness crumbled in her mouth, almost making her forget the reason for Cassie's impromptu visit.

"Whatever it was that's left you with that ridiculous grin on your face."

Megan washed down the pastry with a sip of coffee, and shrugged. "I don't know what you mean."

"Liar!" Cassie said without a trace of malice. "You're practically glowing. Now spill it or I'll take back the scone."

Megan shook her head, amused more than annoyed. "Fine. If you must know, it was fantastic." She took a sip of her coffee then added, "All three times."

Cassie squealed and rounded the table, pulling her into a hug. "I knew it!"

Megan embraced her, laughing. "You did not."

"I did," Cassie insisted, pulling away. "Although I didn't know how many times. When you decide to do something, you really go for it."

"Making up for lost time, I guess." She ate another bite of her pastry. "I have to say, it was worth the wait."

"I bet," Cassie said with a knowing grin. "So, now what?"

She shrugged. "I don't know, exactly. By the time he left, we were too tired to talk about it."

"So he hasn't called yet, I take it?"

Megan glanced at the clock and then over at the counter where her phone was charging. "Not yet. But it's early. And really, it's okay if he doesn't. I'm a big girl, and we didn't make any promises." At least, that was what she'd been telling herself.

"No, it's not okay. If a man gets nookie, he should at the very least call the next day," Cassie insisted, indignation flashing in her eyes. "Better yet, he should send flowers."

Megan was about to argue when the doorbell rang. She settled for rolling her eyes at such an outdated, sexist idea and headed for the front of the house.

Ever curious, Cassie followed right on her heels. "Who do you think it is?"

"Your guess is as good as mine." She reached the door and swung it open, stumbling into Cassie in the process. "Give me some space, will you?" she protested, catching herself on the doorjamb.

"Oh, okay. Sorry. I thought…never mind."

Too late, she looked up. Luke, looking befuddled, stood at her front door with a bouquet of tropical flowers in his hand. Crap.

"Hi," Cassie said in a chipper voice from somewhere over Megan's left shoulder.

"Um, hi. Cassie Santiago, right? Nice to see you." Shifting from one foot to the other, he nodded before turning back to Megan. "I'll just go. You can call me… or not…whatever." He started to turn and then, as if suddenly remembering, he thrust the flowers at her. "These are for you. Do what you want with them."

"Wait, no!"

Misunderstanding, he jerked his head toward Cassie. "Fine if you don't want them, maybe she does."

Frustrated, she grabbed his arm. "I mean no, don't leave."

He shook off her hand, hurt shadowing his features. "It's fine. If you want space, I can do that. I didn't mean to overstep."

This was ridiculous. "I said, don't go." Clearing her throat, Megan started over. "When I said I wanted space, I was talking to her." Megan pointed at Cassie, who was watching the goings on with rapt attention. "She was standing too close and I backed into her trying to open the door."

Cassie waved, looking only slightly embarrassed. "It's true. I was trying to see who was at the door. I thought it might be you, and I was right." She turned to Megan, smirking. "And I was right about the flowers, too."

Luke rubbed a hand over his jaw. Clearly, this hadn't been the welcome he'd expected.

"Please, come in. Cassie was just leaving."

Taking the hint, Cassie nodded. "Right, consider me already gone." She dug in her pocket, pulled out her keys and then scooted by the two of them and out to her car.

Megan watched her drive away then turned to find Luke staring at her. "Let's start over, shall we?" She backed up, breathing a quiet sigh of relief when he followed her inside and mutely handed her the bouquet. "Thank you for the flowers. They weren't necessary, but I love them."

A bit of the tension bunching Luke's shoulders seemed to dissipate. "Good. I was worried you'd be upset, given the whole secrecy thing, but I told the saleswoman they were for my mom. I figured you could tell Owen or whoever that they were to celebrate finishing that big project you'd be working on."

A few of the little bubbles of joy bouncing around inside her popped at the reminder of their unusual arrangement.

Sensing her sudden change in mood, he frowned. "You don't have to keep them, if you think it will cause problems."

She held the flowers to her chest protectively. "Of course I'm keeping them. I just hate having to be dishonest about it."

He grinned. "So you want to tell people I gave them to you in appreciation of the best sex I ever had?"

"Fine, fibbing it is." She laughed, shaking her head

at his audacity. They weren't doing anything wrong, not really, and a few white lies never hurt anyone.

She hoped.

Luke didn't stay long at Megan's. He had work to do and he knew she didn't want Owen wondering about their relationship. Still, it wasn't easy to leave and it didn't get any easier the next time, or any of the times after that.

For the next few weeks, he'd visited under cover of darkness. At school, they maintained the appearance of a polite but professional relationship. Despite the strained secrecy, the sex was amazing, and so was the conversation they shared between bouts of lovemaking. Luke loved hearing about the progress Owen was making or learning more about her growing software development business, and she'd proved insightful when he had issues from his day that he wanted to discuss.

In fact, everything was perfect. So why, with things going exactly as planned, did he feel worse each day? It was like being a kid and wanting a particular toy, and then after you finally got it realized it wasn't so great after all. Except in this case, being with Megan was even better than Luke had imagined. It wasn't her; it was the whole situation that left him feeling hollow, as though something vital was missing. That, of course, was ridiculous. Maybe he just needed someone outside the situation to remind him of that.

Ensuring that his office door was firmly shut, he dialed Grant. If anyone could knock some sense into him and tell him he was being an idiot, his fishing buddy would.

On the second ring, he picked up. "So, did you ask out that hot mom yet, or what?" Grant asked by way of greeting.

Luke rolled his eyes, reminding himself this was why he'd called. He needed Grant's bluntness right now. "Hello is the way normal people start conversations."

"Thank goodness I'm not normal. And you didn't answer the question."

"Yes, I asked her out. Sort of. It's complicated."

"Which is why you're calling me, I assume. If it was all rainbows and unicorns, you'd be busy with her instead of talking to me." There was no censure in his voice, Grant just called it like he saw it.

"I wouldn't put it quite like that," Luke replied, a niggle of guilt reminding him he'd skipped fishing the last three weekends in a row. "In fact, things are going really well. She's smart, and sexy, and I really like her."

"So what's the problem? Is it your job—did some old biddy on the school board find out and throw a fit?"

"No, they don't know anything. In fact, no one does. We agreed to keep things quiet for now."

"So…what, you're sneaking around?"

Luke tapped a pencil against the arm of his chair. "Yeah, actually. I go over there at night, after her son's asleep, and then I leave before he wakes up. Hell, I even park down the street so no one sees my car in front of her house." He hadn't realized how much that bothered him until now. It was worth it to see her, but he was tired of feeling like a teenager trying to avoid curfew.

"Can I assume that these late-night visits are of an adult nature?"

"Yes, but if you repeat that to anyone, I'll kill you and feed your body to the sharks."

"Understood," Grant acknowledged mildly. "So, you are having regular sex with a beautiful woman you like and admire, and that's not working for you, is that right?"

"It's stupid, I know."

"Not really."

Well that wasn't the response he'd expected. "It's not?"

"Not if you want more than that. Seems to me, you got a taste of something good and now you want the whole enchilada."

Luke grimaced. "Can we not refer to Megan as if she's something you can order off the value menu?"

"Sure," Grant conceded with a nod Luke couldn't witness. "But see, that just proves my point."

"Which is what, exactly?" The late nights and lack of sleep must be catching up with him because he was not clueing in to whatever Grant was throwing down.

"That she's not just a means to an end for you. If all you wanted was sex, or some entertainment, you'd be perfectly happy and we wouldn't be having this conversation. But if you value her as a person, if you are looking for a real relationship, then this halfway crap is just going to frustrate you. Giving you a glimpse of what could be, but without actually getting it."

Wow. Luke hated to admit it, but what Grant was describing was exactly how he was feeling. Leaning back in his chair until the springs squeaked in protest, he tried to wrap his head around what this all meant. He'd always known he'd eventually want a real relationship, maybe even settle down, but that was down the road a ways. At least, he'd thought it was. Now that particular off-ramp was suddenly in sight and he didn't know if he was ready for it.

"We've only known each other a few months and you make it sound like I want to pop the question and start putting up a white picket fence," he protested.

"Do you?" Grant countered. When Luke didn't answer right away he chuckled. "Maybe start with asking her out on a real date. Like dinner or something."

Air whooshed out of his lungs. A date was infinitely less intimidating than a lifetime commitment. "I think I could manage that." Asking Megan out would be the easy part. Getting her to agree to take their relationship into the public eye could prove difficult. He hoped not impossible, because despite his initial panic at the idea of forever, he couldn't imagine a future without her.

Having a secret boyfriend was exhausting.

That was the reason Megan was using to justify her trip to the lounge for a fifth cup of coffee today. Between the late-night conversations and even later night bedroom activities, she was running way too many hours on way too little sleep.

Burning the candle at both ends wasn't new to her, but she was starting to feel like the middle was melting, too. And yet, as she stirred cream and a hefty amount of sugar into her cup, she felt happy, despite the constant weariness. Luke made her happy. He was smart, insightful, considerate, and absolutely incredible in bed. But most of all, he made her feel confident in herself, less worried about the bumps of life that used to be a source of nearly constant anxiety. Just knowing she would see him later never failed to give her a bit of strength as she pushed through whatever hard moment came up over the course of a day.

Megan liked him, and she loved who she was becoming now that she was with him. She would have to catch up on sleep later—maybe over the Thanksgiving holiday. That was only a few more days. She could make it that long and then, in a month, she'd be in the mountains with plenty of time to relax while her parents entertained Owen. She just had to hang in there a while longer.

"Is there any left, or do I need to make a new pot?"

Luke's voice brought a smile to her face, chasing away some of the weariness that clung to her. "Enough for one more cup, at least." Turning, she found him leaning against the open door of the lounge, watching her.

"Good." He straightened and headed for the machine. As he filled his cup, she got the impression he had something he wanted to say, so instead of heading back to her table in the conference room, she waited for him. When he just looked at her, opened his mouth and then closed it again, her anxiety rose.

"What is it?" Was he going to break up with her? Because, exhaustion aside, she wasn't ready for things to end. Not yet.

"What is what?"

"Whatever has you so wound up you just put salt in your coffee instead of sugar."

"I did?" He eyes the dark liquid suspiciously and took a cautious taste only to spit it right back into the cup. "It's not funny," he groused as she giggled. "That was really gross." He dumped it in the sink and rinsed his mug, his actions jerky.

"It is, too. Besides, I warned you."

"You did," he admitted with a shrug. "Guess I like to learn things the hard way."

She wanted to say something about how he could have trusted her, but that seemed much too deep for the situation. Especially since he still looked like something was wrong. "Seriously, Luke, what's up? You're kind of freaking me out here." Pressing him might not be the best idea, but if it was bad news, she'd rather get it over with.

He turned the empty mug around in his hands. "I've just been thinking…about our situation."

Here it was. She set her cup down on the table in front of her and braced her hands on the edge so he wouldn't see them shaking. "And?" she prompted.

"And…" He paused, inhaled audibly, and then quickly blurted, "I want to go to dinner."

"Um, okay…" She knew low blood sugar could have weird side effects, but all this because he was hungry?

"I mean I want you to go, too." He pulled on his already loosened tie, undoing it. "With me. Together. Hell." He yanked off the tie altogether, and bunched it in his hands. "What I'm trying to say…to ask, is…will you go out to dinner with me?"

"Like a date?"

"Exactly." He nodded, relief clear in his features. "I know you wanted to see how things went before going out in public, but as far as I'm concerned, the only thing that could be better is not having to sneak around."

Her mind spun, thoughts tripping over one another. "S-so you d-don't want to break up?" she sputtered inanely.

"What? No." He shook his head vehemently. "Do you?"

"No." That was perhaps the only thing she was sure of. "But I don't know if I'm ready for anything more yet, either."

His face fell, and she wanted to kick herself. What was her problem? A sexy, smart, amazing man wanted to take her to dinner. That wasn't a problem worth panicking over and yet she felt completely sideswiped by the idea. "Can I think about it and get back to you?" She tried to soften her answer with a smile, but it felt forced. "You caught me by surprise. Let me figure out some logistics, and we can talk about it tonight."

"Yeah. Sure. Tonight."

Megan could tell from his tone that her answer wasn't what he'd been hoping for, but she couldn't do any better. Not without careful consideration of what it would mean for her, for him, for Owen. This wasn't the kind of decision she could make on a whim. Her heart wasn't the only thing at stake.

"Listen, I've got to go," he said, his expression shuttered. "I'll see you later."

"Okay."

He brushed by her and, for once, the closeness of his body didn't heat her blood. Instead, as she watched him walk away, all she felt was cold.

Chapter Twelve

If there was one thing Luke hated, it was feeling like a fool. And yet even knowing that pushing Megan had been foolish, he'd gone and done it anyway. Worse, he'd sprung the idea on her without warning. Maybe if he'd waited until they were at her house, alone, and had brought it up more carefully, she would have been open to the idea. Instead he'd just blurted it out. Still, he hadn't expected the look of utter shock on her face. Nothing like asking a woman out and her getting that caught-in-the-headlights look to take a guy's ego down a notch.

So, yeah, he was in a foul mood, one that didn't improve when he had to work through lunch again. By the end-of-day bell, he was hungry, disappointed, and ready for a distraction.

"I'm going to go grab a sandwich at the diner," he informed Ms. White at the front desk on his way out of the office. "If anyone needs me, I'll be back in twenty minutes."

A few stragglers meandered the halls, but he was able to make it to the front doors without being stopped by anyone, probably thanks to the frown that felt permanently etched on his face. Pushing out into the open, he dragged in a deep breath of fall air. Florida might not get much in the way of sweater weather, but the break in the humidity was enough for him. The students seemed to feel the same way; an impromptu game of tag had broken out on the front lawn.

He stopped to watch for a moment, letting the simple joy of childhood wash over him. This was why he'd gotten into education in the first place, to see and be a part of that small snippet of life when anything was possible. Being with kids made him believe that, too. At least, most of the time.

Still starving, but with a better attitude, he turned to make the short walk to the restaurant and nearly crashed into someone. Taking a step back, he apologized automatically, recognizing her as Liz Robins, the mother of a student.

"Sorry, I didn't see you there."

She smiled, her brightly painted lips making the gesture garish. Highlighted hair, large dangling earrings, and nails long enough to be considered talons, had him mentally relegating her to the "tries too hard" category in his brain.

"It's okay. No harm done." She ran her hands down

her body as if to illustrate her lack of injuries, or more likely, to show off the skintight athletic shirt and short tennis skirt she was wearing. "In fact, I was hoping to run into you, although not quite so literally." She giggled at her own joke.

He forced a smile. "If you'd like to schedule an appointment, I'm sure Ms. White would be happy to set something up for you," he hinted, stomach growling. "She knows my schedule better than I do."

"Oh, that's not necessary."

Of course not. Sighing, he checked his watch before turning his attention back to her and whatever subject was so important it couldn't wait. "Is there an issue regarding Brian?" Her son was an average student, and not prone to trouble, but sometimes parents tried to get him to change a grade or to overrule a teacher's decision. If that were the case, he'd insist she make an appointment so he could include the teacher in the discussion. He trusted his staff, and wouldn't go over their heads without giving them a chance to defend their decision.

"Brian?" She wrinkled her nose in confusion. "No, I wanted to talk to you about the Scholar's Banquet."

"As soon as the details are finalized, we'll have tickets for sale in the front office. There should be a handout going home about it next week, after the break." He couldn't wait to have that finished and out of the way.

"Right, okay. But what I really want to know is, if you'd like to go with me, as my date." She fluttered her false eyelashes up at him, and he wondered if she knew that one was partially unglued. "This is my first year here in Paradise, and I thought it would just be so nice to attend the biggest event of the year on the arm of the man who makes it all happen."

Was she serious? It was a school fundraiser, and even in a town as small as Paradise, it certainly didn't qualify as the event of the year. But even if it was, he wouldn't want to spend it with her. Of course, he couldn't say that. Especially since he knew she had already made a generous donation to the school scholarship fund. She was rumored to have married well and divorced better; alienating her wouldn't endear him to the powers that be.

"I'm flattered but—"

"Wonderful!"

He shook his head. How had he gone the last year with a nonexistent social life, and now been involved in not one but two dating conversations gone wrong in one day? "No, I mean I'm sorry, but I can't."

She frowned, her perfectly plucked eyebrows forming a narrow vee. "I don't understand. Why can't you?"

The truth would not be helpful, and might cost the school a major donor, so he seized on the first excuse that came to him. "I'm afraid I already have a date."

"Really?" Disbelief heightened her pitch. "I hadn't heard that. With whom?"

Hell. If he didn't give her a name, she'd know he was lying. And Paradise was too small a town to just make one up. Everyone knew everyone in this place. Desperate, he said the only thing he could think of. "Megan Palmer."

"Humph." She straightened her shoulders and tossed

a lock of artificially lightened hair over her shoulder. "That will be nice, I'm sure."

"Yes…well, hopefully I'll see you there."

She made a noncommittal noise and waved to her son. "I'm sorry, I can't keep chatting. Brian will be late for his karate appointment."

Luke nodded. No point in reminding her that she was the one who'd approached him, not the other way around. Checking his watch, he headed back into the school. His twenty minutes were up and he'd lost his appetite anyway. Instead of hunger, anxiety chewed at his belly.

He'd just outed his relationship with Megan, and now he had to warn her before she found out from someone else.

Megan kept her phone within arm's reach all day, hoping Luke would text or call, something to indicate that he wasn't holding on to any resentment after their awkward conversation in the lounge. Still, when it finally buzzed in her pocket, she nearly dropped the plate she was washing. Shaking the suds from her hands, she yanked it out, hoping to see Luke's name on the Caller ID. When she saw Cassie's name, that little bubble of hope burst, just like the ones landing on the floor around her.

"Hey, Cassie, what's up?" She tucked the phone in between her ear and her shoulder and went back to scrubbing the dinner dishes. She wanted to get everything done before Owen went to bed and Luke arrived.

"I think I should be asking you that question. Have any news you want to share?"

"Um, not that I can think of." Megan set the plate in the drying rack and grabbed another. "Why?"

"I don't know, maybe the fact that you and Luke are now an official couple, and he's taking you to the school gala?"

"What?" She straightened so fast her phone slipped from its precarious spot and tumbled toward the sink. Dropping the dish, she bobbled the phone in soap-slicked hands before finally getting a solid grip.

"Are you okay?" Cassie's disembodied voice came from the damp but not destroyed phone as Megan wiped it and her hands with a mostly clean dishtowel.

"I'm fine," she answered automatically as she put the phone back to her ear.

"I heard a crash."

"It was just a plate." Surveying the broken pieces on the floor, Megan mentally calculated how long she had to clean it up before Owen finished his bath and he and Lily came looking for a bedtime snack.

"Are you sure? Did anyone get hurt?"

"Cassie, forget about the plate! Tell me what you heard about Luke and me." She squatted and started picking up the bigger shards of pottery.

"Just what I said, that you and he are going to the Scholar's Banquet together, as a couple. And..." Her friend continued, a hint of recrimination coloring her tone, "I have to say I'm a little annoyed that you didn't tell me first."

"I would have, if it were true."

"It's not?"

"Nope. And, really, you should know better than to believe everything you hear in this town."

"You're right, but this seemed reliable," Cassie protested. "I heard it from a client this afternoon, Joyce Jacob. She's a manicurist over at the Hot Sands Salon, and she said that Liz Robins had been in for a polish change and was complaining that you swooped in and stole Luke right from under her nose."

"I did not!" Megan's hands clenched in outrage, a prickle of pain slicing through her indignation. Looking down, she saw a spot of red pooling in her palm where one of the pottery shards had pierced the skin.

"I know, but that's what she's saying. Apparently, she asked Luke to the banquet, and he told her he couldn't because he was already going with you."

"Well, he's not." She grabbed a paper towel and pressed it to her hand. "So either she made the whole thing up, or he's got some explaining to do."

The doorbell rang before Cassie could weigh in, the possibility of which Megan thought most likely.

"Speak of the devil, that's probably him," she said, glancing at the kitchen clock. "He's early. He never comes before Owen goes to bed." This day was getting stranger and stranger, and she didn't like it one bit. "I've got to go. I'll let you know what happens."

"Promise?"

"Promise," Megan assured her before hanging up. Rushing to the door, she found Owen had beaten her there. Wrapped in a towel and dripping water onto the floor, he peered through the side window.

"Hey, that's Dr. Wright! Mom, Dr. Wright is here." Owen's excitement tugged at her heart. He adored his principal, often coming home from school quoting things Luke had said during assemblies or morning announcements. His obvious admiration fit right in with her own daydreams, making her wonder what if… But dreams and reality were rarely the same thing, and she needed to protect her son from the disappointment that came from confusing the two.

"Well, why don't you go put on your pajamas while I let him in?"

Owen looked down in surprise, as if only now realizing his state of undress. "Okay. But tell him not to leave."

She shook her head, marveling at the change in Owen since the school year had started. She had Luke and his decision to allow Lily in the classroom to thank for much of that. However, after what Cassie had just shared, she wasn't feeling all that thankful.

Opening the door, she noticed the strain around his eyes that said he knew something was wrong. The question was, had he simply heard the rumor or had he started it? Mindful of Owen, she held off asking right away and instead simply stood aside, giving him space to enter without overtly inviting him in.

"I hope it's okay I came so early." Luke cast his eyes around the room, as if looking for something to focus on other than her face. "I wanted to talk to you before—"

"I heard about us attending the banquet together?" Her heart sank even as her anger rose. "I'm afraid you're too late. Cassie called and told me."

"Well, hell."

"You're not supposed to say that. It's a bad word." Owen, now fully clothed, frowned at Luke. "You need to say you're sorry."

Luke looked so uncomfortable, Megan almost, but not quite, felt sorry for him.

"You're right. I'm sorry." He turned to Megan and his tone softened. "I really am sorry. Can you forgive me?"

"Sure!"

Owen's easy absolution brought a slight smile to Luke's mouth, but it vanished when he saw that Megan wasn't going to be so quick to pardon him. Not until she had some idea of what on earth it was that he had done, and how on earth she was going to control the damage. From the guilt written in the lines of his face, he had more to confess, and she wanted to hear everything before she could even consider absolution.

Luke waited, breath held, for Megan to say something. To give him some hope that he hadn't lost her trust totally. Instead, she addressed Owen, reminding him that it was bedtime.

"I want Dr. Wright to tuck me in."

"What?" Megan's shocked question echoed through the small house, but Owen wasn't deterred.

"Please?" He took hold of Luke's hand and pulled, attempting to tug him toward the hall.

Helpless, the boy's small fingers locked around his own, Luke looked to Megan for permission. She was already mad at him for overstepping, but he couldn't bring himself to tell the kid no.

She met his silent entreaty with a sad, nearly wistful smile. "Fine. But be quick about it. One story—no more." Meeting Luke's eyes, she added, "I'm serious. He'll try to talk you into half a dozen if you aren't careful."

Nodding in acknowledgment, he let Owen lead him to his bedroom. Stacks of books about dinosaurs, wild animals, and, of course, sharks, covered the top of a sturdy chest of drawers. Fiction was notably absent, leaving Luke wondering exactly what kind of bedtime story Owen expected him to read.

"So, which one?" He scanned the titles. The first one—*What Happened to the Dinosaurs*—seemed a bit ominous for bedtime. He didn't want to give the kid nightmares about mass extinction. *Fish Species of the Florida Coast* sounded safe, if a bit dry. He turned, holding it up for approval.

"Not those books," Owen admonished from his spot on the bed. "Those are for research. My regular stuff is over here."

"Ah, of course." Because every first-grader kept a stack of research materials. Shaking his head, Luke put the book back and crossed to the nightstand where another, smaller pile of paperbacks vied for space with a startlingly realistic-looking owl lamp.

Picking one that looked familiar, he eased onto the bed. Immediately the boy scooted closer, wiggling into a comfortable position. Comfortable for the boy anyway. Luke's arm was going to be numb with Owen's head pressed against it and he wasn't sure how he would manage holding the book and turning the pages one-handed.

As it turned out, Owen handled the page turning, and they finished the book without Luke suffering any permanent nerve damage. And if he had, it might have been worth it. He'd read to kids hundreds of times in his career, but sitting in front of a classroom was nothing like having a child snuggled peacefully against you. The tension that had gripped him since the encounter with Liz Robins had all but vanished. This was special, and he was smart enough to know it.

If things worked out with Megan, would he do this every night? The thought was dizzying. But he couldn't let himself think in that direction. Not yet. Given the welcome he'd received, he was more likely to be kicked to the curb than to ever be a part of this family.

Until and unless he got Megan to agree to a real relationship, Luke couldn't even pretend they had a future.

Pushing that grim thought aside, he returned the book to the nightstand. "Good night, buddy."

Owen blinked sleepy eyes. "G'night. I liked you reading to me."

Luke swallowed hard. "I liked it, too."

Once alone in the hall, he stopped to gather his thoughts. Today had been a runaway train of emotion, and this evening's conversation with Megan had the potential to send it right off the tracks. His only hope was to keep himself calm, to let her vent the anger she had every right to feel, and to pray she'd be willing to give him a second chance.

He found her in the kitchen standing over an open first-aid kit. "What are you doing?"

Her answer, as she struggled to bandage her own hand, was muffled by a length of medical tape held between her teeth. Probably for the best, as the one word he did make out was the type to earn one of his students a week of detention.

"I probably deserved that, but if you let me help you, I promise you can yell at me afterward, okay?" He gently pulled the tape from her mouth and examined the makeshift bandage. "What happened anyway?"

Glaring, she gestured with her uninjured hand at a pile of pottery pieces on the floor. "If you must know, I was washing the dishes when Cassie called to inform me that I was attending the Scholar's Banquet with you. Given that I hadn't agreed to any such thing, and our agreement to keep things private, I was a bit surprised. I dropped a plate and cut my hand cleaning it up."

Her tone made it clear that the injury was his fault, which, given the circumstances, was probably accurate.

"All the more reason to let me help, right?"

She didn't answer, but let him unwind the tangled tape and gauze without objection. Perhaps she realized that seeing her hurting from an injury he'd caused, however indirectly, was punishment enough. Fresh guilt rose like ire in his throat at the sight of ragged wound, not just for the injury, which thankfully was superficial, but for the much deeper pain he knew he'd caused. Flesh healed swiftly; hearts were more delicate.

When he'd finished, he grabbed the broom and swept

up the broken pottery while she stood and watched, her expression blank.

"You seem to be making a habit of this, you know."

He dumped the dustpan into the trash and set the broom back in the corner, trying to figure out her meaning. He'd screwed up plenty in his life, but his mistakes with Megan seemed to be uncharted territory, each one a new way to mess things up. "How so?"

She nodded at the broom. "Sweeping up my messes. You cleaned up broken glass the first time you came here."

"Oh." He smiled, remembering how flustered she'd been that day. It seemed a lifetime ago, and yet, in so many ways, they'd made very little progress. He was still trying to find the line between too much involvement and not enough, and he was damned tired of it. But what other choice did he have? Maybe this mistake, as badly as he felt about it, was really their chance to make a real move forward.

Or maybe it was the last stop on what had always been a dead-end journey.

Megan hated that such a simple thing like sweeping up broken glass could soften her anger so quickly. She needed to be strong for this conversation, and swooning over a man doing household chores wasn't going to help. She wanted answers, not a cleaning service. "You didn't have to do that."

He shook his head. "It was the least I could do, after everything."

"No argument there." Maybe he was just doing it out

of guilt, not natural chivalry. Still, that he would instinctively step in to help had to be an indication of his character, right? He'd done exactly that from the beginning. That kind of behavior matched with who she'd thought he was…at least until tonight. Now? She wasn't so sure. And worse, she wasn't certain she wanted to find out. Not if the truth was ugly. Hadn't she had enough ugliness to last a lifetime already?

But even if ignorance was bliss, and she wasn't naïve enough to believe it was, there was no ignoring Luke Wright. He took up to much space—in her kitchen and in her heart.

"Can I explain?"

"I sure hope so." He'd stayed on the far side of the room, as if afraid to move for fear of raising her wrath. Smart man. But she'd been on her feet all evening, so she motioned him to the table. Whatever he had to say might hurt, but her feet didn't have to.

He sat across from her, his hands flat on the table in front of him as if he were bracing for something. Probably her reaction. "I want to start by saying I'm sorry. I didn't mean for this to happen."

"For what to happen?" No way was she letting him off the hook that easily. She couldn't accept his apology without knowing what it was he was apologizing for.

"For telling Liz Robins that you were my date for the banquet."

She'd been expecting them, but hearing the words still shook her. Swallowing hard, she asked the next obvious question. "Why?"

"Because she wanted me to take her, and there was

no way that was happening." He grimaced and, for a small, petty moment, she gloated at his obvious lack of interest in the attractive woman. "The only way I could think to put her off was to say I already had a date. But then she wanted to know who it was."

"And you said me."

"What else was I supposed to do?" He leaned in, frustration deepening the lines around his eyes. "Say some other woman and have you think I was dating someone else?"

The heated anger that had been building since she'd spoken to Cassie dropped a few degrees. As bad as this was, hearing that he was involved with another woman would have been worse. Just knowing someone was hitting on him had jealousy twisting her insides—which was ridiculous. She couldn't insist they keep their relationship a secret and then get upset that people thought he was available. She was like a dog who wasn't sure he wanted a bone, but didn't want anyone else to have it, either. Luke was a good-looking man, and because of her insistence on secrecy, as far as anyone knew, he was available.

Logical, but that didn't mean she had to like it. "You could have just made someone up."

He rolled his eyes. "A mystery woman? Even if she'd been willing to believe there was a new person in town she hadn't met or heard of yet, as soon as Liz Robins and her gossip buddies started digging, they'd have realized the truth. Aside from being pointless, lying to a parent isn't exactly a great career move."

"And dating a parent is?"

He shrugged. "Since she'd just asked me out, she'd have been pretty hypocritical to make a fuss about that."

Out of arguments, Megan fell silent, the ticking of the old kitchen wall clock and Lily's soft snores the only sounds. Before Luke, the quiet of the night had been the hardest time for her. Did she want to send him away and go back to that?

As if directed by her thoughts, Luke stood. "I'll go, and let you think things over."

He was being a gentleman, as always. Giving her the space she kept saying she wanted. And yet something told her that if she let him walk out now, he wouldn't be back. That one thought cut through the noise in her head. She may not have everything figured out, but her gut said letting him go would be a mistake she'd always regret.

The realization made her bold. Standing, she stepped in front of him, blocking his path. "I thought you said I should stop overthinking everything."

His slow, sexy smile had her bare toes curling into the worn linoleum. "I did. But I wasn't sure you could."

"I'm trying." She stretched her arms up, wrapping them around his neck as she leaned into him. "Maybe you could help find a way to distract me."

Heat flashed in his eyes, and she tingled in anticipation. But then, instead of pulling her closer, he stepped back. "No."

"What?" *He* was rejecting *her*? "I thought this was what you wanted?"

"Oh, I definitely want you," he rasped, his expression nearly feral. "But taking you to bed right now isn't going to fix this."

A lump formed somewhere behind her breastbone, making it hard to breathe. "I don't know what you want, Luke."

"You. I want you, Megan."

Confusion fed her frustration. "So take me!" They were speaking in circles, and she was too tired to see a way out.

Again, he shook his head. "This isn't about sex. As awesome as that is, it isn't enough, not anymore." He took a breath, and she held hers, not sure she was ready to hear whatever came next.

"I'm not asking you to promise forever. But if you won't even risk being seen in public with me, if you aren't going to give a real relationship a chance, then there's no point to any of this."

"Is that an ultimatum?"

He shrugged, but the movement was stiff. "Call it what you want. But if you don't want to move forward, then I need to move on."

Luke watched Megan digest his challenge and wondered for the thousandth time what the hell was wrong with him. He had a gorgeous, smart, funny, sexy woman who wanted to have sex with him on a regular basis, and he was messing it up for what? To take her to a fundraising banquet in the school auditorium? So he could hold her hand in public when he already had her naked in his arms in private?

Still, even as he mentally prepared himself to walk

away, he knew he was doing the only thing he could. Yes, they had a good thing going here, but he didn't want to settle when he knew it could be better than good. They could be great—if only she'd just trust him enough to try.

Seconds passed. He tried to read her face but her expression had frozen. Whatever reaction he'd been expecting, it wasn't that.

"Megan, whatever you're thinking, just say it."

She blinked twice, fast, as if his voice had startled her out of whatever inner conversation she'd been having, then nodded once. "Okay."

"Okay, what?" Was she agreeing to a more serious relationship or agreeing to end it?

"Okay, I'll be your girlfriend. Or whatever they are calling it these days."

Air whooshed out of him, the sudden deflation leaving him light-headed for a second. Or maybe that was euphoria he was feeling. Like a runner's high but way better. Adrenaline was a funny thing—you never noticed how much was pumping through your veins until it was gone. "You can call it whatever you want," he assured her.

A playful smile danced at the corners of her mouth. "You sure you're ready for this?"

"We still get to have sex, right?" he teased, reaching for her.

She melted into his arms, her body molding against his as if she'd been made to fit him. "We'd better, or I'm going to change my mind."

"Well, we can't have that," he murmured into her

neck, greedily inhaling the sweet scent of her skin. She arched, giving him better access, and he happily complied with the unspoken request, trailing kisses up to the sensitive spot behind her ear. When he nipped at the delicate lobe, she moaned, the sound triggering an instant reaction from his body. "Bedroom," she ordered breathlessly, tugging at his belt buckle. "Now."

He had better things to do with his mouth than answer, so he allowed her to pull him along as she backed toward the hallway. With each step, he teased and tasted her, moving ever so slowly along the deep V of her shirt, stopping only when they reached the safety of her room. There, he released her long enough to turn and lock the door. When he looked back she was already half naked, her shirt and bra tossed to the floor.

"You are so beautiful."

She shook her head at the compliment, one hand coming up to cover her bare chest.

"Beautiful," he insisted, taking her hand in his. Gently, he brushed their joined fingers across the rise and fall of her breasts as he uncovered her. "Just looking at you makes me ache. Seeing you like this…" He dipped down and sucked a rose-colored nipple into his mouth for a brief taste before continuing. "Makes me hot." He knew she was self-conscious about her body and the changes from childbearing, but all he saw was perfection. Softness where there should be softness. Also strength. She might not believe his words, but there were other, more primal ways to communicate how he felt about her. And he was willing to spend as long as it took to make sure she got the message.

Dropping her hand, he quickly stripped. He didn't want to let go for even that long, but once he had her naked, he wasn't going to want to stop for anything. She must have been feeling the same way because she was already nude by the time he kicked the last of his clothes away.

He paused only long enough to grab a condom from the wallet he'd tossed on the nightstand before pulling her to him and onto the bed. She landed on top, straddling him.

He caught her hand as she reached for the condom. "Not so fast."

Before she could argue, he rolled, flipping their positions. "I'm going to take my time enjoying you first."

He wanted to show her she'd made the right call, to show her how much this meant to him, how much she meant to him. And selfishly, he wanted to make it last as long as humanly possible because he wasn't sure he'd be able to hold back once he was inside her. He started with her mouth, kissing her thoroughly before working his way down. His hands traced and smoothed over silken skin, his lips and tongue following, searching out new spots that made her whimper, mapping each inch of her body until he couldn't contain his own need any longer. Rising, he grabbed the condom and quickly covered himself.

As he entered her, he felt not just physical pleasure but a deep satisfaction, a realization that this was no mere sating of lust. This was more. Every part of him vibrated with the certainty that she was his, and he was going to do everything in his power to keep it that way.

He put that energy into their lovemaking and Megan met him thrust for thrust, arching her hips and gripping his body with an intensity that had him unable to hold back. Too soon, he hit the brink and tumbled over, his body shaking as he felt her come with him. Spent, he bent one elbow and rolled to the side, tugging her against him.

And wished to heck he never had to let go.

Chapter Thirteen

Megan leaned against the sturdy railing enclosing the porch of the mountain cabin her parents had rented, a mug of coffee warming her hands in the morning chill. She'd been drawing out this moment, savoring both the custom dark roast and her last chance for one-on-one time with her mother before they had to pack up.

"They look like they're having fun," her mom observed, moving closer for a better view.

Down in the yard, Owen was busy upturning rocks, intently checking the wet grass underneath. Behind him trailed his grandfather, a field guide of North Carolina wildlife in his hands. He'd had it shipped overnight after noting Owen's interest in the creatures they'd found on their daily walks. Together, they were marking each new discovery.

"Definitely. I love seeing how well the two of them get on." Megan took another sip of her coffee and smiled. "And I admit, I enjoy getting a bit of break." She'd felt almost guilty at first, unused to Owen preferring to spend so much time with anyone other than her. But it was important, and normal, for a kid to have role models in his life other than his mother. And that knowledge, plus sheer exhaustion, had overcome any lingering hesitation about sitting on the sidelines while her parents entertained Owen. Or, as was often the case, he entertained them.

"If anyone deserves to relax, you do. Your father and I are so impressed with how well you've handled everything, but I know it's a lot."

Setting her mug down, Megan warmed at the praise. "Thanks. I do the best I can. But I wish he could have more days like this." She took a deep breath of crisp air and continued. "I was hoping you and Dad could start visiting more often?"

"Oh, honey, I would love that. But your father's so busy right now, I just don't know when we'll be back in the country."

"What about Christmas? If Dad is so busy, maybe you could come?" Megan was begging, and she hated it. Especially knowing it was pointless. Even now, her mother was shaking her head, features pinched.

"I'm afraid we're going to be in Switzerland. One of the foreign ministers is organizing some sort of think tank at his chalet, and wants your father to be part of it. They want to work out all the details before the legislative session starts up."

Disappointment, bitter and ugly, rose inside her, stealing the peace she'd been feeling a moment ago. She shouldn't have gotten her hopes up. It had been years since they'd opened presents together. Still, was it so wrong to want her son to have a big, family Christmas?

Her mother fussed with the chain holding her reading glasses, avoiding eye contact. "Perhaps you and that man you were telling me about can do something this year? You did say that he and Owen get along so well."

"They do." Megan picked up her mug and, realizing it was empty, set it back down again. "But I thought if you and Dad were there, it would give you a chance to meet him. I think you'd like him."

"I'm sure we will…just as soon as we can get there."

Megan fought the urge to push harder. She wasn't a little girl upset about her parents missing a recital. She was a grown woman. And if her parents still didn't want to make their only family a priority, she wasn't going to beg and plead to try to change their minds. But the rejection—because that's what it felt like—stung.

She shrugged and started for the door. "Well, let me know where to send your present, I guess."

"Megan, don't you walk away from me like that."

That tone of voice would have stopped her in her tracks only a few years ago. But one of the benefits of living through hell is realizing your own strength. So her footsteps didn't falter on the old oak boards. "Sorry, Mom. It was great seeing you, but I've got to pack."

She didn't have time for melodrama or hurt feelings. She was busy enough, what with her job, Owen, and now a boyfriend. That was plenty. It had to be. Yes, it would be good for Owen to spend more time with his grandparents. And yes, having them around would make her newfound social life easier to manage. And maybe she had hoped to finally make up for the time she'd missed with her parents. Oh well.

Life didn't get easier just because you wanted it to.

She was moving forward now, and if her parents were not part of her future, she wasn't about to let them drag her backward.

Luke was equal parts impressed and horrified when he found Megan perched precariously on a rickety ladder leaning against the equally rickety eaves of her house. She was obviously trying to clean out the gutters, but the ladder was about a foot too short, leaving her standing on her tippy toes and stretching dangerously as she dug her gloved hand into the clogged metal. A pile of rotten leaves and debris sat on the ground beneath her. Evidence of her hard work if not her good judgment.

Ever since she'd returned from her Thanksgiving trip to the mountains, she'd become even more self-sufficient, if that were possible. He didn't know what had happened; she'd refused to talk about it other than to say that her parents would not be in town for Christmas. He'd heard the hurt in her voice. There was more going on there, but family stuff could be tricky and he didn't want to push her if she wasn't ready. Earning Megan's trust had been accomplished one step at a time and he wasn't going to undo all that progress by focusing on something that didn't really involve him.

However, letting her handle her family issues was one thing. Letting her break her neck doing home maintenance was another.

Afraid to call out and risk startling her, he stood quietly, chest tight, waiting for her to look down. When she did, she rewarded him with a weary smile.

"You know there are easier ways to do that, right?"

"Yeah, but they all involve paying someone else to do it or buying equipment that costs more than I'm willing to spend." She gingerly eased herself down the ladder. It was clear that she knew she'd be even sorer tomorrow. "But I will admit, the videos on the internet made this seem a lot easier."

"They always do." Luke glanced through the sliding-glass door and saw Owen occupied with his Lego toys on the floor, Lily right beside him. Taking advantage of the relative privacy, he grabbed Megan's arm and tugged her around the corner of the house before planting a kiss right on her surprised mouth. She tasted like sunshine and lemonade, and he wasn't sure he'd ever get his fill of her.

Too soon, Megan pulled away. "Stop it," she protested, laughing. "I'm filthy!"

He shrugged. "So? Guys like girls who get dirty."

She wrinkled her nose. "Really?"

"Sure, haven't you ever heard of mud wrestling?" To be honest, it wasn't something that had ever appealed to him, and still didn't, but when it came to Megan, he was speaking the truth. She was grimy and sweaty, mud striping her face and arms, and her tank top sticking to her in places... And she was still the sexiest thing he had ever seen. Pulling her hips to his, he made sure to show her exactly how hot she made him with another sizzling kiss.

When they broke to take a breath, he was pleased to see the dazed look in her eyes. In the two weeks since she agreed to officially be his girlfriend, they hadn't managed time for even one real date. He'd spent the Thanksgiving break at his mother's, helping her with some maintenance around the house. Since his return, they'd both been slammed with work. Moments like this proved he wasn't the only one who wished they had more time together. But Megan never forgot her main priority. Even now, she was stepping back, looking in the direction of the rear of the house.

"Owen—"

"Is playing with his Lego. If anything was wrong, Lily would have let us know." Indeed, he'd only ever heard the perfectly mannered dog bark once, and that was when Owen's shirt had gotten stuck on a branch while he'd been climbing a tree at the park. Both Luke and Megan had been within eyesight but hadn't realized the predicament until Lily had sounded the alarm. Megan had explained at the time that Lily's primary job was to calm Owen before he got upset, but that if that didn't work, she would bark until someone arrived. Truly, the dog was a miracle.

Yet Megan still worried, and right now that could work in Luke's favor. "But hey, why don't you go check on him? Maybe grab us some cold drinks while you're in there."

Megan crossed her arms and glared at him. "You

aren't fooling me. As soon as I am inside, you're planning to take over and finish cleaning the gutters, aren't you?"

He shrugged. "Maybe."

"That's so sexist. Just because you're a man, you think you should do the dirty jobs?"

"Hey, we already established that I have no problem with you getting dirty. What I do have a problem with is you being unsafe. There's a reason those ladders have a warning label saying you shouldn't stand on the very top. It's too easy to overbalance. So, unless you have a taller ladder somewhere, you need someone with a longer reach. Besides," he added with a wink, "if you end up in the hospital, who will I take to the banquet?"

"Well, there's always Liz Robins," Megan quipped, smirking.

Luke grimaced. "Definitely not an option." He'd rather clean all the gutters in the neighborhood than spend one evening with that man-eater.

"Fine. Knock yourself out." She tipped her head toward the house. "I'll go make some lemonade while you prove your masculinity."

He took the time to watch her walk away, enjoying the view before she rounded the house and he was left with only the sad-looking ladder for company. The thing was even more decrepit than he'd first thought. The old wood was bleached and splintered from who knew how many years of Florida heat and humidity. Still, he'd rather risk a rung crumbling under his weight than have Megan topple off the top. And not because he cared about the stupid fundraiser, but because he cared about her.

Luke didn't think that made him sexist. Dumb, maybe, given the way the first rung of the ladder creaked under his foot. He did have a longer reach than Megan, but he also weighed significantly more. He hoped no more than the dilapidated contraption could hold. Still, he eased upward, gripping the hot, sun-scorched side rails as tightly as he dared—a tumble from the ladder was nothing compared to how hard he'd fallen for Megan.

Chapter Fourteen

Megan held her breath, eyes closed, as Cassie zipped up the back of the dress. She'd had to order it online and, thanks to a shipping snafu, it had just arrived— only hours before Luke was due to pick her up for the banquet. If it didn't fit, she was sunk.

"So, are you going to look?"

Dipping her head in embarrassment, she dared a quick glance in the full-length mirror hanging on the bathroom door. Another last-minute online purchase; until recently she hadn't cared about her appearance to need one. For years, she'd settled for clean and hope- fully unwrinkled, which made the woman staring back at her nearly impossible to recognize.

"Wow."

"Definitely wow," Cassie agreed. "That dress was positively worth waiting for."

"It's not too tight?" Megan smoothed her hands down her sides, loving the feel of the sleek red fabric. She'd chosen it, hoping the stretchy material would be comfortable. Though, she had to admit, the snug fit and above the knee length, while perfectly appropriate, left very little to the imagination.

Cassie shook her head. "It's perfect. Luke is going to trip over his tongue when he sees you in it."

The mental image of Luke panting after her like Lily begging for a treat was ridiculous enough to break through her worries about the dress.

Cassie was right. She looked amazing. She felt amazing. As if when she'd wiggled into the dress a piece of herself had fallen into place, as well. A piece she'd almost forgotten existed.

She'd been taking baby steps to…something…ever since she and Luke had started dating. But this dress felt like a giant leap toward the woman she wanted to be. Confident, sexy, and hopeful for the future. A woman who didn't spend her life in crisis mode, waiting for the other shoe to drop, for the next problem to surface. She and Luke had a good thing going, and she wasn't going to second-guess it anymore. At least, not tonight.

Feeling a bit like Cinderella getting ready for the ball, she slid on the matching sky-high heels Cassie had loaned to the cause. Unfortunately, that had been the only clothing size they'd had in common, or she could have avoided the entire shopping debacle.

Although, seeing herself now, Megan had to admit

she was glad she'd gone to the trouble. This was the start of a new chapter in their relationship, and in her life. A new outfit was practically required. And wearing it, she looked like a whole new person.

"Mom, is dinner ready yet? Lily and I are starving!"

Owen's voice broke the spell. She might have a boyfriend and the beginnings of a social life, but she was still a mom. Maybe she'd find a better balance over time, but right now her kid needed dinner. Turning from the mirror and the vision of what might be, she kicked off the heels and faced the present.

Two sets of eyes, one human, one canine, stared accusingly at her, as if five minutes past mealtime was a crime of epic proportion. She was about to point out the unlikely odds of starving to death in such a short time when Cassie placed a hand on her arm.

"Hungry enough for the Salty Chicken?" Cassie asked.

Owen's eyes lit up at the mention of his favorite takeout restaurant. "With extra sauce?"

Cassie agreed before Megan, off kilter in her cocktail dress and bare feet, could call time-out on whatever was happening. "Sure, as soon as you're packed, we can head straight there."

"But I was going to drop him off after dinner," Megan protested once Owen had darted down the hall. "You're already watching him overnight. You don't have to take him out to eat, too."

"Whatever." Her friend blew off the concern with a shrug of her shoulders. "I was going to pick up food on the way home anyway. Might as well save you the trip. Besides, this way you can take your time getting ready, do your hair, all that stuff." Cassie ran a hand over her own no-nonsense ponytail. "I don't know that I even remember what that involves, but I do know it will be easier if you're not darting back and forth to the kitchen while doing it."

Unexpected tears stung Megan's eyes. A few months ago, she'd thought she had no one in her life to rely on. Now, she not only had an amazingly hot boyfriend, but a really good friend. She wasn't quite sure which was better. "Thank you." She sniffed and wiped at her eyes. "For the shoes, and watching Owen, and…" Emotion clogged her throat, stopping whatever words she might have used to express the importance Cassie's friendship and support had come to mean to her.

"Stop." Cassie shook her finger in warning, a suspicious glint of moisture in her eyes. "It's not a big deal."

Megan wanted to argue, but Owen was already back, overnight bag and plastic container of kibble in tow.

"People food makes Lily puke," he advised Cassie. "She has to have her own food."

"Good to know," she answered soberly, as if learning brand-new information and not an experienced veterinarian. "I'll be careful."

"Okay. We can go then."

"Can I get a hug goodbye at least?" Megan was glad he was becoming more independent. A year ago, he'd never have been able to spend a whole night away. But Lily, and his recent social growth at school, had given him the confidence to try new things. Including a sleepover with his friend Emma. Megan had no doubt he'd have a great time, which was something else to be grateful for. She'd still worry, but he was in good hands, and she couldn't ask for more than that.

"Too tight!" Her son squirmed in her embrace and, even though part of her wanted to hold on forever, she took a deep breath and let him go.

He was moving forward, growing and embracing new relationships and adventures. If she needed any inspiration for her own life, all she had to do was to look at her son and hope to live up to his example.

Luke gripped the steering wheel tightly, willing his hands to keep the car on course even as his eyes drifted from the road. He'd been stealing glances at Megan since he'd picked her up. He hadn't thought he could be any more attracted to her than he already was. He'd been wrong. So very wrong.

When she'd opened the door in that dress, the impact had hit him like a rogue wave, leaving him speechless for a full minute. Finally finding his tongue, he'd mumbled something trite he couldn't remember now. But a guy couldn't be expected to form a coherent sentence when all the blood had rushed from his brain to regions south. It was as though some switch had been thrown and all his dormant caveman genes had woken to demand he take this woman as his mate. Now. Forever. And that revelation, on top of the overwhelming lust clouding his head, was rocking his world.

"Are you okay?"

"Hmm?" He kept his eyes on the road, as if he'd been fully concentrating on it and not her the whole time.

"You're all flushed. And you keep making a weird face."

He turned his eyes toward her in time to catch her imitation of his scowl before checking for himself in the rearview mirror. "I am not," he fibbed.

"Yes, you are," she insisted. "And I don't know what that steering wheel ever did to you, but if you squeeze it any harder, it's liable to break apart."

He glanced down and eased his grip enough for blood flow to return to his whitened knuckles. "I'm nervous about the banquet going well, I guess." That was true. Before his sudden testosterone overdose and subsequent "Megan is the one" realization that had been his main concern for the night. Now he was trying to figure out when he could get her alone and if their first real date was too soon for a marriage proposal, an absurdity that would be completely unbelievable if he wasn't experiencing it firsthand.

She laughed and, for a startled moment, he was afraid he'd spoken his thoughts aloud. But she didn't look like she was making fun of him, if the smile he caught in his peripheral vision could be believed.

"It's an elementary school function. It's probably going to be unbearably boring."

"Not helping," he grumbled between clenched teeth.

"But," she continued, ignoring him, "it will raise a bunch of money and everyone will see how well you are running things."

"I hope you're right."

"I am. Unless…"

His hands tightened on the wheel again. "Unless what?"

"You keep looking at me instead of where you're going." Her lighthearted tone took the sting out of the rebuke, and he felt a bit of the tension ease from his body.

"Sorry, but that dress…"

"Isn't going anywhere. You'll be sick of looking at it by the end of the night. So just get us there in one piece, okay?"

He'd never get sick of looking at her, in or out of that dress, but he nodded and kept his eyes forward for the rest of the drive to make sure they lived long enough to test the theory. Besides, his recently discovered inner cave dweller possessed a primal urge to protect his desired mate at any cost. The realization that he was putting her at risk, not just himself, was enough to temporarily quash the urge to stare.

Only when he had the car safely tucked into a faculty spot behind the school gym did he give in to the need to look his fill. He thought he was prepared; surely the initial impact had been a one-time thing. Now that he knew what to expect, he'd be fine.

He wasn't fine.

He was so far from fine, he'd need a map and a compass to find it again.

Just as before, his breath caught in his chest until he had to consciously will his lungs to start working again. His heart, on the other hand, was working overtime, his pulse pounding like a runaway stallion that had tossed its rider and was hell-bent for home. The only thing saving his dignity: he hadn't actually started drooling. Yet.

"Um, are we going to get out?" Megan waved to where his hands still rested on the steering wheel, and he realized he hadn't even turned the car off.

"Yeah, sorry. Just…thinking."

"I told you, it's going to be great. Boring," she added, with a wink, "but great."

Her smile, so full of confidence, somehow got through to the part of his brain still capable of higher-level thought. She was right; this was going to be great. He'd worked hard to put everything in place, and this was his chance to enjoy the end product—and to enjoy a real night out with the woman he loved.

There was no doubt in his mind now that it *was* love. Not the kind that celebrities gushed about two weeks before announcing yet another breakup, or that greeting cards described in flowery phrases that meant less than the paper they were printed on. No, this was deeper. More real. Every cell in his body resonated with it.

He wanted to tell her. The words hovered at the tip of his tongue, waiting to burst free. But that wasn't a pronouncement to make in a parking lot, and he certainly wasn't going to expose his innermost thoughts and feelings in the middle of a crowded gymnasium-turned-banquet-hall. But after tonight, with their relationship out in the open, he wouldn't hide how he felt. And if she didn't feel the same way? Well…he'd just have to wait until she did.

But when he finally got out of the car and opened

her door, she looked up at him in a way that made him think it might not be a long wait at all.

As they walked hand in hand into the school, he was confident that everything he'd been working and hoping for was about to come true.

Less than an hour later, crammed into the dimly lit equipment room with four prominent members of the school board, the hopes and dreams Luke had been so sure of were deflating faster than the lopsided basketball puddled in the corner beside him.

Taking a deep breath of stale air that reeked of rubber and disinfectant, he tried, again, to make sense of what he was hearing.

"You want me to step down as principal?" When all four started to reply at once, talking over each other, he held up a hand. "Rob, can you please explain what on earth is going on?"

Robert Swanson, a former bank officer and the most senior of the board members, both in age and length of term, nodded. "You see, we heard— I mean…" He paused, wiping at the sweat that dotted his liver-spotted forehead. "That is to say, um…" He looked to the others, as if for a reprieve. Finding none, he shoved his hands in the pockets of his suit pants and, with the air of a man doing a necessary but distasteful task, continued without ever meeting Luke's eyes. "There has been an allegation of impropriety. Given the circumstances, stepping down quietly seems the best choice for everyone. I'm sure you understand."

Luke bit his tongue to keep from explaining in

graphic detail just how much he didn't understand. Only when he was sure none of his words would be of the four-letter variety did he allow himself to respond.

"What kind of allegation? By whom?" Holy crap, had someone accused him of being inappropriate with a student? The idea was preposterous. He'd taken every precaution, followed every guideline. Everyone he knew did, because a false accusation, although rare, could ruin a career. And, by the time the truth came out, the court of public opinion would have already made up its mind.

Sweat pooled under his heavy suit jacket, and Luke wondered if part of the stink in the room was the scent of his own fear. Still, he kept his voice calm. Acting impulsively wouldn't help anything. "I can assure you that I follow all the proper precautions regarding student-staff interactions. So if someone is saying otherwise—"

"This doesn't concern the children. At least, not in that way," Rob assured him, as if that somehow made everything okay.

Relieved but confused, Luke turned to the woman standing nearest the door. "Melinda, fill me in. Please." Melinda Harris, one of the newest members of the school board, was the one he knew best because—unlike the others—she still had a child enrolled. Her son, a talented artist, was in the sixth grade. Luke had recently written a recommendation for the boy as part of his application to a fine arts middle school on the mainland and had expressed to Melinda his hope that she'd stay on the board even after her son had moved on. If anyone here could bring some clarity to the situation, it was Melinda.

"Nothing has been decided. There will need to be an investigation," she started, her hands twisting nervously as a few of the others scowled at her. "But one of the parents has accused you of showing favoritism to a student due to an inappropriate relationship with his mother."

Clarity hit in an instant. He should have expected this—hell, part of him had been preparing for such a confrontation from the beginning. He just hadn't anticipated being ambushed in the supply closet while top dance hits played in the background.

That begged the question why now.

The answer was as obvious as the woman herself. Liz Robins. He'd seen her—more of her than he'd wanted to given her low-cut minidress—smirking a few minutes before Rob had corralled him. Now he knew why. Apparently, if she couldn't be his date to the Scholar's Banquet, she'd sabotage it for him instead. Classy.

"So, because of one person's accusation, you want me to resign?" Now that he understood the situation, his bewilderment shifted to anger. "Do you seriously expect me to just up and quit right now? What, do you want me to write my resignation letter on a scorecard or something?"

Stepping forward, he strode through the group that had pressed him into the equipment room a few minutes ago. "In case you hadn't noticed, we are in the middle of the biggest fundraising event of the year. The school that you all represent depends on what happens tonight. Those donors expect me to be out there, running things, and if they get wind of a scandal, you can kiss those big fat checks goodbye."

"Is that a threat?" Rich Dillard, another of the old guard, demanded, his face reddening in indignation.

Beside him, Alice Bell, a small, round, nearly silent woman tsk-tsked. "We hoped you would have the decency not to cause a scene."

Nick laughed bitterly. "Too late for that. You already created one when the four of you dragged me in here. You think people didn't notice?" He tipped his head at the still closed door. "Every gossip in town is out there right now coming up with their best conspiracy theories and, trust me, every one of them will be juicier than me dating a parent." He watched the faces of the board members as the truth of what he was saying sank in. "If I walk out now, with no explanation, they're going to have a field day. You'll have parents pulling their kids out left and right—and demanding their tuition be refunded, too."

"He's right," Melinda said, voicing what the others refused or were too stubborn to admit. "I told you we should wait, call a meeting of the board, and deal with things properly."

"But she said if we didn't do it now, she'd tell everyone!" Rich insisted, his voice rising. "That she'd make sure not a single donation came in."

"And you fell for that?" Luke let his disappointment in the older man's judgment show through, just like he did when lecturing a student who'd let peer pressure push him into a rash decision. "Really, Rich? You're a lawyer. You know she can't do that without legal implications. She faked you out. She faked you all out."

Shaking his head, Luke opened the door, letting the festive music seep in.

"Wait!" Alice shouted, confusion and a touch of panic lending a shrillness to the exclamation. "We haven't settled anything."

"And we aren't going to. Not here. Not tonight. If you want to get rid of me, you can call a meeting of the board and follow the procedures spelled out in my contract. But first, you might want to figure out what you're going to say to those people out there, and you'd better do it quick."

"Us? What about you? What are you going to do?"

"My job." That, it seemed, had just become a heck of a lot more complicated. And he wasn't sure who to blame. Liz for her dramatic stunt? The board members for going off half-cocked? Or himself, for naïvely thinking he could have it all.

Megan hadn't thought anything of it when a few of the board members had asked to speak to Luke privately. They might be on a date, but this was a school function and he was, technically, on duty. So while he went to deal with whatever minor issue they wanted to address, she roamed the room, trying to look like she belonged.

And that was silly, really, because she had as much right to be there as anyone else. More, maybe, since she not only had a child at the school but was also the plus-one for the principal. Yet, being allowed entry wasn't the same as feeling welcome. Most of the attendees there so far—early arrivals like herself and Luke—were members of the faculty or on the decoration committee. The former were huddled in groups discussing standardized testing and an upcoming teacher-training workshop, not exactly her areas of expertise. Decorating wasn't, either, but it beat standing alone in the corner, reenacting her memories of middle school dances.

Bypassing a very serious woman with a clipboard and a frown, she headed for a group of women about her age huddled around a table full of empty vases. "Need some help?" she offered.

"Oh my goodness, yes!" A statuesque woman with pale skin, even paler hair, and impossible blue eyes thrust an open box of assorted seashells toward her. She looked like a Viking, if Vikings had elaborate updos and wore black cocktail dresses. "These centerpieces were supposed to be done last night, but the supplies got put in the art closet instead of in the PTA closet, and none of us had a key. Now people are already arriving and Lisa over there is hopping mad."

So clipboard lady was Lisa. "Gotcha. Well, I'm here, just show me what to do."

"It's simple. Each vase gets a scoop of sand from the bucket over there, and then some shells, with a candle in the middle. Jillian's on sand duty, and I've got the candles, so if you could do the shells, that would be great."

"Shells it is." Megan grabbed a few and placed herself in the center spot of the little assembly line. Turning to her left, she offered a smile. "Jillian, you're friends with Cassie, right? She mentioned that you offered to hold the banquet up at the Sandpiper Inn, but the board turned you down."

Jillian nodded vehemently, sending her dark curls into a riot of motion. "We were going to donate the space, and we already have the linens, centerpieces, et cetera. It would have saved the school a bundle."

"And we wouldn't be standing here shoveling sand instead of enjoying the party," the Viking woman added ruefully. "But Lisa didn't want to lose control, or let Jillian here get a share of the limelight. She's running for PTA president next year, and since half the school board is related to either her or her husband, she gets what she wants."

"And Mrs. Cristoff wouldn't have gotten her chartreuse tablecloths," Megan said.

The women all laughed. "True," the Viking said. "And if you want a friend for life, just tell her how much you love them." She looked around. "She should be here shortly. Just look for a little old woman in a bright green dress." She paused. "I'm Kirstin, by the way."

Setting aside a finished centerpiece, Megan extended a slightly sandy hand and smiled up at the taller woman. "Hi, Kirstin. I'm Megan. Nice to meet you."

"Oh, we know who you are," Kirstin said with a laugh. "Everyone does."

Megan's hand tightened around the shell she'd just picked up, the delicate edge digging into her palm. "Excuse me?"

Kirstin's pale face blanched even whiter, her eyes going wide. "Oh, I didn't mean it like that! Not like people are talking about you behind your back or something. I mean, some are, but—"

"She means, all the kids know who Lily is," Jillian interjected, rolling her eyes at Kirstin. "So, by extension, everyone knows who you and Owen are."

"Right," Kirstin hastily agreed, blushing. "I didn't mean it in a creepy way, I swear." The woman's complexion was like a virtual traffic light signaling her emotions. Megan felt a flash of sympathy at the thought, and forgave her on the spot for the poor choice of wording.

"It's fine." She reassured her with as much of a smile as she could muster. "It's just that…well, Owen has had his difficulties, and sometimes people haven't been very kind about it, or about me keeping him in this school. He's doing a lot better, but I guess I'm still a bit defensive."

"Of course." Jillian handed her another sand-filled vase ready for shells. "But everything I'm hearing has been positive. I'd say Lily and Owen are practically celebrities at this point." She hesitated and then, after exchanging a loaded look with Kirstin, continued more quietly. "That said, I did hear something about you and Dr. Wright…?"

Megan shrugged, trying to look like it was no big deal. "We're dating, if that's what you mean. I'm here with him tonight." Looking up from the finished centerpiece in her hands, she searched Jillian's face for any sign she was holding back. "Why, what are people saying?"

"Not much," the brunette assured her.

Kirstin nodded in agreement, chiming in to add, "A few of the single moms were talking about it last week at my yoga class, just saying how lucky you are if it's true."

"Well, it is, and I definitely am," Megan admitted with a grin.

"I bet. And the good news is, once a rumor is confirmed, it stops being interesting. So you two being out in public tonight will probably put an end to most of it, at least for a while."

"Good." It seems her worries about their relationship causing drama had been overblown. It wouldn't be the first time she'd overthought something and she was more than happy to be proved wrong. Setting down what looked to be the last of the centerpieces, she scanned the room again. She was enjoying the women's company, more than she'd expected, but surely Luke was almost done with whatever he'd been called away for by now.

"Speaking of our esteemed principal..." Kirstin pointed with a stubby candle somewhere over Megan's shoulder. "He seems to be looking for you."

Spinning around, Megan spotted him walking away, toward the place where he'd left her. She frowned. "He must not have seen me over here."

"So go after him," Jillian admonished, shooing her away. "We're all done with these."

Megan didn't need to be told twice. Waving a quick thank-you, she made her way through the now crowded room as fast as her borrowed heels would let her.

Luke had one goal in mind when he stepped into the gym. Damage control. Once Liz realized her plan hadn't worked, she was going to explode, and he needed to be sure Megan didn't get caught in the blast. Luckily, she was easy to spot, having strategically positioned herself to keep an eye on the action. At least she had the sense to look away when she saw him head her way. After all, even snakes had an instinct for self-preservation.

"We need to talk," he stormed, struggling to keep his voice low. Causing a scene would only feed her ego.

"Oh, did you want to say goodbye? I heard that you might be leaving."

"You heard wrong," he stated flatly, refusing to be baited. "But I'm happy to explain the misunderstanding—outside." Without waiting for her reaction, he strode for the door. The sound of her shoes on the pavement outside told him she'd followed. He'd known she would, if only because she didn't want him to have the last word.

"So did Rob wuss out? Or are you just hoping to get me to change my mind?" She tipped her head, looking him up and down. "You do look awfully good in that monkey suit you've got on…maybe we should find somewhere private and you could try to persuade me."

His stomach roiled at her insinuation. No doubt some men would be more than happy to take her up on the offer, but a tight dress and red lips weren't enough to make up for ugly behavior. "I'm not going anywhere with you. Not now, not ever."

Liz's perfectly plucked eyebrows narrowed, and he had the random thought that the Botox must be wearing off. "Pretty big talk from a guy about to lose his job."

"Maybe," he acknowledged with a shrug. "But right now, I'm still in charge of this school. And I'm not going to have you stirring up drama that hurts the school just because I hurt your feelings." He took deep breath and tried to sound as sincere as possible. "So let me say that I'm sorry I upset you. I didn't mean to."

Liz's slow clap echoed in the night air. "Very impressive, Luke. I almost believe you."

"Believe what you want. I'm just trying to do the right thing here."

"This from a guy giving special favors to a student just so he can get a woman in his bed? Spare me the sermon."

Luke shook his head, knowing that was exactly how she'd spin it. "That isn't what happened."

"Really? Because from where I stand, not only did you let that troublemaker stay, now he gets to bring his mutt with him." Her lips twisted into a cruel smirk. "And maybe that's not the only perk. For all I know, Megan could be working off that tuition bill the old-fashioned way."

If looks could kill, he'd have murdered her on the spot. Rage and helplessness churned in his gut. For a split second, he thought he might actually throw up. Never had he felt so frustrated. Or so helpless. And not just because of the very real threat this woman posed to his career. What had his insides revolting was the idea of her jealousy and hatred hurting Megan—or even worse, Owen.

Luke could try to find another job, although it might be hard if the accusations were put in writing. But if Owen got kicked out of school, then what? Would he have to go to a school on the mainland, one that likely

wouldn't allow him to bring a service dog? Would
Megan have to move if the commute got to be too much,
adding one more disruption into the little boy's life? All
because he'd turned this woman down for a date? If it
was the plot of a sitcom, he would have said it was too
farfetched to be real. And yet he was living it. And the
consequences were much too real.

"Hate me if you want. But don't go slandering innocent people," he warned. "There are legal implications to this that go beyond my job, or your love life. I
get that you are angry. Fine, be angry at me. Slash my
tires or put poop on my doorstep or something. But if
you hurt this school or anyone involved, I'll make sure
every possible action is taken to stop you."

"Is that a threat?" She was trying to look tough, but
her posture wasn't quite as confident as it had been a
minute before. Good.

"Why don't you ask your lawyer? 'Cause, honey,
you keep this up, and you're going to need a good one."

"You know what, I don't have to put up with this
kind of treatment. Enjoy your stupid banquet—I've got
better places to be."

He half expected her to say something else, to dig
herself deeper and just to drag him down with her. But
she just muttered something unladylike about what he
could do with his precious school, and flounced off toward the parking lot. A full retreat, although he knew
she'd never admit as much.

"You know she's not done, right?"

The question came from behind him, and he knew
the voice even before he turned to see Megan standing

just outside the heavy double doors. With her face in the shadows, he couldn't read her expression.

How long had she been standing there, listening to Liz spew her venom?

He started toward her, stopping short when she took a step back. "How much of that did you hear?"

She shrugged. "Enough to know this isn't going to work."

"What do you mean?" His pulse pounded in his ears, maybe his body's attempt to drown out her answer. "She left. She knows she can't prove anything."

"She doesn't have to prove it to cause trouble. All she has to do is get enough people talking. Some of them will have sympathy for her—or at least pretend to if they think it might get them somewhere."

Luke wanted to tell Megan how wrong she was, that the world didn't work that way. But he couldn't. A rumored scandal didn't need to be true to be believed. Still, that didn't mean they should just give up. "My friend Grant is a lawyer. He can help, maybe write some kind of cease and desist letter or something. Stop her in her tracks. We can fight this, Megan."

The harsh glow of the security lights glinted off the tear tracks on her cheeks, the only giveaway that she was crying. Her voice held steady, unlike his, and he had to wonder how, when he was ready to crumple to the ground. "Don't you get it? It's too late. She's already won."

"You can't mean that."

"I have to. You heard her, she's out for revenge, and she doesn't care who she hurts in the process."

He could sense her resignation, but he couldn't—wouldn't—accept it. "Megan, I'm in love with you."

Her bitter laugh was somehow even sadder than her tears. "You know how they say 'all's fair in love and war'?"

He nodded, unable to speak past the knot of pain blocking his throat.

"Well, I lost my husband in a war. And I'm not going to let my son be collateral damage just because we fell in love. So, fair or not, this thing between us is over." She shrugged, as if this was all no big deal and she hadn't just torn his still beating heart from his chest. "It has to be."

"At least let me drive you home." Maybe once they were away from here, and she'd had some time to calm down, she'd feel differently.

"Are you kidding me? What do you think people will say if you vanish in the middle of the fundraiser, and it comes out that you left with me? Liz wouldn't even have to say a word, the scandal will write itself."

"Then how will you get home?"

"Don't worry. That's why God made taxis. I've been taking care of myself for a long time. I'm used to it."

Luke watched as Megan marched off. He knew he should have called the cab himself, but he suspected Megan wouldn't accept any semblance of help from him. As she disappeared around the corner of the building, her phone to her ear, he tried to pull his chaotic thoughts and emotions under control. Every fiber in his body was screaming at him to run after her.

But Megan didn't want that. And after everything, he owed it to her to respect her wishes.

So he turned, put one foot in front of the other, and walked back into the building, away from the only woman he'd ever loved.

Megan decided not to call a cab, after all—too much money, and it wouldn't be that far a walk. But the borrowed shoes didn't make it past the first half mile of the trek home. Kicking them off, she stretched her cramped toes on the chilly sidewalk and wished she'd had the forethought to bring a jacket.

Of course, she hadn't thought she'd be outside longer than it took to walk from Luke's heated car to the gym, and given Florida's mild winters and her own lackluster social life, she'd never bothered to invest in the kind of outerwear suitable for a formal event. And given how well tonight had gone, she wasn't planning to do so in the future. Rubbing at the goose bumps studding her arms she picked up her pace. The faster she walked, the warmer she'd be, and the sooner she could curl up in bed and cry.

She'd made it another quarter mile or so when one of the cars cruising by slowed and pulled up alongside her. Instinctively, she gripped her purse tighter. Paradise wasn't known for random crime, but occasionally the tourists got a bit rowdy. With the local colleges out for the holidays, there were a few more of those than usual. A glance up and down the street showed nothing but dark storefronts. She'd have to call 9-1-1 if she needed help.

The sound of the car door opening prompted her to action, her fingers fumbling over the pass code in her haste. She'd just found the bypass when a feminine voice called out.

"Megan! It's me."

The voice was familiar, but not enough to identify who "me" was. Her thumb hovering over the call button, Megan slowly turned, shielding her eyes from the glare of the idling car's headlights. "Kirstin? What are you doing here?"

"Rescuing you?" She looked up and down the empty street. "That sounds a bit dramatic, when I say it aloud. But it is cold out, and I thought you might want a ride."

"But…you don't even know me. Why would you—"

"Grab any excuse to ditch the world's most boring gala?" Her laugh rang out over the deserted street. "I only go to that thing because, as an employee, it's expected. I hate that kind of thing." She leaned across the hood, a conspiratorial grin making her look more like a rambunctious teen than the model Megan had likened her to earlier. "Really, I could say you are rescuing me. I said a friend had an emergency, and bounced. As long as you get in the car, it's the truth."

A friend? They had just met. Still, Kirstin had gone to all the trouble of finding her. It would be rude to turn her down; besides, her toes were going numb.

"Well, I wouldn't want to make a liar out of you," Megan said, forcing her face into what she hoped was a smile. Surely, she could keep up some semblance of normalcy for a few minutes, and then she'd be free to fall apart in the privacy of her own room.

Kirstin's car, an older model compact hatchback that had definitely seen better days, was blessedly warm. "Thank you," Megan sighed, holding her fingers up to the vent. "I didn't realize how cold it was."

"Yeah, this front sure blew in quickly. I heard it might drop down near freezing in the morning. Of course," she said with a roll of her eyes, "I didn't bother to check the forecast until after I'd already left the house in this." She pulled at the wispy material of her little black dress. "So you aren't the only one that got fooled by Mother Nature."

"No, but you weren't trying to walk across town barefoot."

"Well, I don't think that was your original plan for the evening, either."

"No, I guess not." She'd expected to be with Luke all night. A lump formed in Megan's throat. Darn it, she was not going to cry. Not yet. Still, her eyes filled and one traitorous tear spilled over. Furiously she wiped at it, but another one followed right behind. When had she become a crier?

Kirstin dug one hand into the jumble of sunglasses and receipts in the center console. Pulling out a travel-size package of tissues, she handed it over silently.

Grateful for the lack of commentary, as well as the ability to wipe away her smeared mascara, Megan managed to say "Thank you" around the catch in her throat.

"No need. Like I said, just helping out a friend."

There it was again. "You keep saying that. Why?" Maybe she just wanted to focus on something other than

Luke, but the casual use of the term didn't fit with Megan's understanding of the word.

"Why am I saying what?" Kirstin brow furrowed. "Wait, that didn't make sense. I mean... Actually, I don't know what I mean. What did you mean?"

Megan laughed, even as a few more tears fell. "You called me your friend. Twice. But we just met, like an hour ago. You don't know anything about me."

"Oh." Kirstin nodded slowly, as if processing. "I see what you mean. I guess it is a little weird, when you put it that way."

"A little."

"Sorry." She shrugged self-consciously. "I guess potential friend is more accurate, but that's a mouthful, and makes it sound like a job interview or something. Or a blind date." Her nose wrinkled. "But I know plenty about you. I know that you care about your son, enough to fight for him to get the services he needs. And you've done a great job with him. He's an amazing kid."

"Wait, how do you know Owen? Do you have a kid in his class?"

"No, I don't have kids." There was a sadness in her voice that had Megan regretting the question. "I'm the school's reading specialist. Dr. Wright finally got the board to approve the budget to hire one, and he had me perform an initial evaluation with every student when I started."

"Oh." Thinking back, she had said something about being an employee, but Megan had been too caught up in her own drama to pay attention.

"And I know you've got great taste in clothes," Kirstin

continued easily. "That dress is a killer. And you jumped in to help with the centerpieces without anyone asking, and were fun to talk to while you did it. But—" she quirked an eyebrow dramatically "—there is one thing I don't know about you. Something pretty important."

"What's that?" Megan asked warily, mentally bracing herself for whatever personal question Kirstin was waiting to lob at her.

"Your address. Unless you want me to just keep driving in circles?"

Chapter Fifteen

Kirstin's comment about going in circles stayed in Megan's head over the weeks that followed. Her friend—and she had truly become one—had been speaking literally, but it also served as a reminder of what could happen if she let the breakup with Luke be her excuse for falling back into old patterns. Retreating to the way things were before, when her world had been small enough to shelter only her, Owen, and Lily, would be easy. She'd been lonely, but she'd also been safe. Now, in less than a month, she'd had her heart hammered twice.

Finding out she still wasn't top priority with her parents had been upsetting, but breaking up with Luke had nearly brought her to her knees. Hence the temptation to just stop putting herself out there. To stop putting herself in a position to be hurt. It was what she'd done after Tim had died.

But what kind of example would that be for Owen? He'd worked so hard to improve his social skills and make friends. If she wanted him to continue, she had to walk the talk. Besides, she doubted Cassie and Kirstin would have let her wallow at home like a hermit anyway.

That night of the banquet, Kirstin hadn't just driven her home, she'd stayed and offered a supportive shoulder to cry on, literally and figuratively. Since then she'd been a regular visitor, often showing up with ice cream or a rented movie, as if knowing the nights were the hardest. She also brought books, lots of them, insisting that the best escape was a good novel. As it turned out, she was right. Megan hadn't ever been much of a bookworm but she'd been flying through the paperbacks Kirstin supplied, forgetting her own pain as she immersed herself in the drama contained within their pages.

Eyeing the stack Kirstin was carrying in now, she whistled appreciatively. "I don't know if you are helping or enabling me. I was up way too late last night finishing that one about the ex marine."

"If book hangovers are wrong, I don't want to be right." Walking to the kitchen without being asked, Kirstin set the new stash on the table, sorting through and grabbing out one in the middle. "And here, this is the sequel. It's about his brother."

"The fireman?"

"That's him. He gets framed for arson and has to clear his name."

"Oh man. I'm never going to catch up on my sleep now!"

"Well, if you don't want it…" Kirstin moved as if to put the book in the oversize tote she always carried.

"Gimme!" Snatching the book, Megan glanced appreciatively at the shirtless hunk on the cover before opening it up, looking for the excerpt at the front of the book. Flipping through the pages, she did a double-take, her fingers, pausing at the copyright page.

"That's weird."

"A fireman framed for arson?" Kirstin asked, her head buried in the fridge. "I don't know, I mean, arsonists like fires, firemen spend a lot of time around fires…it could happen."

"No, I mean the publication date."

"Who cares about when it was published, a good story is timeless, right?" Kirstin's glib comment rang false. When she returned to the table with a pitcher of tea, her face was pink.

"Where did you get this? Wait, do you know the author?" If so, maybe Kirstin could get a signed copy.

"Um, you could say that." Cheeks flaming, she lifted her thick blond hair off her neck before letting it fall back down. "Say, is it hot in here?"

"No." Why was Kirstin being so weird about this? Did the author swear her to secrecy or something? "I promise I won't tell anyone you let me read it, if that's what you're worried about." A thought hit her. "Oh, are you part of one of those fan clubs, or whatever they call them, where you get early copies and write reviews or whatever?"

"Street team," Kirstin corrected. "And no."

"Okay then…" Megan shrugged. "Never mind, forget I asked."

Kirstin sighed and sank into one of the old wooden chairs. "No, it's okay. It's just not something I talk about."

Curiouser and curiouser. Pulling out the adjacent chair, Megan eased down and studied her friend, who looked uncomfortable and even…embarrassed? Setting the book aside, she laid a hand on Kirstin's arm, shocked to feel her trembling. "Hey, it's okay. I didn't mean to upset you. I don't know what's going on, but whatever it is, we don't have to talk about it." Kirstin had been nothing but supportive, and Megan wasn't going to ruin their new friendship over a paperback, of all things.

"Thanks, but it's okay. I'm just being silly." She blew out a breath, blond strands of hair floating off her forehead. "I have an advanced copy because the publisher sends me a stack of them before they officially hit the shelves." Grabbing the book from the table, she pointed to the name printed in heavy font on the glossy cover. "I wrote it."

"What?" Megan's eyes flicked from the printed words to her friend's face and back again. "You're Jared Reeves?"

"In the flesh." She offered a tentative smile. "Is that too weird?"

"Weird?" Megan's voice rose. "Are you kidding? That's so cool! Have you written anything else, other than this series?" Not waiting for an answer, she grabbed her phone from her back pocket and pulled up a search engine, entering Kirstin's pen name and the word *author*. In less than a second, she was looking at a list of nearly a dozen titles, several of which she recognized as bestsellers. "Oh my God. Kirstin, you're famous!"

Her friend shook her head, laughing. "No, Jared is famous. I'm just me. And I'd really like to keep it that way."

"Of course, if that's what you want." Megan shook her head, still stunned by the discovery. "But I'm warning you, my silence comes at a price."

Kirstin's eyes widened and this time it was Megan's turn to laugh. "Don't look at me like that! I just want you to sign the book. Er, I want Jared to sign it. However that works."

Her friend grinned. "That I can do. Got a pen?"

"One sec." Jumping up, she went to the junk drawer and rummaged through the assorted odds and ends until she found a pen, her mind still processing Kirstin's double life. She'd managed to balance two careers, one practical, one creative, and it appeared she was doing it well. Megan had hoped to find a similar balance between her role as Owen's mom and her relationship with Luke. It just hadn't worked out.

And no matter how good Kirstin's books were, reading about happily-ever-after wasn't the same as living it.

Twenty-four steps. That's how many it took for Luke to pace from one end of the small hallway to the other

and back again. Stopping in front of the double doors
that led into the library meeting room the All Saint's
board of directors utilized for meetings, he strained to
hear what was being said on the other side.

Unfortunately for him, the library had been designed
to minimize sound, not wanting whatever functions
took place to disrupt the quiet reading of the regular
patrons. Frustrated, he resumed pacing, only to nearly
trip when Grant, seated in one of the two chairs flanking the doors, stretched a long leg directly into his path.

"What the heck?" He grabbed the wall to keep from
falling face-first into the maroon industrial carpeting.

"You're giving me whiplash, pacing like that." Grant
stretched his neck until it cracked. "Plus, it makes you
look guilty."

"I thought you were on my side." Maybe bringing
Grant along to the meeting had been a bad idea.

"I am. Which is why I'm telling you to sit your butt
down and stop acting like you did something wrong."

Luke hissed out a breath, but sat, shifting in the uncomfortable chair probably donated from some rich
person's estate decades ago. Definitely meant more for
looks than comfort, but it didn't matter. The thing could
have been a butter-soft leather recliner and he wouldn't
have been comfortable. Inside the end-of-year board
meeting was happening, and he'd been notified that the
allegation made by Liz Robbins was on the agenda. It
was total crap, but sometimes crap had a way of sticking to you, which was why he'd brought Grant.

A lawyer was overkill, that's what he'd told himself,
but when Grant had offered, he'd accepted anyway. Bet-

ter to have backup and not need it than the other way around. And unlike him, Grant was a local boy. That mattered in a place like Paradise. It would be harder for the old guard to dismiss the arguments of one of their own. At least, he hoped so. He'd already lost Megan to this nonsense, now his very livelihood was on the line.

He'd nearly stared a hole through the doors by the time they finally opened, the polished wood making a soft whooshing sound as it rubbed across the carpeting. "Dr. Wright, please come in." Melinda offered him a smile as she let him pass. He returned it with gratitude. At least he had one ally in this thing.

Inside, the ten members of the board sat around a conference table. Behind it, opposite the door, late-afternoon sunlight leaked through the gaps of the dated vertical blinds covering the large window. Flanking the table, floor-to-ceiling bookcases lined the walls, holding the more valuable or delicate books that could only be read on site. At some point, he'd enjoy perusing them, seeing what hidden treasures might be found. But today his attention was on the matter at hand.

"Thank you for joining us," Alice Bell said in greeting, as if this was a social call rather than what could be the beginning of the end of his career. "But I'm afraid this is a closed meeting," she continued. "Your visitor is welcome to wait outside."

"My *lawyer* will be staying," he informed her, making sure to emphasize the word he knew would matter to them.

"I hardly think an attorney is necessary," Robert Swanson said with a broad grin from the end of the table. "Surely, we can handle this matter among our-selves."

"That's the goal," Grant said smoothly, stepping forward and introducing himself. "Think of me more as a consultant, someone familiar with the terms of Dr. Wright's contract as well as the relevant statutes."

"Statues? What statues?" demanded Elijah Reed, his bushy eyebrows drawing together to give the appearance of a graying caterpillar perched on his brow. "I thought we were going to talk about some hanky-panky going on with him and that pretty lady."

"*Statutes,*" Melinda said to the septuagenarian, lips twitching. "He means laws. Not *statues.*"

"Well, then he should have said so," the old man grumbled.

Great. This was the group he was supposed to trust with his future? Luke was tempted to just walk out, and keep going until he hit the mainland. Resigning would be less painful than having his personal and professional actions judged by a group of self-righteous, out of touch busybodies. They could take their job and—

"Let's have a seat, shall we?" Grant pulled out the nearest empty chair and half steered, half shoved Luke into it, effectively quashing any ill-advised attempts to flee.

When Luke glared at him, Grant just smiled wider. Despite his annoyance, Luke found himself relaxing a bit. He didn't trust himself right now, but he trusted Grant to protect his interests.

Sitting, as well, Grant managed a commanding presence, and all eyes were on him as he pulled a file folder from his briefcase and set it on the table in front of him. Leaving it closed, he made eye contact with each board member before beginning, his voice clear but authoritative.

"As I said, I've familiarized myself with Dr. Wright's contract and, as I'm sure you are all aware, there is nothing in it that precludes relationships of any kind, including those involving—" he cleared his throat "—'hanky-panky' with a relative of a student. So that leads me to ask what this proceeding is about." He grinned, working the charm that won him dates and court cases alike. "Not that I don't enjoy meeting y'all, but I'm sure you busy people have better things to attend to than a schoolhouse rumor."

A few heads nodded, eating up Grant's good-ole-boy routine. Or maybe they didn't care either way, and just wanted to get home, where they could gossip in comfort. Whatever worked, Luke didn't care. But of course, it couldn't be that easy.

"But he's the principal! He can't date a parent!" Alice Bell insisted petulantly.

"According to his contract, he can." Grant opened the folder and removed a stapled set of papers. "I've got a copy here, if you'd like to take a look, but I assure you, there is no such restriction anywhere in it." He passed the paperwork down the table to her.

Pulling a pair of glasses from her purse, she read, her lips moving silently. As the minutes stretched by, her cheeks flushed in fury.

"Would anyone else like to look?" When no one said yes, Grant closed the folder and replaced it in his briefcase before resting his elbows on the table, his posture showing he was more than happy to let the board make the next move.

"What about the accusation that he's been favoring the woman's son?" asked someone along the table.

Luke bristled. "That woman has a name," he growled, leaning forward to try to see who had spoken.

Grant kicked him under the table, the sharp motion at odds with the smoothness of his words. "Is there any evidence to that effect? My understanding is that the person making that allegation does not have a child in Owen Palmer's class, nor does she have any direct knowledge of any interactions involving him. And as schools that follow the Americans with Disabilities Act have demonstrated, providing help to a special needs student is *not* favoritism."

Grant's less than subtle hint landed with the intended impact.

Silence followed, and tension in Luke's shoulders eased slightly.

"Well, then, let me thank you for your time, and your diligence." Grant started to rise. "As there seems to be no actual misconduct, I'm sure we all agree that you will continue to honor the employment terms spelled out in Dr. Wright's contract, and to conduct his end-of-year evaluation in a manner consistent with the terms therein."

"What about the kid?" Rob Swanson spoke again, his baritone echoing in the low-ceilinged room.

This time Grant anticipated Luke's reaction, gripping his arm firmly enough to forestall a retort. But even

Grant's voice had an edge to it when he replied, "I'm sorry, can you be more specific? What about Owen?"

"Well, he doesn't have a contract, right? So we could kick him out, and any other kid whose mama Luke gets a hankering for."

Luke had to grip the arms of the chair to keep from leaping up and grabbing the smug banker by his fancy golf shirt. But pummeling the old man wouldn't help, so he dug his nails into the wood and let Grant handle it, praying his friend had anticipated this.

"Not in the same way, but I assume his parent signed an enrollment agreement. I'm afraid I haven't had an opportunity to familiarize myself with the terms of it, but they would be binding."

Alice, apparently eager to redeem herself, popped out of her seat. "Even so, what matters is the precedent it sets. We need to be sure this doesn't happen again. And the enrollment agreement just says that if a student is asked to leave, we have to refund them any remaining tuition balance."

Crap. She was right. Luke had reviewed the agreement himself back when he'd planned to expel Owen. When Grant looked to him for confirmation, he nodded, afraid if he opened his mouth to speak, he might throw up. He should have anticipated this, but he'd stubbornly held on to the idea that reason would prevail and he and Megan could go back to being a couple. But it didn't look as though that was going to be an option. Swallowing heavily, he stood. "You don't have to do this. We aren't dating anymore."

"Still, I think it's important to set an example. To

prevent this from happening again," Alice argued stubbornly. When Rob slowly nodded in agreement, the rest followed.

And it hit him. This was no longer about doing right by the students, if it ever had been. This was about power, and them not wanting to be proved wrong. He knew how the petty politics of this group worked, and thought they might make his own life difficult, but even then, he'd been sure that any ire would be directed at him, not at Owen or Megan.

But Megan had known.

That was why she'd wanted to keep things secret. It was why she'd broken up with him.

And even that hadn't been enough.

Grant tried to persuade the board to reevaluate at a later date, but Luke knew it was over.

Because of him, Megan's worst fears had come true.

Standing forcefully enough to knock his chair back several inches, he said the only thing left he could.

"Effective immediately, I quit."

"Megan! Wait up!"

Megan stopped at Kirstin's request, already partway out the double doors of the school entrance. She'd just dropped Lily off at Owen's classroom after taking her for a bathroom break. Since the gala, she'd gone back to working in the park, or at a café, knowing that using the conference area would just fan the flames of any gossip about her. Besides, she really wasn't ready to run into Luke yet—hence her mad dash from the building as soon as Lily was settled. Still, she wasn't going to blow off a friend, either.

"What's up?"

Kirstin looked up and down the hall before motioning Megan closer. "Did you hear about the school board meeting yesterday?"

"No, did you?" She'd never been one to stay up on that stuff, and trying to plan a half decent Christmas for Owen was draining all her mental energy. She had none to spare for school board politics, and now that she and Luke had broken up, and Liz hadn't started any more trouble, it hadn't seemed important.

Nodding, Kirstin again checked the hall. "They're trying to keep it quiet until after the winter holidays," she said, referring to the two-week break that started tomorrow. "But I was in the office to turn in some evaluations and heard one of the admins on the phone complaining about how hard it was going to be to get a new principal midyear."

"What?" Megan's legs weakened. "They fired him? Even though we broke up?"

"No, that's the strange thing. From what I heard, his contract didn't give them any grounds to fire him."

"Then why do they need a new principal?" Either she was missing something or Kirstin wasn't making any sense.

"Because he quit."

"What?" Forgetting to be quiet, Megan's voice filled the empty corridor. "Why would he go and do a stupid thing like that?" He loved his job; had wanted so badly to prove he could do it well.

"I don't know, exactly, but I did hear your name mentioned. And then she said something about how she'd always known Dr. Wright was hot, but she didn't realize he was such a romantic."

"What on earth is that supposed to mean?"

Kirstin shrugged. "I don't know, but maybe you should find out."

"You mean…like, talk to him?" Her stupid heart fluttered at the thought.

"Unless you know sign language, or have mental telepathy abilities you've been hiding, yeah, that's probably the best approach."

Megan closed her eyes, considering. She really didn't want to get involved. But from what Kirstin was saying, she already was. And breakup or not, she'd rather get the scoop from Luke than one of the board members.

Opening her eyes again, she sighed. "Fine. I'll go."

"Good." Kirstin smiled in approval, likely imagining some romantic reunion scene like in the books she wrote. That would not be happening. Still, Megan needed to find out what was going on, for her own peace of mind. And she needed to do it before the gossip brigade started spinning a hundred different versions of what had actually happened and it was impossible to untangle what was and wasn't true.

"If I'm not back—"

"Can I walk Lily for you? Sure, I can do it during my planning period."

"Thanks." Impulsively, Megan gave her friend a quick hug. "I'll let you know what I find out."

* * *

The drive to Luke's home took only a few minutes. Not nearly enough time for her to figure out what she was going to say. Or to build up the courage to say it. And that was why she was passing his driveway for the third time instead of parking and getting it over with. If she kept this up, the neighbors were likely to report her for suspicious activity.

The fear of being arrested for stalking was finally what had her pulling into his driveway on the next go-round. But it was sheer curiosity that got her out of the car and walking to the door. Why on earth would he have quit?

A thought struck her as she pressed the doorbell. What if he'd quit to avoid her? Was he so hurt, or on the flipside, so angry, that he couldn't stand to be in the same building anymore?

Sweat tickled her brow despite the cool December breeze. Would he even speak with her, if he hated her that much?

This was a mistake. She was sure of it. But before she could leave, the door opened.

"Megan." Luke rubbed a hand over the dark stubble along his jaw. "I was going to call you."

"You were?" Her voice sounded weird, high and breathy, like some Marilyn Monroe impersonator. Not good. But speaking was difficult when just seeing him knocked the breath out of her.

"Yeah. I mean I think so."

She arched an eyebrow. "You don't know?"

His shoulders drooped, his hands falling to his sides.

"Hell, I don't know anything anymore. But yeah, I wanted to call. I just…hadn't yet."

Given her multiple laps around the block, she couldn't really fault him for that. "I can leave—"

"No!"

She wasn't sure who his shout startled more, him or her. But when he stepped back and motioned her in, she went. He led her to the living room, where he plopped down on one of the easy chairs, his elbows on his knees as if he was too tired to hold himself up. By the look of the circles under his eyes, he might be. Better to cut to the chase, ask what she needed to ask, and get out.

"I heard that you quit."

His shoulders tightened but he kept his gaze on a spot of carpet a few feet in front of him. "I did."

Frustrated at the lack of detail, she sucked in a breath and just went for it. "Do you really hate me that badly?"

Luke's head snapped up at the accusation, his eyes searching for a clue that he'd misheard her. "Hate you? Why would I hate you?"

She shrugged, twisting her hands in front of her. "Because I broke up with you?"

"Honey, I couldn't hate you if I tried." Feeling every minute of the sleepless night he'd had, he pushed into a standing position and headed for the kitchen. "Can I get you some coffee? Or whatever?"

She shook her head, trailing after him but keeping her distance.

He grabbed a mug from the drying rack by the sink and then a pod of whatever dark brew had been on sale.

A press of a button and a rich aroma filled the air as the single-serve coffee machine did its thing. Not the world's best coffee, but for a single guy it made more sense than brewing a full pot.

He took a sip, scalding his tongue. Still, after tossing and turning until the wee hours of the morning, the caffeine was worth the pain. Seemed like a lot of life was like that lately—a matter of balancing priorities and pain.

Megan had watched him silently as he drank, but he could see her getting restless, and knew he wasn't going to be granted any longer of a reprieve. "I don't hate you," he repeated, because it deserved to be said twice. "Was I angry when you just walked away the night of the gala? Yeah, I was." He shook his head, trying to banish the memory and the lingering emotion. "But I know you did what you thought was right. I know it wasn't about me, it was about protecting Owen."

"Right." She nodded, and the relief in her face was like a stab to his heart. How long had she been carrying around that burden, worried that he'd felt that way? "But then, why quit?"

He sighed. She wasn't going to take this well. And he didn't have any way of softening the blow. "They were going to kick Owen out of the school. They said they wanted to set an example, so no other parent would be willing to date me."

Her jaw dropped, and he said a few choice words under his breath. If he didn't know it would make things worse, he'd have made life a living hell for those people.

As it was, he'd done the only thing he could. "I figured they wanted to get rid of me, so if I gave them what they wanted, they'd leave you and Owen alone."

"And did it work?"

"I don't know."

She trembled, her face blanching, and this time he didn't bother to stay quiet when he cursed. Pulling out one of the stools at the breakfast bar, he motioned for her to sit. "You okay?"

She nodded, stopped, and shook her head. "No, not really, but it's not your fault."

That was debatable. He'd been the one to push her into a relationship against her better judgment. And he'd been the one to insist they take their relationship public. So, yeah, from where he stood, it absolutely was his fault. "The board isn't going to kick Owen out right now. With me gone, they don't have grounds. But there is a chance the new principal, whomever it is, won't want to allow Lily on campus."

"But that's not fair!"

"I know. And Grant is already looking up any legal precedents he can use—"

"I can't afford a lawyer," Megan protested, pushing off her bar stool.

"He offered to do it pro bono," Luke assured her. Technically, he hadn't actually said that, but he knew Grant had more money than he needed, and would be willing to write off his fees to help a single mom and kid. And if not, Luke would pay the legal fees himself. It was the least he could do. "He's already looking into any relevant case law, and he's pretty sure that a sternly worded letter will handle things. If not, he's prepared to file an injunction retaining the status quo until it can be decided by the courts."

"An injunction. That's temporary, right?"

"It is." God, he hated raining bad news on her, yet she needed to know. "But a lawsuit would cost the school money, and Grant said he was pretty sure that, plus the threat of bad publicity, would be enough to stop them from doing anything dumb."

"What's dumb is you up and quitting without even talking to me first," she countered, anger bringing some color into her pale cheeks.

"Hey, I'm not the enemy here." He raised his hands in surrender. "I'm just trying to do right by Owen, same as you."

She bit her lip, worrying it, and another chunk of his heart crumbled. Unable to take it, he put his hands on her shoulders, careful to try to keep the contact firmly in the realm of friendly rather than romantic. "We're on the same team. I don't regret quitting, if it helps Owen."

She looked up at him and he swore he could feel electricity flow from her into his body, lighting up the part of him that had gone dark without her.

When she spoke, he felt more than heard the words. "Do you regret us?"

"Never." He whispered the word, and then, as gently as he could, he kissed her. Just a taste to remember her by, and even that brief press of lips nearly overwhelmed him.

* * *

He'd kissed her. He'd kissed her and then he'd told her to leave.

Megan still couldn't believe it. Any of it. From him sacrificing his career to the kiss to the abrupt and final goodbye. The whole darned thing made no sense.

What she needed was a sanity check. Glancing at the dashboard display, she saw it was just after noon. Kirstin would be with a student at this time of day, but if she was lucky, Cassie would be on her lunch break and available to talk.

The clinic parking lot was mostly empty, but Cassie's car was tucked into its spot at the back. Thank heaven for small favors. At least one thing was going her way today.

Inside she found Cassie crouched in front of the complimentary coffee station, wiping down the front of the cabinet.

"Don't you have staff for that kind of stuff?"

Grinning, her friend straightened and, setting down the rag she'd been using, pulled Megan into a quick hug. "I do, but they're on lunch and I noticed some drips when I was walking by. It's faster to just clean it off quick than to wait and try to remember to tell someone else to do it later."

Typical Cassie, she was about practicality not her own ego. A bit of her no-nonsense attitude was just what Megan needed right now. If anyone could sort through the mess her life had become, Cassie could. "Do you have a minute?" she asked, not sure what she'd do if Cassie said no.

"Sure, if you don't mind me eating while we talk. I've got a frozen dinner heating up in the microwave." She started toward the break room, pausing to ask, "Are you hungry? I'm sure I've got some more in the freezer if you want one."

"No thanks, I'm good. You go ahead." The last thing on her mind was food. Her stomach was so twisted in knots that nothing would stay down even if she tried.

Cassie retrieved her lunch and sat behind the reception desk. "I'm on phones until someone comes back from break," she explained, motioning for Megan to take the other chair. "But we're really slow right now. People are spending their money on Christmas gifts, not routine vet visits." She took a bite of her pasta and then pointed at Megan with her fork. "So spill it. What's up?"

Megan took a breath, ready to relay the entire story, but before she could start, the front door to the clinic opened.

"Mrs. Cristoff, how can I help you?" Cassie pushed her meal aside and smiled at the elderly woman as she walked inside. Dressed in a lime-green velour tracksuit with hot-pink trim, pink high-tops, and a pair of rhinestone sunglasses, she looked like a Florida postcard gone wrong. But her wide smile more than made up for any fashion shortcomings—*short* being the operative word given her tiny stature.

"I need a bag of those low-fat treats for my son's dog," she said, shaking her head in disapproval. "I've told him and told him to stop overfeeding the poor thing, but he won't listen. That dog is as fat as a tick.

So I figure I'll switch out his regular treats for the diet ones and no one will be the wiser."

Cassie chuckled. "Of course. Megan, could you get them for me? They are on the top shelf, above the dog food."

As she rose to fetch the treats, Mrs. Cristoff's attention turned her way. "Megan Palmer? You're the one who was dating the school principal, right?"

Megan bristled. "I don't think that's anyone's business." Not her most tactful moment, but she was sick and tired of being the latest item on the menu for the local gossip. Still, this was Cassie's client. If she got offended and—

A thin, veiny hand slapped the counter with a loud smack. "Darn straight! That's just what I told that old Rob Swanson when I beat him at bridge last night. I told him that what went on behind closed doors was none of his never-mind, and that unless he wanted the ladies' auxiliary digging into his closet, dragging out some rather shabby-looking skeletons, he'd back off."

Stunned, Megan fell back a step, clutching the cellophane bag of treats like they were her lifeline to sanity. "You...you said that?"

Her unlikely champion nodded vehemently. "You bet I did. I also reminded him that I know a few disability advocates—at my age, you meet more than a few—who would have a field day with this in the press. A little harmless gossip is one thing, but to stand in the way of love? And then to bring that precious little boy of yours into it?" Her dark eyes snapped in anger. "That's just wrong, and I made sure he and Alice and the others all knew it. You won't have any more trouble with them, don't you worry.

"If your man wants his job back, and I wouldn't blame him one minute if he didn't after all this, it's his for the asking." With that, she patted Megan on the cheek as if she were a long-lost relative and not a total stranger, and took the treats right from her hand before waltzing out. "Just put it on my card, Cassie dear. And give my best to your family."

"Did that just happen?" Megan blinked, wondering if she'd had some kind of hallucination. "Did a total stranger just waltz in, buy dog treats, and mention she'd taken over fixing my love life?"

Cassie grinned. "It definitely happened. And not a total stranger. Mrs. C. knows everything that goes on in that school. My guess is she's been following the gossip mill for weeks about you two. Now I guess I don't need to ask what you wanted to talk about. Sounds like things finally reached a head with the school board?"

"You could say that." Megan sat, her head spinning with all that had just happened. "Luke brought a lawyer, and when they realized they couldn't fire him, they decided to expel Owen instead."

"No!" Cassie gasped, her fork halfway to her mouth. "That's awful! No wonder Mrs. Cristoff laid into them. She's tough as nails, but a big softie when it comes to kids and animals."

"Too bad she isn't on the school board," Megan mused wryly.

"She was for a while," Cassie said between bites. "But she got bored. She still controls pretty much everything on this island, but she prefers working behind the scenes. Anyway, what about Luke? What did Mrs. Cristoff mean when she said he could have his job back? I thought you said they couldn't fire him."

"They didn't. He quit. He thought that if he was gone, they'd let Owen stay."

"Oh my goodness, that's so romantic!" Cassie gushed. "I mean it's terrible, but still, he gave up his career for you. Not many guys would do that." Her eyes widened. "Have you seen him? Are you back together yet? Is that what you wanted to tell me?"

"Whoa, slow down." Megan held a hand up to stop Cassie before she got any further ahead of herself. "Yes, I saw him. He's devastated." The way he'd sat, with his shoulders hunched as if the weight of the world was crushing them, would haunt her for a long time. "And no, we are not back together."

Cassie's brow creased. "I don't get it. If he's not the principal, there's nothing keeping you apart now, right?"

If only it were that simple. "The last thing he needs is me around, reminding him of what he lost. The sooner he moves on and forgets me, the sooner he can rebuild his life."

When Cassie opened her mouth to argue, Megan shook her head. "I ruined the man's life. There's no going back from that."

Chapter Sixteen

"Are you sure this is a good idea?" Grant asked for what had to be the twelfth time in the last half hour.

"Yes," Luke grunted, reaching to untie the last strap holding a gargantuan Frasier fir to the roof of his car. "Just shut up and don't drop the tree."

"Your precious tree is fine," he said, easily guiding it to the ground. "It's you I'm worried about. A week ago, you swore you were going to move to the mainland and never see Megan again. Now you're showing up on her doorstep with an instant Christmas party, ready to beg her to take you back. I like her, you know I do, but you gotta admit, this is unusual."

Luke shrugged. "Probably." If anything, that was an understatement. But they were past the point of half measures. Time to go big or go home.

"Don't listen to that grinch." Mrs. Cristoff adjusted the pointed ears attached to her headband. He'd balked when he'd first seen the elderly woman in her elf outfit, but after her miraculous intervention into his job situation, he couldn't tell her not to come along. Cassie was there, too, and Kirstin, whom he'd liked since he'd hired her as the school's reading specialist.

The three women had staged what could only be called an intervention a few days ago, showing up at his house with a six-pack and a pizza. That got them in the door, where they proceeded to tell him how much Megan missed him. That she was brokenhearted, and lonely, and it was his duty to make up with her before Christmas was ruined. That last part was from Mrs. Cristoff, who, to his knowledge, had never spoken to Megan about any of this.

But it was their secret weapon, a handwritten note from Owen, that had propelled him to this moment. Luke had it tucked in his pocket for good luck, but he didn't need to pull it out to know what it said; the words were permanently etched in his mind.

Dear Principal Luke,
I hope you aren't too mad about me and Lily getting you in trouble. We didn't mean to. The kids at school miss you. If I stop bringing Lily, can you come back? I kinda hoped you might be my stepdad one day, but if you can't, I wish you could at least be my principal.
Sincerely,
Owen

P.S. Mom misses you, too. She cries a lot, but says she isn't. I asked if she loved you, and she said yes, but it didn't matter. But I think it does matter. And she is so nice, and pretty, maybe you could love her, too?

Owen had given the note to Cassie when she was at the house one day, and asked her to deliver it. She'd done so, but not before calling Kirstin in as reinforcement.

Mrs. Cristoff, seeing the two women arrive on his doorstep from her window in the house across the street from his, had showed up soon after with the excuse of needing to borrow a cup of sugar. Before he'd even made it to the pantry, she'd gotten the scoop and inserted herself into the scheme. In one fell swoop, she'd gone from fundraising pest to champion ally!

Cassie and Kirstin had backed up Owen's take on things. Megan really was in love with him. He'd barely heard anything after that, his mind caught up in that one amazing fact. When he was finally able to focus, the pizza was mostly gone—for such a tiny person little Mrs. Cristoff could really pack it away—and the conversation had turned to Christmas.

He'd remembered Megan talking about how she always tried to make a big deal out of the holiday for Owen's sake, but that she always felt let down with it just being the two of them.

According to Kirstin and Cassie, this year was even worse. He'd cringed, guilt curdling the cheesy pizza in his gut. He'd promised to get the boxes of decorations down from the attic for her, and they'd had big plans to trim the tree together. To make it a real party. Instead, he hadn't so much as offered a helping hand. Breakup or not, he could have at least made sure she'd had help lugging the heavy stuff.

That's why he'd invited Grant. If Cassie and Kirstin were wrong, and Megan had no interest in getting back together, then his friend would bring down whatever was in the attic and make sure the tree got set up. But he really hoped they weren't wrong.

He wanted to give Megan a Christmas to remember. He'd brought friends, and food, and the biggest fir on the lot, but what he really wanted—for both of them—was a second chance. Because all he wanted for Christmas, and for the rest of his life, was to call Megan and Owen family.

"Mom, there's something at the door," Owen yelled, his voice carrying from the front of the house to the kitchen where she was mixing up what she hoped would be a batch of Christmas cookies. The burned remnants of her first attempt were already in the trash.

"Like a package?" She was pretty sure all the gifts she'd ordered online had arrived, but it could be something from her parents.

"No. Like a tree."

"A what?" Resting the gooey spoon on the edge of the bowl, she headed for the front door. Had a tree blown over onto the front porch? Or maybe the wreath she'd hung had fallen? That might look like a tree from a little boy's perspective. Either way, her curiosity was piqued.

Shooing Lily and Owen out of the way, she pulled the door open and found, as he'd said, a tree. Blinking, she briefly wondered if somehow she'd ordered *that* during one of her late-night shopping binges.

"Principal Luke!" Owen's joy-filled shout drew her gaze from the branches in front of her to the man behind them.

"Hey, buddy!" Luke tousled the boy's hair, genuine affection in his voice. "I've missed you."

"Me, too!" Owen stuck his head between the branches, inspecting the tree. "Is this tree for us?"

"Uh-huh."

"Cool. And did Miss Cassie give you my letter?"

"I did."

Megan's head swiveled in the direction of the answer, realizing for the first time that Luke wasn't the only person standing on her porch. Cassie was there. And Kirstin. And Luke's friend Grant. And… Mrs. Cristoff?

"What letter are you talking about?" she asked her son. "What's going on?"

Immediately, everyone started talking at once. Something about a letter, and Christmas, and her attic…it all kind of ran together. Even Lily got in on the action, her excited barking adding to the cacophony.

"Stop!" Megan held up a hand, needing to take back at least a semblance of control. "One at a time." She pointed to Owen. "You wrote Principal Luke a letter?"

He nodded. "Uh-huh. I wanted to tell him I was sorry

we messed up his job, and that even if he couldn't be my dad, maybe he could be my principal again."

Pain, sharp and full of regret, bloomed in her chest. "Oh, baby, you didn't do anything to mess up anything."

"That's right." Luke bent and put his hand on Owen's shoulder. "None of what happened was your fault. And I was never, ever, angry with you." He lifted his eyes to Megan. "Or your mom."

Needing to look away from the intensity in his gaze, Megan turned to Cassie. "You knew about this, and didn't say anything?"

"He swore me to secrecy." She grinned, not looking at all repentant. "And it wasn't addressed to you. Tampering with the mail is a crime."

So much for loyalty. Although, part of her was secretly pleased that her son had good people to turn to when he needed help. Even if it wasn't her. Still, she didn't like being kept out of the loop. Shifting her eyes to the next person, Grant raised his hands in surrender. "I just helped with the tree. I swear."

Shaking her head, she narrowed in on Kirstin, who stood partially hidden behind everyone else. "And are you going to claim innocence, as well?"

"Nope." She shook her head, blue eyes snapping merrily. "I fully confess to being a partner in the Santa Scheme."

"Santa...what?"

"See, I told you to wear the costume!" Mrs. Cristoff scolded Luke, her plastic elf ears wiggling as she talked. "Without that, it doesn't make sense."

Somehow, Megan doubted that Luke in a Santa suit would have added clarity to anything. But before she could ask any more questions, Luke stepped forward.

"Don't be mad at them, they were just trying to help."

"So I should be angry at you, instead," she asked, hands on her hips.

"If you want. You've got reason enough to be. But I'm hoping you'll let me in, and we can talk."

Hell. She couldn't turn him away now, not without looking like a scrooge. "Fine."

She stepped aside to allow everyone to troop in, one by one, realizing that, aside from the tree, they'd also brought two big shopping bags full of food and drink. Minutes later, there were carols playing on the radio as the smell of warming cider wafted through the house.

"Where do you want it?" Grant held the tree up in the middle of the room. "I've got the stand all ready, just tell me where it goes."

"Um, over there, in front of the window."

He nodded and went to work, leaving her at a bit of a loss. Owen was in the kitchen being fed and fussed over by the women. Luke was somewhere in the attic, searching for the decorations. The house was filled with the sounds and smells of Christmas, and she…she had no idea how any of it had happened. "Now what?" she asked Lily, who was proudly sporting a red-and-green Christmas collar.

"You forgive me?"

She spun around and came face-to-face with Luke,

a dusty cardboard box in his arms. "For what, bringing me an instant Christmas?"

He shook his head, his dark eyes as serious as she'd ever seen them. "For pushing you to go public. For not listening to you when you were worried about the fallout. And most of all…for letting you walk away. I should have gone after you. I should have fought for you, fought for us."

What was he saying? "But your job. You lost everything because of me. Being with me ruined your life."

He shook his head. "No. You and Owen—you're my everything. You're my life. You mean more to me than any job ever could."

"You can't mean that."

Could he? A seed of hope she'd thought long buried began to blossom. Her father's career had always come first, and then she'd gotten married and the military came first. She'd understood, she really had, but the idea that, for this man, she might come first… The idea was dazzling. She couldn't quite wrap her mind around it.

Luke set down the box, and gently, as if afraid she might bolt if he moved to fast, took hold of her shoulders. Looking her in the eyes, he smiled. "I have never meant anything more. I'd rather be out of work and have you, than lose you forever because of my career. I love you, Megan."

Warmth, from his hands and his words spread over her, heating the parts of her that had grown so cold in his absence, making her bold. "I love you, too," she echoed, the words on her tongue almost as sweet as the taste of his lips as he pulled her into a kiss.

"Wait! We haven't hung the mistletoe yet!" Mrs. Cristoff chided. Megan ignored her. They'd already waited too long for this. She didn't want to waste another minute.

"I can't believe tomorrow is Christmas," Owen said, staring at the stack of presents under the tree.

"Me, either," Megan agreed, snuggling closer to Luke on the couch. Actually, her entire life seemed too good to believe. This past week had been a happy blur of holiday preparations by day, and lovemaking at night. Luke had even taken Owen out shopping, just the two of them.

They were going to visit Luke's mother tomorrow afternoon, and part of her was nervous, but she was too gloriously happy to consider it would go anything but well. The only thing that would make it better would be if her parents had come. That still stung. But Luke's presence at her side more than made up for it. In fact, she was so content, she was half asleep when a knock at the door had her jerking upright.

"Do you think that's Santa?" Owen asked, jumping to his feet.

"Pretty sure he doesn't knock on doors, big guy," Megan said, laughing. But her laughter died the minute she opened the door. In truth, she'd have been less shocked if it had been old St. Nick himself.

"Mom! Dad! You came!" Megan stepped back as Owen crowded in for his hug. "But how? I thought… I mean you said…" Megan threw her hands up in confusion, too excited to string a full sentence together.

Her mother, unfazed by the lack of proper diction, tipped her head toward the other side of the room where her father and Luke were stacking presents beside the tree. "Luke called me, and said you and Owen needed us." She swallowed, a look of regret cloudy in her still vibrant blue eyes. "I know it doesn't excuse anything, but until he called, I didn't really think of it that way. You've always been so independent..." Her voice cracked, and Megan couldn't take it anymore.

"Hey, it's okay. What matters now is that you're here. I still can't believe it. How'd you even manage to find a flight at this late date?"

"Your father called in a favor and got us on a private flight. Remember all those fundraisers and charity golf tournaments he said he had to go to, to make contacts and build relationships? Well, I told him it was time those connections were good for something other than a bigger paycheck or better promotion."

Megan felt her mouth drop open. "You told him that?"

"She did." Her father threw an arm around her shoulders, pulling her in for a gruff hug. "And let me tell you, your mother doesn't put her foot down often, but when she does, I know better than to argue. She insisted I either find her a flight to get her to her daughter, or she'd find someone who could."

"Wow."

Her mother shrugged as if it were no big deal, but there was a glint of triumph in her eyes. "I've spent years traipsing from one end of the earth to the other. I think I've earned my chance to set the destination."

Megan looked for her father's reaction to that statement, but instead of appearing put out, he grinned and pulled his wife in for a quick kiss. "You certainly have. And I look forward to seeing what other plans you have for us, now that I'm retiring."

"Excuse me?"

"You heard me. My bride and I had a long talk on the flight here, and she pointed out a few things that I should have realized on my own." He blinked rapidly. Was that a tear in his eye? No way was her tough-as-nails father crying.

"I'm sure you would have…eventually," her mom interjected, lightening the suddenly emotional moment. "But rather than wait for whenever that would be, I reminded him that he's been of great service to his country, and given that we only get so many years on this planet, he might want to spend the rest of them in service to his family."

"It seems I'm needed on a new assignment," her father added with a wry grin. "A transfer, you might say. Right here to Florida."

"You're going to live here, Pops?" Owen asked, his quick mind grasping what her father was saying before she'd fully absorbed the meaning of his words.

"Yes, sir. I sent my notice of resignation as soon as we hit the ground. By the time your nana has the house packed up, I'll be ready to go."

Megan tipped her head in admiration of her mother's genius. Nothing meant more to Gregory Paine than duty. Asking him to turn his back on duty had always been futile. But in what may be a true Christmas miracle, her mom's new tactic, replacing one mission with another, seemed to have worked.

"What do you think, baby girl? You okay with having your parents hanging around a lot more?"

Megan opened her mouth to say of course, but an unexpected surge of emotion had her choking back a sob instead. Swallowing around the lump in her throat, she settled for nodding so hard her head felt like it might fall off.

"Good," he answered, pulling her into a hug. "Because I have a lot of missed time to make up for."

"We both do," her mom agreed. "I know we can't just jump in as if we'd been here all along, but I'm hoping once Owen becomes more comfortable with us you'll let us babysit sometimes."

"Of course. That would be…" Megan paused as her scrambled brain searched for the right way to express her gratitude.

"Amazing. And greatly appreciated," Luke supplied, stepping up to join the group.

Megan blushed, knowing exactly how Luke would want to spend the alone time they would finally now be able to have. "Right. Sorry. I'm still so shocked that you're here. And now to find out you're going to be moving here… It's more than I ever expected. It's overwhelming—but in a good way."

She turned to Owen, who was trying to pull his grandfather toward the backyard. "I think having you guys move here is the very best Christmas present we could get, don't you, Owen?"

Owen stopped and, to her surprise, slowly shook his head.

"Well, I suppose Santa might have some pretty cool stuff in his sack, but I bet none of it is better than having Nana and Pops here," she insisted, trying to keep the embarrassment out of her voice.

"I know," Owen acknowledged with an offended huff.

Thank goodness. She hadn't really wanted to add a talk about gratitude to her post-holiday to-do list.

"But Mr. Wright has a better one. Don't you?" He looked up at a suddenly flustered-looking Luke. "Tell her yours is better, isn't it?"

"Well, um…"

"Owen! Whatever Mr. Wright brought for you is a secret until tomorrow."

"It's fine." Her mother smiled. "I remember what it's like to be a kid, even if it was a hundred years ago. I would have been more excited for a new toy myself at that age."

"But it's not a toy!" Her son's shout echoed off the terrazzo floors. "And it isn't for me. It's for Mom!" Turning his flushed face to Luke, his body nearly vibrated with indignation. "Show her!"

Luke, rather than looking put out by the demand, just grinned sheepishly as he squatted to whisper something in Owen's ear. Megan couldn't make out what he said, but from Owen's smile she could tell Owen was about to get his way. She probably should be annoyed at being overruled, but the Christmas spirit and her son's sheer joy made that impossible. Not only did she have Luke, but her family was here, together, for Christmas.

"Fine, but I've already got my Christmas wish," she insisted, smiling at her parents.

"Then I guess you don't want this?"

Megan looked back to where Luke had been standing, and then down, to where he knelt on one knee, an open jeweler's box in his outstretched hand.

"Yes, she does! Don't you, Mom? Say you do!" Owen begged, jumping up and down beside Luke. "Say you'll marry him."

"Yeah, say it," repeated Luke, a teasing grin on his face, and all the love she could ever want in his eyes.

"I'm not going to agree to marry you just because I'm outvoted," she protested.

"Then say it because you love me, and you want us to be a family," he countered, his deep voice thick with emotion. "Say it because you mean it."

What better reason could there be? "Yes, I'll marry you." She reached her hand out, eager for him to slide on the ring that would mark the next step in their lives together. "And, Luke?"

"Yes?" He looked up, her hand in his.

"Merry Christmas."

* * * * *

WE HOPE YOU ENJOYED
THIS BOOK FROM

⊕ HARLEQUIN
SPECIAL
EDITION

Believe in love. Overcome obstacles. Find happiness.

Relate to finding comfort and strength in the
support of loved ones and enjoy the journey
no matter what life throws your way.

6 NEW BOOKS AVAILABLE EVERY MONTH!

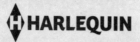
HARLEQUIN

*Uplifting or passionate,
heartfelt or thrilling—
Harlequin has your
happily-ever-after.*

With a wide range of romance series that each
offer new books every month, you are sure to
find the satisfying escape you deserve.

**Look for all Harlequin series
new releases on the
last Tuesday of each month
in stores and online!**

Harlequin.com

#2863 A RANCHER'S TOUCH
Return to the Double C • by Allison Leigh

Rosalind Pastore is starting over: new town, new career, new lease on life. And when she buys a dog grooming business, she gets a new neighbor in gruff rancher Trace Powell. Does giving in to their feelings mean a chance to heal...or will Ros's old life come back to haunt her?

#2864 GRAND-PRIZE COWBOY
Montana Mavericks: The Real Cowboys of Bronco Heights
by Heatherly Bell

Rancher Boone Dalton has felt like an outsider in Bronco Heights ever since his family moved to town. When a prank lands him a makeover with Sofia Sanchez, he's determined to say "Hell no!" Sofia is planning a life beyond Bronco Heights, and she's not looking for a forever cowboy. But what if her heart is telling her Boone might just be The One?

#2865 HER CHRISTMAS FUTURE
The Parent Portal • by Tara Taylor Quinn

Dr. Olivia Wainwright is the accomplished neonatologist she is today because she never wants another parent to feel the loss that she did. Her marriage never recovered, but one night with her ex-husband, Martin, leaves her fighting to save a pregnancy she never thought possible. Can Olivia and Martin heal the past and find family with this unexpected Christmas blessing?

#2866 THE LIGHTS ON KNOCKBRIDGE LANE
Garnet Run • by Roan Parrish

Raising a family was always Adam Mills' dream, although solo parenting and moving back to tiny Garnet Run certainly were not. Adam is doing his best to give his daughter the life she deserves—including accepting help from their new, reclusive neighbor Wes Mobray to fulfill her Christmas wish...

#2867 A CHILD'S CHRISTMAS WISH
Home to Oak Hollow • by Makenna Lee

Eric McKnight's only priority is his disabled daughter's happiness. Her temporary nanny, Jenny Winslet, is eager to help make Lilly's Christmas wishes come true. She'll even teach grinchy Eric how to do the season right! It isn't long before visions of family dance in Eric's head. But when Jenny leaves them for New York City... there's still one Christmas wish he has yet to fulfill.

#2868 RECIPE FOR A HOMECOMING
The Stirling Ranch • by Sabrina York

To heal from her abusive marriage, Veronica James returns to her grandmother's bookshop. But she has to steel her heart against the charms of her first love, rancher Mark Stirling. He's never stopped longing for a second chance with the girl who got away—but when their "friends with benefits" deal reveals emotions that run deep, Mark is determined to convince Veronica that they're the perfect blend.